CIRCULATE

Walking Money

Walking Money

James O. Born

ROBERT HALE · LONDON

ISBN 10: 0-7090-7987-7
ISBN 13: 978-0-7090-7987-3

Robert Hale Limited
Clerkenwell House
Clerkenwell Green
London EC1R 0HT

The right of James O. Born to be identified as author
of this work has been asserted by him in accordance with the
Copyright, Designs and Patents Act 1988

2 4 6 8 10 9 7 5 3 1

Typeset in 10½/12½pt Janson
Printed in Great Britain by St Edmundsbury Press,
Bury St Edmunds, Suffolk.
Bound by Woolnough Bookbinding Ltd.

For Donna, John and Emily

acknowledgments

Several people made this book possible:

Thanks to Dutch for his guidance and critiques. Gregg Sutter for his unending support. Neil Nyren and Peter Rubie for seeing the value in this effort. James O. Wade for everything.

This is a work of fiction. It is the type of thing a cop thinks about on surveillance late at night. I am proud of the profession I have chosen and particularly proud of my agency, the Florida Department of Law Enforcement. No events or characters in this book are real.

one

B ILL TASKER massaged the cramp in his thigh as he peered
out the small rectangular window cut into the door of the
walk-in freezer. His leg pain took his mind off the black eye he'd
gotten a few hours before. His breath formed clouds on the thick,
pockmarked glass that looked out on the main floor of Remy's
Quick Stop. The thirty-degree air kept the others quiet, waiting
for the FBI's information to pan out. Tasker thought, Some big-
time task force on robbery. Four grown men spending the past
two hours waiting for someone to rob a convenience store. This
sucked. As the only state cop on the task force, he fell somewhere
in the middle of the natural friction between the locals and the
Feds.

'Tell us about your eye, Billy,' said Tom Dooley, the FBI representative on the task force.

'Just an accident,' Tasker said, not turning from the window.

Dooley laughed. 'Yeah, I had an accident like that once. My
wife accidentally caught me with my girlfriend.'

Even Tasker laughed at that one.

Dooley tapped him on the shoulder and asked, 'How old was
she?'

'Ten.'

'Ten, that's not right.'

'It was my daughter.'

'I guess that's all right in Florida, but we find it unacceptable.'

Tasker waited for the other cops to stop laughing and said, 'I
was showing her how to fast-pitch a softball and she caught on
quick.'

Dooley said, 'Or you can't catch for shit.'

Tasker nodded, chuckling a little as he kept his watch.

A minute later, Tasker saw a young white gangbanger, wearing a ripped, hooded sweatshirt, stride in through the front door. Wearing something like this in Miami's eighty-degree night air meant you were either on a serious weight-loss program or an armed robber hiding your Smith & Wesson ATM card.

Tasker let a small smile spread across his face as he realized at least they'd make an arrest. The little moments like this were what made him glad he hadn't followed his dad into the dry-cleaning business. He felt the almost comfortable sensation of his heart picking up a beat.

'Stand by. We may have a live one,' croaked Tasker, his face plastered to the tiny window.

The other three men sprang up toward the door, jockeying for position.

'Look out, Rick, I'm the one who needs to see what the hell is going on,' Dooley said, elbowing past the Metro-Dade cop. He already had his Smith & Wesson model 13 in his hand. Dooley tried to muscle Tasker out of the way, too.

'Hang on, Tom,' Tasker said, still staring out the window. 'I know I'm not a Fed, but I think I'm capable of watching a damn street robber.' A slight shift of his six-foot frame sent the portly FBI man back a step, slipping on a pebble of ice. Turning his attention back to the store, Tasker watched the suspect act like he was looking at a magazine while the last customer paid for her gigantic soda and microwaved burrito. The suspected robber's sweatshirt had pockets up front and the sleeves whacked off. A tattoo of a pitchfork on his right arm identified him as a member of the Folk Nation of street gangs. No way this jerk-off would be interested in *PC Computing*. His eyes darted toward the clerk over the top of the magazine. A big lump filled the right pocket of the ratty sweatshirt.

In a calm, almost sleepy voice, City of Miami Detective Derrick Sutter asked, 'What's it look like, Bill?'

Tasker's right hand tightened on the grip of his Beretta still locked in his leather hip holster. 'The clerk even knows this is the one. We'll wait a second to let him move up to the counter, then give him the shock of his life.' Tasker's heart raced like it did anytime he had a couple of minutes to think about things like this. 'He's making his move. Get ready.' Tasker made sure he said it slow and steady. He didn't want these guys too hyper when they popped out of the freezer.

The robber walked to the counter, dropping his hand to his pocket. Tasker shoved the door wide, shouting, 'Police, don't move.'

Immediately, three shots echoed in the little store, slugging his eardrum like a fist. What did this guy have, a cannon? Tasker slid to a stop and dove for cover behind a low ice-cream cooler as Rick Bema fell in behind him, unashamed of pushing his face hard into the seat of Tasker's jeans. Dooley pivoted on the heels of his penny loafers, his girth shifting, giving him momentum, and leaped back into the freezer, his belly jiggling under his button-down oxford shirt and cheap polyester-blend sport coat. He yelled from inside, 'The son-of-a-bitch cocksucker is shooting.'

Tasker ignored the flustered FBI man. He turned his head, still down low behind the image of a big DoveBar, and barked in a harsh whisper, 'Rick, cover the end of the aisle.' He watched the Metro-Dade detective scurry down the aisle, keeping his head well below the top shelf of candy.

Tasker gripped his Beretta tight in both hands and peeked around the cooler quickly. As he dropped back behind his cover, he analyzed the image he'd just seen. The clerk was still standing and *he* had the gun. A big gun. 'Hold your fire,' yelled Tasker. He looked to make certain Bema had heard him. No one moved in the freezer. Tasker popped out from the cooler again, making sure of what he saw. The dark-skinned clerk had a blue steel .44 Magnum revolver in his hand, pointing at the ceiling, smoke drifting up from the barrel in a light wisp.

Tasker stayed behind the DoveBar and spoke very precisely. 'Put the gun on the counter and step away from it.'

'No, no. It is okay, Officer. I handle the situation,' said the man in a heavy singsong Pakistani accent.

'Listen to me. Drop the gun right now,' Tasker said, slowly articulating each syllable.

The clerk tossed the gun on the countertop and moved toward the register. 'You don't need to be nasty. I am not the criminal.'

Tasker stood up, seeing Sutter and Dooley at the freezer opening and Bema coming up the other aisle. The young guy in the sweat suit lay on the floor with blood gushing from what was left of the top of his head. Tasker kicked the small revolver from the dead man's hand and watched it spin across the floor as he thought about the other three times he had taken a gun from a dead man's hand.

'Fuck me,' Sutter said quietly from behind him.

Rick Bema crossed himself with the barrel of his gun.

Tasker felt something on his neck and looked up at the clumps of flesh and blood stuck to the ceiling, dripping down in swirling little wads. This hadn't worked out like they had planned.

'What the fuck you do that for, Hadji?' Dooley asked, stepping toward the tall, thin clerk.

'I was thinking I would be of assistance and save you the trouble of shooting this boil of a man.' The clerk smiled.

'You should have waited for us.' Tasker didn't want to get into it right now, but he had given the clerk explicit instructions. This would cause him some stomach trouble when he sat down to explain it.

'I do not even get a thanks for my civic duty?'

'You might get a foot up your damn ass is what you might get,' said Derrick Sutter, slamming his Glock with silver-painted grips into his holster.

Tasker heard the sirens coming toward them. The getaway car was long gone. The outside surveillance had missed them altogether. A crowd gathered at the front door.

Tom Dooley looked up from the corpse to his partners. 'On the bright side, it's an early night.'

TASKER CUT ACROSS two lanes of traffic, then punched the brand new Buick Century into the lot. The first year after being transferred from the West Palm Beach field office of the Florida Department of Law Enforcement to the Miami Regional Operations Center, he'd been continually stuck in the slow lane or missing turns. Now, after four years of experience and some tutoring from the Cuban agents he could drive anywhere. Anywhere but Hialeah. No one who didn't live there ever drove there. A suburb of Miami, Hialeah had no established traffic laws, or at least that was the general perception. You never hit your brakes; it was a sign of weakness.

'Where'd you get the wheels?' asked another agent as Tasker hopped out of the car in the parking lot of the Miami FDLE office.

'Rental. FBI gave it to me for the robbery task force. We all got white Centuries. Great for surveillance, huh.'

'I forgot you're on that task force. Nice job last night.' The older man smiled.

'I claimed the arrest even though the dipshit died.' Tasker held up the arrest sheet in his hand.

'A stat's a stat.' The other man nodded and headed on his way.

Miami was the largest of the seven operations centers. Tallahassee, Tampa, Orlando and Jacksonville claimed the other major offices, but Tasker liked Miami. Things moved faster in South Florida, crime was more spectacular and no other office would take him now. Not since his 'severe lack of judgment,' as the internal investigation report had said. In his opinion, they had been kind. Severe lack of judgment was buying Lucent at eighty bucks. Getting a cop killed was a fuck-up, plain and simple.

The operations center sat west of the Miami International Airport just off the turnpike, a twenty-five-minute drive from Tasker's town house in Kendall. One of the few good areas left in Dade County. He felt safe leaving his ten- and twelve-year-old daughters there while he cleared up his paperwork. By this afternoon, their mother would be down from West Palm to pick them up and he'd have to wait anxiously for another two weeks to see them. He'd pretty much given up winning Donna back, but he still got a thrill out of seeing her every few weeks. At least living ninety minutes away he didn't have to see her dating. Even though the girls let out a hint now and then.

Physically this office bore no resemblance to the old West Palm Beach police department where Tasker had spent the first seven years of his career. At thirty-four, he was approaching the age when a cop talked a lot about how things used to be. His squad bay looked out at a mall from the third floor, and as he walked through the door, he froze. Tasker had expected it, but not so soon. Someone had used a computer to print 'Informant Recruiter' and hung the banner over his desk. He tried not to smile. You couldn't encourage these smart-asses. The other agents never looked up. Only the secretary let out a little snicker.

'Funny,' Tasker said, sifting through the paperwork on his desk. In addition to the usual reports and forms, he found a Circle K convenience store employment application. The job title of 'Clerk' had been marked out and 'Firearms Instructor' typed in its place.

Tasker smiled, said, 'That's two.' Then he saw the *Miami Herald* article on the shooting with the clerk's comments highlighted in green: 'The police told me to shoot him dead if I was in danger.' The picture next to it showed Tasker talking to the clerk. 'Great,' he mumbled. His partners may think it's funny, but Tallahassee wasn't going to see the humor.

'Billy, *mi amigo*, what's new?' asked a Cuban man, his graying temples showing the only signs of middle age.

'Nothing. I was going to tell you about my surveillance last night, but it looks like you already heard about it.'

'Oh, that little thing. I seem to recall hearing 'bout a shooting or something.' He smiled. His Cuban accent made everything he said sound like a joke. 'Rick Bema called me. He's my wife's sister-in-law's cousin.'

'So you guys are family?'

'Zactly. Anyways, he call me last night and tell me you did a good job and he likes you.' Thirty-five years in Florida hadn't affected his accent from fifteen years in Cuba.

'It's a tough detail to make friends on.'

'Bema say the FBI guy is a fucking asshole.'

'Aren't they all?'

'You got that right.' The older man let out a hoarse, loud laugh and slapped Tasker on the back, showing that Latin flair for melodrama at every opportunity. 'Bema say he don't like the black guy on the detail neither. The Miami cop.'

'Sutter? He's okay. Rick thinks he's too slick. You Cubans don't trust anyone smarter than you.'

'Billy, *mi amigo*, there is no one smarter than a Cuban.' He smiled.

Tasker knew the older man believed it.

AFTER BEING GRILLED by the regional director of the Miami office, the chief of investigations and his own supervisor on everything from the clerk's comments in the *Herald* to why outside surveillance let the second robber get away, Tasker settled into his squad bay to sort out the nightmare of paperwork on the incident. He wished it really was *Miami Vice* and all he had to do was walk away from the corpse. Miami reality was another story. How many hours a year were wasted writing about dead guys who couldn't be arrested or crimes no one would ever solve? He was lucky his bosses were cops and knew how things could get screwed up in the street. They realized agents had to take some risks to make decent cases, and supported them. That was the problem at some agencies – the bosses had forgotten what it meant to be a cop. Tasker heard the agent at the desk next to him slam down the phone.

'Problem?' asked Tasker.

'There's a protest in Liberty City tonight and I gotta cover it,' the former Broward County sheriff's detective said. 'Why protest at night? The goddamn trial runs from nine to five.' His creased, tanned face was more a result of boating than years of road patrol.

Tasker asked, 'Think anything will happen if they acquit him?'

The Cuban agent strutted back over. 'Acquit who? Hernandez?'

Tasker said, 'Yeah. Mike's got to cover a protest tonight.'

The Cuban said, 'Goddamn blacks. Protesting what? A cop doing his job? If Hernandez had been black, they never would've indicted him.'

Mike said, 'They would if Janet Reno were still here. She always indicted the cops. If she'd showed half the interest in crooks she showed in cops, the county would be cleaned up.'

Tasker interrupted. 'You never answered my question. If Hernandez beats this thing, will there be trouble?'

Mike said, 'The Committee for Community Relief, now known on the street as the CCR, says no. The gangbangers seem more interested in trouble. The Black Gangster Disciples have been storing up weapons and recruiting hard off Sixty-second Street.'

'The warranties on the TVs and VCRs they looted three years ago are running out. If they have the chance, they'll smash some stores,' said the Cuban, stomping away.

Mike leaned in close to Tasker. 'You know we didn't mean nothing by our jokes about CI recruiter or the killing.'

'I know.'

'I mean, there was no hidden reference to your problems in West Palm Beach. We were just laughing about your potential snitch gettin' capped by the raghead last night.'

'Forget it.' His face flushed red. Now he remembered why he'd kept the beard for so long. 'It's a good gag, really.'

'Hi, boys,' said a young woman in a long skirt and a business jacket, coming through the door.

Thank God, thought Tasker. She'll get this old fart off the subject. Everyone noticed Tina Wiggins making an entrance.

'Hello, Legs,' said the other agent, smiling, his crow's-feet filling his leathery face.

'How would you like it if I called you by a part of your anatomy. How 'bout "Turkey Neck" or "Belly"?' the twenty-eight-year-old agent said, releasing a vicious smile.

Tasker gazed at her. That smile could cut right through you. She had brains, looks and some awesome legs. He wouldn't risk telling her right now, but she had them.

'You okay, Bill?' She looked him in the eye.

He couldn't open his mouth as he stared into those clear, dark eyes. 'Huh?'

'Are you all right after last night?' Then she added, 'You get that shiner last night?'

'Yeah. Just a witness, not a participant.' How could he make it sound more interesting?

'What about your eye?'

Tasker shrugged. 'Accident.'

'What kind?'

The other agent, Mike, cut in, saying, 'Masturbation accident.' Then cackled wildly.

Tasker just said, 'Softball.'

Mike, still chuckling at his wit, said to Tina, 'I'm gonna cover a CCR rally tonight. Wanna come?'

'Creedence Clearwater Revival?'

'Reverend Al Watson's revival.'

Tina said, 'I thought he was in charge of the African-American Alliance.'

'They changed the name to avoid a lawsuit from the American Automobile Association. Once everyone started calling the alliance the AAA, the car club insisted on a name change.'

'It wasn't an alliance anyway. Watson's in control alone, isn't he?'

'He's the spokesman and chairman of the board. His attorney is the treasurer.' The older man sat on Tasker's ancient wooden desk. 'He's settin' himself up as peacemaker if Hernandez is acquitted. Makes it look like he's an activist, but he doesn't want trouble. He'll claim all the credit if there's no riot. What about it, Legs, you gonna come with me tonight?'

'Sorry, Turkey Neck. I'm shaving these babies tonight.' She placed her foot on the desk, pulling her skirt to her hip, exposing her leg. Then ran her hand over it slowly. She stood up, blew a kiss at the older agent, turned and winked at Tasker, then strutted to her desk.

What a woman, thought Tasker.

THE REVEREND Alvin T. Watson stood at the corner of North-west Fifty-fourth Street and Seventh Avenue with a giant mural of Martin Luther King rising twenty-five feet on the wall of a building behind him. The pulpit before him was carefully constructed to look rickety and thrown together, but actually had been custom-made for the reverend for occasions like this. Two freight pallets under his feet allowed him to tower above the crowd of seven hundred. He knew the city officials were too chickenshit to bother him about a parade permit. The police had even stopped traffic for the rally. It had been years since something had gotten the spotlight like the Hernandez shooting. Reverend Al loved it. The CCR was growing by leaps and bounds, with membership and donations beyond his wildest dreams. At forty-one, he had it all. The good Lord provides for those who provide for themselves.

As he waited for the crowd's undivided attention, he straightened his tie and ran his hand over his tightly cropped hair. In the eighties he had let it grow long and used straightener, but you had to change with the times. This hair was a hell of a lot easier to manage. He gazed at the crowd. The shepherd and his flock. Sheep ready to be fleeced. The Lord was generous indeed. He noticed the news crew from Channel Eleven give him the thumbs-up.

'Friends.' He paused. 'We meet in fellowship here this fine evening to show our interest in justice. A justice that has eluded us for so many, many years. We intend to show our interest by our presence, our cries and our anger, if necessary.' He listened to his own voice resonate so clearly. Even though he'd been born in Detroit, his southern accent was perfect. Folks from Alabama claimed him. Georgians said he grew up there. He claimed Florida.

'A jury in our county, at our courthouse, listens to evidence our tax dollars paid for. A costly investigation into an incident we already know was wrong. By a member of the Miami police force we paid to put through the academy. Who is responsible? Who do the police answer to?' He paused to hear the crowd shout out 'No one,' and 'To themselves.' Then a couple of 'Amens.' Thank God for good Baptists.

'That's right. No one. Not one person, until now.' He slowly looked around the crowd, then to the TV camera. 'Now they must answer to us. That trial is not about one man, one incident. It is about police tactics against us. About the targeting of African-Americans based on the color of our skin. If Officer Jesus Hernandez had stopped a white man for speeding, he would have apologized and let him go. Instead he stops a black man and automatically suspects him of an armed robbery. Then shoots that man dead for no reason.' They knew the story. 'I am here to say – we will not stand for it. Not today, not tomorrow, never again. I hope that jury hears me – we won't stand by and let that killer walk free.' He slammed his fist to the specially padded top of his pulpit. The sheep roared with approval.

'Now, I'm not advocating violence. But we are only human. Faced with what we have been through, I'm not sure even the great man behind me could object to a demonstration of displeasure, an exercise in our right to free speech, if Jesus Hernandez leaves the courthouse a free man.' Mumbles of approval rumbled through the throngs of people. 'The Committee for Community Relief is your voice and your hope. What the city can't provide, the CCR can. I hope those of you who cared enough to show up here tonight will care enough to support the CCR with real power. The fuel that guides the world. I'm not talkin' about love, which fuels the spiritual world; I'm talkin' about cash. In the real world, money gets results. It can get our small businesses running to hire more of our people. It will build centers to get our young people off the streets. It will give us a future. Not one dictated to us by others, but a future we can build and we can claim responsibility for.' He stepped back and raised his arms like he had just scored a touchdown. A couple of his assistants jumped up to lift their hands to his. The street echoed with cheers. Al Watson thought, Good take tonight.

WALKING INTO the four-room office of the CCR on the fifth floor of one of the most expensive buildings on Brickell Avenue, the Reverend Watson glanced at the stack of cash sitting on the antique oak desk. He looked at his lawyer, Cole Hodges, and said, 'That all from tonight?'

'Since Sunday. I like to make only one trip to the bank a week now,' the fifty-year-old black man said. With the sleeves of Hodges's Brooks Brothers shirt rolled up, Watson could see his massive forearms. There was a hideous scar over the right elbow, with ridges of scar tissue forming tan mountains and valleys over his dark brown skin.

'Cole, my friend, we are truly blessed. The good Lord has provided for us in a heavenly way.'

'Cut the shit, Al, and help me dump these ones and fives into the deposit bag.' The lawyer pushed stacks of five- and one-dollar bills wrapped in rubber bands off the edge of the desk into a bank bag the reverend held open.

'What's the total?'

'In keeping with your directives, I kept the twenties and fifties and gave the fives and ones. We split the tens down the middle and use the coins for the coffee fund.' He looked at a tally sheet. 'This week the CCR has earned sixteen-thousand-four. We pocketed twenty-two and change.'

'And your legal fee?'

'I'm no greedier than any other attorney. At Broward University they taught me to claim thirty-three percent, but take half. We're partners, Al. We split it down the middle.'

'I don't have to remind you that they give because of me, not you.' The reverend had had all he could stand of this shyster. A two-year law course at a second-rate school didn't teach you how to do anything but steal better. He'd work a new deal with the lawyer when the time was right. Maybe a brick in the head.

'Al, we been together a long time. Don't make me list the things you could go to jail for.'

'Don't threaten me, you—'

'Fraud, grand theft ...'

'Cole, I don't even like that kind of talk.'

'Arson, sodomy of a minor, child molestation...'

'Cole ...'

'They hate child molesters in jail, Al. Especially guys who like little boys.'

'Fifty-fifty' said the reverend.

Cole said, 'That's fair.'

three

COLE HODGES WALKED through the less than stately front entrance of the Alpha National Bank of Miami, Overtown branch, at precisely ten in the morning. His bank business had become a Thursday morning ritual. He'd hold the cash from the weekend and add the usually hefty Wednesday night take, then deposit it here, no hitches, no problems. He walked past the toughest cats in Miami and all they ever said was, 'Morning, Mr. Hodges.' He loved it. The real Mr. Hodges would have loved it, too, if he hadn't been resting at the bottom of a canal in his beat-up Volkswagen the last fourteen years. Hodges had to laugh at life's little jokes. From hitch-hiking escaped con to law student in one night. All because the law professors at Broward University couldn't tell one black man from another. He had been through enough court proceedings to understand what the hell was going on in class. It was pure luck that the real Cole Hodges had had no family and had been working so hard to put himself through law school he hadn't had time for friends. The Missouri State prison still listed the lawyer as their only successful escape. If they'd only known how well he'd used his life since riding out the front gate strapped to the bottom of a garbage truck.

The interior of the bank fit the entrance, looking like it had once been a dime store or maybe a liquor store. It had a glass facade and cheap linoleum floors with a giant vault that looked like someone's afterthought. There was no fine antique wood around the tellers or pretty murals on the walls like in the banks downtown. The loan department was a desk in the corner.

Hodges looked at the lines in front of the two fat, nasty tellers. One with long, gnarled fingernails, the other with a purple tinge to her hair. He didn't need this shit.

'Mr. Hodges!'

He snapped at the sound of his name. A pudgy little white man in a cheap, polyester three-piece suit hurried from an office. Hodges smiled at the pig-like features of the little pink bank manager. Not just his weight or shape, but his facial features. A stubby nose and sloppy grin. The nasal sounds he was constantly making. Hodges thought of the word 'cute' as he approached, then thought of 'disgusting' as he got closer. Sweat dripped off the man's small chin and his hair stuck in wild positions from the sweet-smelling gel he had smeared on his head.

Hodges summoned his best James Earl Jones voice. 'Good morning, Mr. Kerpal.'

'How is my best customer today?' asked the little pig man.

Hodges glanced around at the street people waiting in line and the old wino filling out a deposit slip from his windshield-washing business. He wondered, Was that a compliment?

'Can you help me with my deposit this morning?'

'Of course. Which do you want first today, the deposit or the box?' He mopped his head.

'Deposit, please.' He handed the bank manager two envelopes and a deposit slip. 'We have sixteen thousand four hundred dollars for the good people of Miami.'

'Excellent. You guys do excellent work. Let me get this taken care of, then I'll let you into the boxes.'

Hodges waited at the safe-deposit entrance while the bank manager scurried around the two giant tellers, making the deposit. He had about eighteen grand for the box after taking his private fee of four thousand and an extra hundred for a hooker the night before. The box was approaching one and a half mil. In a few weeks, he'd disappear with the cash and find another man's life to slip into. He had hated being a lawyer this long. Next he would be an accountant. Put him closer to people's money. Definitely stay in Florida. With the old folks and new arrivals, this was truly the Promised Land.

The bank manager waddled over. 'Sorry, Mr. Hodges, computer's a little slow today.'

'Think nothing of it.' Hodges smiled.

As usual, the manager stood just outside the door as Hodges took the money from his briefcase. He picked up the eight-inch stack of bundled twenties and slid them into the box with the other cash, then did the same with the smaller pack of fifties. He knew the little fat fucker was peeking, like at a sex show, sneaking a glance every time Hodges came in. He didn't care. One mean look and that tub of Jell-O wouldn't say boo to the cops.

Hodges knew the FBI man had been by the bank. What was his name? Dooley. That horse's ass had cornered him once about the CCR's collections. He was just like any Fed: insulated from the street and way overconfident. Hodges had shaken him off with talk about civil rights and a lawsuit, reminding him the FBI would not approve of one of its agents harassing a hardworking member of the African-American community. He hadn't seen him since.

'All set,' Hodges called out, like the manager wasn't a few feet away.

After an appropriate pause, the manager came to the gate. 'Fine, fine. See you next Thursday, then.'

'You can count on it.' Hodges smiled as he strutted out of the bank.

TASKER SWERVED his Century wide to miss the blue Camaro turning next to him.

Derrick Sutter, sitting in the passenger seat, said, 'Goddamn Cubans. Don't drive any better than they talk.' The thirty-year-old Miami cop kept looking out the window, following the Camaro with his dark eyes as they peered over his Ray-Ban knockoffs.

'What crawled up your ass and died?' asked Tasker.

'This whole task force and that fat-ass Dooley. We've done nothing I couldn't do easier workin' with my own squad. I thought we were gonna go after the big-time robbers. Banks, serial robbers, not this chickenshit stuff.'

'We'll get there.' Tasker said it but didn't believe it. He could already tell the FBI was after stats, not quality arrests. And Dooley had gone out of his way to treat Sutter and Bema like junior partners. Tasker didn't know if it was racial or because they were locals. In the day since the shooting, the task force had done absolutely nothing, but Tasker had avoided a confrontation with Dooley over the slow pace. He rationalized that it would do no good.

Sutter shrugged his shoulders. 'You got nothin' to worry

about. FDLE gets to work decent cases. You guys travel, get the choice of investigations. Good cars, good bosses. I'm stuck here in the city. Outside of Miami, I got no authority. But inside the city limits, this really is my town. I take it personal when shit happens here and I don't know about it.' Sutter folded his lean arms and stared out the window at the passing buildings.

'You don't like Dooley controlling some of our cases, do you?' Tasker smiled, trying to provoke a response.

'I don't like that Boston butthead, period. And Bema's a typical, conceited Cuban asshole, too.'

'Hate to think what you say about me.' Tasker smiled but he wondered about the answer.

'You're a cracker, but you been okay. You're our interpreter for Dooley. You're useful for now. It'd help if you stood up to him a little more. You're too laid-back.'

'Just like the low profile,' was all Tasker said.

'No, man, you need to get in the fat man's face. Otherwise the man gonna keep treating all of us like shit.'

Tasker kept quiet, deciding how much to share with his new partner. 'I know what you mean. I was raised on cop shows where the detectives don't take any shit. But in real life, shit happens.'

Sutter changed his tone. 'That how you became a cop – TV shows? You seem more like, I dunno …'

'An accountant?'

'A tennis pro.'

'What? How'd you get that?'

'You know. Good shape, laid-back. You look like a tennis pro.'

Tasker laughed. 'Nope, in high school I worked in my dad's dry cleaners. Every Saturday, five in the morning, start the boilers and get to work on the stains. I knew I had to do something else.'

'You'd be a good dry cleaner.'

'Now my brother is a good dry cleaner. You trying to tell me something?'

Looking at Tasker's black eye, Sutter said, 'Yeah. Don't try out as a catcher for the Marlins.'

Tasker touched his fading black eye, now more yellow. 'What about you? How'd you become a cop?'

'TV really did make me a cop. I lived through the old reruns. What shows you watch growin' up?'

'Usuals. *Dragnet* and *Adam-12* reruns, *Miami Vice*, but my all-time favorite was *Hill Street Blues*.'

Sutter laughed. 'I liked the sergeant, the one who died.'

'Yeah, but no one stole the show like Belker.'

'The little crazy one?'

'Tough, honest, above reproach.' He liked the sound of that.

Sutter looked at him. 'I prefer tough, rich and a pussy magnet.'

'As a cop, you might get two of those three.'

Sutter smiled and said, 'You never know.'

THEY DROVE in silence through Liberty City, then under I-95. Most of the buildings needed major repairs, with gaping holes and missing doors exposing the people sitting inside, trying to stay cool. Some buildings even had scars from the last riot, bullet holes and scorched walls. As was the custom in Miami, the riots were named after the cop who'd shot someone. The last one had been called the Lozano riot after the cop who'd shot a motorcyclist on Martin Luther King's birthday. Junk cars littered the parking lots of the two-story tenements. Most of the fences had long since been smashed to the ground and were starting to look like part of the natural landscape. Tasker noticed that no grass grew in the shell rock yards. Mostly weeds. Dark patches of oil spotted the front yards where old junkers leaked or people changed the oil in their cars and let it run into the porous ground.

Tasker smiled at some kids using an old mattress as a trampoline. He turned to his passenger. 'You see any action during the last riot?'

Sutter pointed to a small white scar on his forehead. 'Bottle over at Third and Fifteenth. What about you?'

Tasker said, 'I was brand-new. They needed a warm body on the special operations team and I got recruited. They gave me a black uniform and an MP-5, then we cruised around in our van drawing fire.'

'Anyone hurt?'

'Nope. The van still has a couple of forty-five holes, but that was the only casualty.' Tasker smiled, thinking back on his adventure. 'We dumped a lot of gas into the building the shots came from.'

'Our brass wouldn't let us return fire unless the shooter was isolated, aiming at us, wearing a target and against a brick wall. That's why things got so out of hand; we weren't allowed to defend ourselves. They'd throw a few bottles and rocks and we'd pull back. Gave the crowd courage.'

Tasker said, 'We're better trained this time. After the hurricane duty and a lot more practice, we're ready this time.'

'Ready to deal with violence but not to deal with people.'

'What's that supposed to mean?'

'None of you guys want to see what the community is upset about, only that they're gonna riot. If you looked deeper, you might agree with their outrage.'

'Not my job, man. I work for the Department of Law Enforcement, not the Florida Department of Understanding Everyone's Gripes.'

'Go ahead and joke, but if it's like last time, twenty to fifty people are going to die over a stupid verdict on a minor incident.'

'You think Hernandez was wrong?'

'He suckered the man into a fight he couldn't win.'

'How do you mean?'

'Hernandez had time and cover. He didn't have to open up on Jackson so quickly.'

'Jackson had just robbed a liquor store and was armed.'

'Hernandez didn't know that. Shit, he didn't actually see the gun until after the shooting was over. I think he suckered the man so he could be a hero.'

'I think cops need to be left to do their jobs. Charging a guy like Hernandez sends the message that we shouldn't do our jobs and use our common sense.'

'That's depending on how much common sense you have. Some of these Cubans don't have common sense. Shit, half can't talk English good. We used to have the patrol zones here in the city numbered ten, twenty, thirty, forty, fifty, sixty, seventy. Now they eliminated sixty and added eighty. Know why?'

'No idea.'

'The Cubans couldn't say sixty clearly enough on the radio. They'd call for backup in zone 'fisty.' The city didn't make them learn to say it right, they just changed the numbers.'

'Big deal.'

'That's what everyone says. No one cares 'cause it's the blacks that lose the jobs to them. In my academy class, there were twenty-two Miami recruits. Of the eleven Cubans, nine are in jail. All river cops.'

'That was one situation that sucked all of them into corruption. White or black cops could've been trapped in that kind of dope deal. They didn't push those security guards in the river, they jumped. That's not a Cuban thing.'

'I think you're wrong, Bill. They had protection and the advantage of a foreign language to insulate them. It was definitely a Cuban thing.'

Tasker said, 'They reprimanded a Cuban sergeant for using his cruiser off-duty.'

'If it were a black cop, he would've been thrown on a desk and left there.'

Tasker didn't answer. Sutter had made up his mind.

FBI SPECIAL AGENT Tom Dooley sat in his government Buick Century as he burped up his breakfast chili dog and watched Cole Hodges walk into the Alpha National Bank of Miami. He carried his big briefcase and met with the fat little manager. Same thing every Thursday. At least he was consistent. Dooley needed some consistency. Aside from his boy, everything else in his life was fucked up. Thursday was his day to dream.

Dooley spent most Thursdays watching Hodges. It gave him time to think about life in retirement with that nice little windfall he expected. Probably over a million in cash by now. A snitch had told him Hodges took more than half of all donations. That meant one heavy safe-deposit box. Other guys around the Miami FBI office knew the CCR was a scam, but no one wanted to get mixed up working a civil rights leader, even if he was a crook. The office was full of rumors about this box, but Dooley was the only one with balls enough to do something about it. He felt some pride in that knowledge. Not too much, because over the years the spines of most FBI agents slowly dissolved into a fine mush, geared toward nothing but making it to retirement without a lawsuit. At least that was how Dooley saw it. He'd seen plenty of good guys kick ass when they were new, then get slapped down by administration so much they just gave up.

He also thought about how to hide the money, because Swiss

banks weren't what they used to be. Maybe the Cayman Islands. He could ask one of the DEA agents. They were always rooting out dope money. They'd know what was safe. Maybe the FDLE guy Tasker. They do a lot of drug work.

The robbery task force was the perfect place for him now. Out of the office, seeing what was going on. He could take Hodges anytime and teach that smart-ass a lesson. The only drawbacks were the nigger from the City and the Metro-Dade spic always hanging around. It wasn't like the old days when J. Edgar didn't let his boys work with the darker races. Commies and bank robbers, man it was great. No legal problems or civil liberties lawyers to worry about. Even though he'd missed the old cross-dresser by a few years, Hoover's legacy still benefited Dooley. Now it was time to get out. He loved his time with the Bureau but wondered what kind of loot he could have had stashed away if he had stayed a Boston vice cop. When he'd left in the seventies, it was all penny-ante stuff. Now a smart cop could shake down the dealers for thirty, forty grand a month. Instead, he sat around in freezers with these local morons waiting for robbers. He'd given the Bureau twenty-six good years; he deserved a retirement bonus. Something to go with the awards and citations for cases during the years. That was one thing he'd always have, the knowledge that on at least a few occasions he'd done what needed to be done. He could follow little Katie Smorsen's scholastic career since he grabbed her from kidnappers in 1985, and know he was responsible. Or he smiled whenever he heard about the Timmons family of bankers, because he'd locked-up the youngest brother for defrauding sixty old couples of their life savings. Sure, he had helped some people, but now it was time to help himself.

Dooley snapped out of his haze, hearing a voice say, 'Why chu here, man?'

He looked out his side window at a scrawny black guy in baggy pants, a knit ski cap and a shirt with Africa on it and a slogan saying 'It's a black thing.' He held a half-filled McDonald's Coke that looked like it'd been dribbled down his shirt. He had a long face with huge eyes that looked like they'd been popped out of his head. A light scar skittered down the side of his chin. Dooley gave him a good stare and said, 'What's your name?'

The man hesitated, then said with pride, 'The people call me Spill.'

Dooley shrugged and nodded, seeing the reason behind the handle and said, 'Okay, Spill, you got three seconds to disappear before I spill some of your blood.'

The man said, 'Why don't you go hassle the big guys? You scaring away my customers. Why you here?'

Dooley fixed a stern stare on the man. 'Walk away now or I'll arrest your ass.' All good humor was washed from his voice.

The man straightened like he was standing up at a protest. 'I don't know the meaning of the word "arrest." It's a white man's term.'

'Do you know the meaning of the words "excruciating pain"?' Dooley watched as the man moved down the street toward the intracoastal, muttering under his breath.

As the crack dealer disappeared around the corner, Dooley saw Hodges walk out of the bank swinging his case. He'd emptied it into that damn box again. First chance Dooley got, that box and eight grand would be in evidence. What would the good reverend and his lawyer say? 'We stole a hell of a lot more than eight thousand dollars.' Dooley doubted it.

Dooley looked at his watch and realized he'd have to hump it to get over to the U.S. attorney's office. The locals were raising another stink about the need to go after bank robbers. It was like their damn mantra, bank robbers, bank robbers; it was starting to annoy the shit out of Dooley. He'd make them understand that he intended to handle any bank robberies personally.

TASKER LOOKED OUT the eighth-floor window of the U.S. attorney's office. 1-95 curved to its unceremonious end a few blocks south, and Little Havana sprang up to the west. Nice little houses and clean apartments. No scars from civil unrest. The Cubans wouldn't allow it. The only times they'd almost rioted were when Bill Clinton hinted Castro might not be such an asshole and when the INS grabbed little Elián Gonzalez.

After listening to Sutter bitch during the ride over, he felt like pushing the fact that they weren't going after big enough fish. No one wanted Dooley in charge, but everyone wanted to work on bankrobbers. They had to take the good with the bad. The Feds went after bank robbers and that was all there was to it.

Rick Bema, wearing a polo shirt with a Metro-Dade badge

patch on it that accentuated his biceps, sat talking with Tom Dooley.

Dooley nodded, saying, 'You don't think twenty-eight is too old to live at home?'

Bema said, 'Oh no, no. My brother is thirty-three and he lives at home. My mama loves us.'

Sutter cut into the conversation. 'Rick, you live at home, like with your folks?'

Bema nodded. 'Yes, they live with me.'

Sutter stayed on him. 'Who owns the house?'

Bema bowed his head slightly. 'My dad.'

Sutter asked, 'Your mama do your laundry?'

Before Bema answered, the man behind the desk who had been reviewing a report spoke up. 'Let's get started,' said the short, squat assistant U.S. attorney, running his hand through the few strands of hair he had left. 'I hear you gentlemen aren't happy with the task force.'

'We want more important cases,' Rick Bema said, rising out of the overstuffed leather chair. Derrick Sutter smiled as he beat Bill Tasker to the empty throne.

'Gotta walk before you can run, Ricky,' offered Tom Dooley with a smile.

'Gotta get off your ass to catch a bad guy, Tommy.'

'Saying I'm lazy?'

'No, I saying the FBI is lazy.'

'Listen to me, you shit-eating, ass-licking, jerk-off little Cuban—'

'Gentlemen, save it for the street. I have other matters to deal with,' said the attorney.

This little guy can handle himself, thought Tasker. Nice job. But Rick's right.

'I got intel that the Eighth Street Boyz might hit a bank if there's a riot,' said Sutter.

Dooley stood up. 'Where?'

'In Tampa, you idiot. Where the hell you think? Overtown.'

'That's bullshit.'

'The FBI knows what the Miami gangs are up to?' asked Sutter.

'There isn't nothing worth taking out of an Overtown bank,' said Dooley.

Sutter continued, 'We could still start some surveillance if there's trouble.'

'That's just stupid. If we followed that logic, we could just watch every bank all the time.' Dooley shook his head.

'What'd you want, Mr. FBI, more convenience stores?'

Tasker chimed in. 'We need something more, Tom. A bank might be a good start. I could sit on it for a few days. See if anyone else is watching it. Maybe Sutter could keep track of some of the Eighth Street Boyz, I could watch the bank and Bema could keep up with the other stuff over at the task force.'

'I said no.' Dooley didn't blink.

Tasker stiffened. He usually avoided wasting time arguing with idiots but this guy was out of line. 'What are you, my mother? Last I checked, you were just an agent with the FBI. Aside from a little jurisdiction, that doesn't give you any right to dictate what we do.'

Dooley remained silent as he stared down each of his fellow task force members. It didn't bother Tasker; he'd been glared at by the best of them. Finally, the heavy FBI man said, 'Why not more commercial robbery targets?'

'We need bigger targets. We could start a daytime surveillance of Alpha National of Overtown.' Tasker now felt like this was a control issue.

Dooley backed off a little. 'What's the big deal about a bank anyway? All robberies are felonies.'

Tasker said, 'We're supposed to go after high-profile robbers. To me that sounds like bank robbers.'

Bema jumped in with, 'The Eighth Street Boyz, they cause shit all over the county, not just the city. Be sweet to pinch some of them.'

Then Sutter said, 'Only a few of them would try a bank. They been trying to turn their image around and be some kind of role models.'

Dooley snorted. 'What kind of role models would those mopes be?'

Sutter answered, 'Best the kids got right now. These guys have been real serious lately. That's why there's a split in the gang.' He paused and turned his charcoal eyes onto Dooley. 'What about bank robbers?'

Dooley's ruddy face turned red. 'Well, maybe, with better

intelligence, we could work on a bank. But we're not wasting our time in Overtown.'

Just then the door to the big office swung open. A Cuban guy in a silk pin-striped suit said, 'Jury's in.'

four

THE FDLE Special Operations Team huddled around a tiny TV screen, watching the court proceedings from the back of their van. The four-hour delay before the verdict was read had given the Miami Police Department parking lot time to become an absolute zoo. Uniformed cops searching for extra vests, commanders briefing small groups, detectives squeezing into old uniforms that no longer fit. It had taken Tasker the full four hours to drive out to his office, grab some gear out of the empty building, get some gas, then drive back to meet the rest of the team. The traffic reminded him of an African refugee flood, with lines and lines of cars flowing in the same direction. The verdict was about to be read and no one wanted to be at ground zero if the jury dropped a bombshell. The FDLE Special Operations van had been left at the Miami police station the night before just for this reason. That still meant each agent had to find his own way to the lot.

As Tasker fumbled with a magazine to his M-16 rifle and chatted with other agents, he noticed a small, courtly looking sergeant walking toward him. Sergeant Walter 'Deac' Kowal was a legend in the Overtown community. When others cracked heads, he turned the neighborhoods around with youth programs through the church where he was a deacon. The older black man smiled.

Tasker said, 'Hey, Deac.'

The older uniformed cop said, 'Billy, what happened to your eye?'

Tasker said, 'Athletic daughter.'

Deac let it slide. 'You still trying to work yourself to death?'

'Just gettin' by. What about you? Thought you were on your way out.'

Deac nodded and said, 'Supposed to be two more days, but I told 'em I'd put off retirement till things settle down. They want me talking to the folks. Calm 'em down.'

'Not like Reverend Watson.'

Deac shook his head. 'He makes me sad more'n anything else. He could do so much with that CCR. But all he's good for is speeches and lookin' pretty.' The older man's creased face looked up at the sound of a gunshot somewhere out in the city. 'You know, I tried to take the CCR over once. Me and my church. We were gonna use it to fund some youth programs in Liberty City.'

'What happened?' Tasker watched the light in the man's eyes.

'He sicced that back-stabbing attorney of his on me. Cole Hodges, you boys with the State should remember that name. He's no good.'

'Good luck, Deac,' Tasker said, turning to listen to his team commander. 'Take extra care your last few days on the job.'

'You too, Billy. Remember, you boys are here to restore order, not go on safari.'

Tasker thought about the older man's comment. It did seem like a lot of the cops were looking forward to trouble.

TASKER FOCUSED ON the tiny figures on the TV sitting at an angle on the dash of the step van. 'Turn it up,' someone behind him shouted. When the judge asked for the verdict, the entire parking lot froze for a moment, making the little TV suddenly sound like an amplifier. On the screen, a fat man in a brown shirt stood up and started to read in a wavering voice, 'We the jury find the defendant, Jesus Hernandez, as to count one, manslaughter ...' Tasker could hear his heart beat in his ears. 'Not guilty.' The cheers of the cops drowned out the 'Not guilty' on count two, reckless endangerment.

'Looks like we work tonight,' said the agent next to Tasker.

The commander leaned out of the van. 'Let's move out. Things'll be hot real soon.'

As he started to jump into the van, Tasker felt a tug on his leg.

'You look good in black,' Tina Wiggins said with a smile. 'What do they have you doing?'

She shrugged. 'Intel with the squad and a few of the black agents from upstate.'

'Out there?' He pointed past the ten-foot walls of the station. Like a fort from the old west.

'The black agents are out in the community. I'm coordinating the info for the field forces here at the station.'

Tasker said, as the van pulled away, 'Wish I could stay with you.'

'Me too,' Tina said, as the van turned onto the street.

Tasker broke into a broad grin.

THE REVEREND Al Watson watched the exodus from his business office in the Brickell Avenue office building. He had his arm around a thin white boy about thirteen years old. 'There is opportunity in this situation, Cole. After talking about showing our anger, no one is going to label me an Uncle Tom when I ask for calm.'

Cole Hodges sat on a leather couch, glued to the big-screen TV. The only opportunity he wanted was an opportunity to grab the box before the Reverend Al did.

The newscaster talked to a correspondent on Third Street. Crowds grew behind the casually dressed man. 'What's the situation, Jason?' asked the anchorman. 'Well, Rick, the word that springs to mind is "tense," ' said the correspondent. The camera swept the area, showing a group starting to toss rocks and bottles at the police. A car ignited as some young men ran from it. The anchor came on screen again. 'We'll continue our coverage of "Miami Under Siege" after these messages.' Hodges stood up to switch off the set, just catching a man in a plaid jacket saying, 'At Big Tony's Appliances, you can just walk in, anytime!'

Hodges smiled. They'll be walking in real soon, dumbass.

'What d'you think, Cole? Should I speak from the scene or from City Hall?' He stroked the boy's hair while looking at Hodges.

'Definitely the street. But leave Scott at home.' He loved those little digs.

Watson's voice boomed. 'I shall speak from the scene of the original shooting.' Then much quieter, 'Where was that again, Cole, Fifth or Sixth?'

'Third and Thirtieth.'

'Whatever. I'll head over there. You man the phones here. Call me on the cellular if you hear anything good.'

'Later, Al.' Cole had a few plans of his own.

TOM DOOLEY SAT in the robbery task force office watching the court proceedings, but not following them. He concentrated on his best plan to liberate Cole Hodges's money from the bank in Overtown. The TV showed the crowds in the 'hood getting nastier by the minute. No one would expect him to show up now. If questioned about his visit, he could point to the intelligence about the bank being hit during the riot. If he had to hurt the fat little manager, he could throw that off on the local wild men, too. Perfect. Now he just wanted to get there. The only other thing he needed was a scapegoat, and the rioters looked like they'd do nicely, unless someone better came along.

Dooley jumped at the sound of a door slamming and loud voices. He heard Derrick Sutter say, 'You don't know shit. We stopped the Lozano riot. Metro-Dade didn't do jack.'

Then Rick Bema growled, 'They kicked your ass. The county kept things from spreading west.' His thick accent made Dooley smile.

Dooley looked up at them as they came in the room. 'Well, if it isn't Amos and Alejandro. Where are you boys headed all dressed up?'

Bema, adjusting his heavy ballistic vest, didn't look up but said clearly, 'Kiss my ass, Tom.'

'Ignore him, Bema,' Sutter said. He kept talking like Dooley wasn't around. 'Like I was sayin', the city can handle the big shit. That's why we're the best.'

Bema said, 'We got better cops. Better training. Shit, we even got better cars than you guys.'

'The county spends more money, but the city sees all the action. Without Miami, Dade County ain't shit.'

'Without Miami, Dade County is paradise.' He adjusted his gun belt, then Sutter helped him attach a face shield to his helmet.

Dooley didn't move from the large, padded swivel chair. 'You boys are loaded for bear.'

'We got work to do,' Bema said, still not looking at the pudgy FBI agent.

Sutter held his Kevlar helmet under his arm. 'What's the FBI going to do if this turns bad and the city burns?'

'Not a federal problem. I keep my usual routine till you get back.'

Bema said, 'That mean you won't do a fucking thing?'

'You'd be surprised at what I'll do.' Dooley grinned from ear to ear.

'THAT WAS CLOSE,' an FDLE Special Operations agent said, reacting to an explosion a block or two away.

Eight agents, dressed in black, waited in the back of their van for the fifty-man Miami police field force to move into the troubled areas.

Tasker grew anxious, listening to the noise and watching the little TV. All the evidence convinced him that every minute they waited things would get further and further out of hand. They needed to move now. The Miami cops seemed content to mill around and casually get their gear in order. He'd been sitting in a thick, hot, bullet-proof vest and black fatigues with an M-16 strapped around his neck for an hour and these jerk-offs were just now getting off their asses. Then everyone turned toward the TV.

'Quiet down, let's listen up,' shouted the special ops commander. Jesus Hernandez came on-screen to make his first statement after his acquittal an hour before.

Tasker squeezed in close to the set. Hernandez's eyes were puffy. His loose tie hung from an unbuttoned collar. He held a small piece of paper as he stepped to the gigantic bank of microphones.

Hernandez waited for the flashbulbs to subside, then slowly started to speak. 'I wish to tank my freends and family who support me through this crises. My attorneys do a berry good job.'

He sounds just like Rick Bema, thought Tasker.

'They tell me to trust in the system, and I feel it was a fair trial.'

One of the FDLE agents mocked him, 'America been berry, berry good to me.'

Hernandez put down the prepared statement. 'Now I wish to say zomething else.'

'Look out,' an agent in the van said.

'I think the people who causing trouble in Miami should be shot like dogs. They nothsing but animals. They don respect the law or nothsing and I think is time to get tough with these thugs. I hope the mayor has the balls to do somesing this time and not let them burn down the city.' An arm from off camera grabbed Hernandez by the shoulder. 'But I not finished,' he insisted. The arm tugged him off-stage anyway. His lawyers restrained him from going back to the cameras.

five

TOM DOOLEY CURSED the new Bureau rental cars, small and efficient. He could barely squeeze his bulky frame into the new Buick Century's narrow vinyl seats. His heart pounded as he considered the score he was about to make. With the city going to shit, now was the time to pay the Alpha National Bank in Overtown a visit. He had dreamed about how he'd take off a bank. Watching people get caught for the last fifteen years had taught him what mistakes to avoid. He knew it could be done. Knew! The hundreds of open bank robbery cases the Bureau had all across the country proved it could be done. Dooley always thought about a good disguise, maybe a biker with tattoos or a spook with shoe polish all over his face. The security cameras weren't set up for too much detail, not in the smaller banks. The problem Dooley always faced was the size of the haul. After all the risk of a straight-up robbery, he'd only walk away with three, maybe four grand. If he were lucky, he'd be assigned to investigate the robbery himself. That would be a hoot. Of all his ideas, this riot presented him with his best chance. The big score. One shot to secure retirement, his son's college and a little something left over. He stomped on the gas, not wanting to risk having the little fat manager close early, making him miss his chance for early retirement.

The traffic moving away from Overtown filled both lanes of Dixie Highway going south. This was outrageous at two in the afternoon, even for Miami. This was America, or at least South Florida, not some backward African country with refugees flowing one way then the other. He breezed toward the old section of Miami until Tenth Street, where it looked like people were panicking and starting to flow into all four lanes, both southbound and northbound.

Dooley yelped, 'Oh shit,' and swerved hard into a pawnshop parking lot as the oncoming traffic grew to a flood. His stomach tightened as he realized he wouldn't be at the bank for at least an hour. He pulled the car to the edge of the road and reached for the siren. Shit, they didn't install them on all the cars anymore. He laid on the horn, trying to force his way back onto Dixie and to his retirement nest egg.

LOUIS KERPAL, manager of the Alpha National Bank of Miami, Overtown branch, tried not to fidget as the last employee gathered her things to leave. Lilly Dane, the loan manager and assistant general manager, grabbed things off her desk she wouldn't normally take home. Mementos, a calculator and some photos. Louis especially liked the photograph of her in Acapulco in a bikini before she had her boob job. People had to wonder when they saw the before picture and the after product sitting in front of them. He wondered how she stayed upright.

'C'mon, Lilly, while it's still clear.' He kept his voice calm.

'I'm trying, Louie. I don't want to lose anything if those animals get inside.' She scooped everything into her purse, stood and straightened her suit top. She was magnificent.

He opened the door for her.

'Aren't you coming, too?' she asked, not slowing much.

'No, I've gotta call the main office and then check the alarm.'

She hesitated. 'I'll wait with you.'

'No, don't be silly. You need to get out of here before anything starts. I'll be along in a few minutes.'

She didn't need to hear that twice and started toward her car. 'Please be careful, Louie.'

He watched her hips sway as she hustled to her car. 'I will, dear, don't worry.' He waited until her blue Mustang cleared the lot and headed east toward Biscayne Boulevard, then locked the door and went to work.

Louis Kerpal scurried around the empty bank, grabbing peeks of the outside to see how bad things were getting. Smoke poured from the building across the street and only a couple of cars now drove past the front of the bank. He had to be the last white man left in Overtown. He glanced at his plastic Timex, then out the front glass door. It seemed dark for three o'clock. This was the first time he had ever closed the bank early and he didn't care that it wasn't a holiday. The other reason he'd closed and sent everyone home was to be alone in the bank for a few minutes. Although he would have liked to be alone with Lilly Dane in the bank, inspecting the silicone additions she so proudly displayed, right now he needed complete privacy. He'd figured out a long time ago that embezzlers always got caught. But if he punched the right safe-deposit boxes, no one would say a word. A crook wouldn't call the cops about being robbed. Besides, with any luck the bank would be looted during the riot and they'd never suspect him.

After grabbing the master key and his personal spare, something he never mentioned to clients, Kerpal entered the safe-deposit-box room. When some of the dope dealers who liked this branch because it was inconspicuous came by to open a box account, Kerpal led them to the older section of boxes in the back. Unlike the rest, he could use the master key and his spare key to open any box. He'd never done it, but now it seemed like the best possible chance he'd ever have.

He pulled out four boxes from the bottom row and lined them up on the table inside the room. He had grabbed them at random because they were easy to reach, but it was worth a try. He unlatched all four without looking in any of them, pausing to savor the anticipation. Then, one at a time, he flipped open the long lids.

The first two had nothing but papers. He didn't even look to see if they were bearer bonds. He wanted something more market-able. He looked in the third box and found something closer to his goal: nice antique jewelry. Nothing too fancy, but nice. He'd see what else he came up with before deciding whether or not to take it. The last box had more papers. Did everyone think their family papers were more important than anyone else's? This was infuriating. With a new attitude, Kerpal checked his list and went after boxes that he knew didn't just have papers.

The first box was up high, over Kerpal's five-five frame. He remembered the Cuban gentlemen dressed in white. They had visited the box only four or five times in the last year. He hoped they had cash because he wouldn't have a clue what to do with cocaine. As he slid the box out, he could tell it wasn't too heavy. Not a good sign unless it held jewelry.

He ran his tongue over his dry, fat lips as he quivered with excitement. Placing the box on the table on top of the other four, he yanked it open like a kid with a birthday present and stared for a moment, then picked up the crucifix with a hook on the bottom for hanging upside down. Damn Santería. He looked at the only other thing in the box. A human finger. Looked like an index, sealed in plastic. No, thanks. He left it and, on an impulse, grabbed the CCR's box. He knew it had cash but no idea how much. That slick attorney Cole Hodges always dropped in some cash on Thursdays, but he took some out, too. Maybe not the big win, but it'd be a start.

After putting the heavy box on the rickety table with the other five and opening it, one word came to his mind, then he said it out loud as a grin spread across his wide face. 'Jackpot.'

He decided that it was enough cash, over a million, easily, that he didn't need to hit any other boxes. Kerpal was so excited he couldn't think straight. He dumped the whole box into a leather satchel that was also in the box and that looked like a big purse. The cash and a couple of letters, as well as a CCR patch and T-shirt, all fit into the roomy pouch. He decided to run it out to his car, come back and clean up and act like nothing had happened. If the bank got looted, fine; if not, Hodges wouldn't admit he was skimming money from the till. He hefted the satchel, feeling the weight against his arm. Time to go.

Kerpal hustled through the front door. The streets were quiet, but in the distance he could hear sirens. He set all the alarms and turned to check the door one last time. All secure.

As he spun back around to head to his car, he found himself facing the barrel of a blue steel revolver. Then he heard the man behind the gun say, 'Closing early today?'

'NOTHING THIS EXCITING back in West Palm, is there, Bill?' bellowed one of the FDLE agents sitting in the back of the van as it moved slowly through the street filled with people. The eight agents, dressed in black from head to toe, each carrying a rifle of some kind, were on edge as pedestrians shot angry looks at them. The men gripped their guns. Five had MP-5 submachine guns, two had scoped .308-caliber sniper rifles and Tasker had his trusty M-16. In addition to the rifles, each man carried about forty pounds in other equipment and a Beretta nine-millimeter handgun. The gear and some extra training made them the special operations team that got to wear the black special operations uniform and respond to fun events like riots and hostage situations. Two cars burned at the end of the block, as a Miami police cruiser with four cops in it pulled up alongside the big blue FDLE Special Operations van. Tasker sat on the end of the bench next to the open rear doors, watching as the fifty Miami cops started to organize into a field force.

Tasker thought about a quick cell phone call to the girls. He'd like to hear about their day and let them know he was fine. The girls wouldn't understand the danger, and Donna might not care, but the call would make him feel better. A closer eye on Jack Sandersen during the arrest and he'd have been watching this from his house in West Palm Beach. A split second's difference in timing and he'd have an entirely different life. A voice rang in his head, breaking his concentration.

The team commander leaned back from the front passenger seat and shouted, 'This is it. When we hear the "Mount up" command, we'll fall out and form up behind the field force. Remember, we're the only ones who can fire so keep your eyes out for guns. The field force will handle the crowds and we protect them from snipers.' The commander looked out the front at the crowds and then out the back at the field force. 'Lock and load.'

As Tasker reached for his M-16, he heard three shots and three hollow thumps against the van. The man across from Tasker yelled out and grabbed his arm as his MP-5 tumbled to the floor of the van. Blood spurted into Tasker's eyes, giving the scene a momentary red haze. He leaned back instinctively, his hands checking his face for a wound. In a second, he realized it was the other man's blood.

The commander twisted in his seat. 'Everyone out. Watch Steve's arm.'

Tasker scrambled out first, his rifle to his shoulder before his feet hit the ground, still blinking hard to clear the blood from his eyes. Two FDLE agents tried to stop the bleeding on the right arm of the wounded man. The Miami cops were in chaos, scrambling for cover. He saw a flash on the roof of the building across a small playground at the same time as another shot rang out.

Before Tasker could react, his ears were pounding with the fire of fifty weapons. The windows of the building shattered and the plaster along the roof crumbled under the withering fire. Every uniformed cop jerked the trigger of his Glock nine-millimeter. Some not even aiming, just raising their hand and shooting over the roofs of the cruisers.

'Cease fire, cease fire, cease fucking fire,' screamed a huge black uniformed sergeant. 'You knuckleheads ain't supposed to shoot. Only the SWAT guys.'

The FDLE commander barked a couple of quick orders, then turned to Tasker. 'Bill, you go up with the Miami unit to make sure they got that son of a bitch. You probably won't be able to identify him, just ensure they neutralized the threat.'

Tasker nodded, put his hands on his legs to keep them still for a second, and looked over at the wounded man being tended by a medic before he moved toward the group of eight cops getting ready to enter the building.

'YOU GONNA BE our cover at the building?' asked the young white sergeant forming up his team. He wore a uniform tailored to fit tight around the biceps, like most of the Miami cops.

Tasker nodded and fell in next to the last man. Tasker still liked action but he remembered when he'd thrived on it. As a new cop he'd have jumped at the chance to do something like this. Now he appreciated the fact that he could get shot. Although a few years ago he wouldn't have cared, now he had things going his way again. He held his M-16 close to his chest and took a deep breath as the sergeant said, 'Let's get this done,' and all eight men hustled toward the building, weaving past an old rusty swing set with no swings and a slide that rotted before it hit the ground.

Making his way across the open field and road, Tasker felt completely exposed and on edge. A bottle breaking near them made him jump. He kept an eye up high on the three-story building's roof even though he doubted anyone could've survived the counterfire laid down by the cops.

No one peeked out a door as the small squad rushed down the first-floor hallway. Tasker figured anyone not already outside didn't want anything to do with the madness that was brewing in the streets. The old building's wooden floors creaked under his boots as he kept pace with the Miami unit. The smell of stale beer, urine and rotten wood filled his nostrils.

At the base of the stairs, they paused. The sergeant said, 'FDLE, can you cover up the stairs as we take each landing?'

Tasker said, 'No sweat,' and pushed ahead to the front of the group. He liked the feeling of having a job to do with a bunch of cops who just took him at face value: another cop doing his job. Looking back at the sergeant, he said, 'Whenever you're ready.' Then he sighted the long barrel of the M-16 on the door to the roof, three floors above. He could just see it through the railings.

The sergeant said, 'Anyone coming in that door is yours.'

Tasker nodded and kept the rifle to his shoulder.

The sergeant took three men and rushed up the stairs, leaving two men on the second-floor landing, then positioning himself near the door to the roof. He called, 'The rest of you come on up.'

Tasker led the remaining four men up to the sergeant and they lined up to the side of the door, with one man on the other side ready to jerk it open. Tasker's throat was dry. What if they hadn't got the guy and he was waiting for them? What if the whole roof is full of people? He knew there was only one way to find out.

The lone cop jerked open the door and the sergeant rushed through to the right with the second cop jumping to the left. Tasker was the next man through, so he followed the sergeant. He quickly surveyed all of the roof in his path. Nothing. They darted around the little building with the door that sat on the roof, its walls pock-marked by bullet holes, and saw only crates and an old refrigerator.

'Where is he?' asked one of the cops.

'Maybe he slipped back inside,' answered another.

Tasker kept the rifle to his shoulder as he scanned the area. He just caught the movement and yelled, 'There, by the refrigerator.'

Everyone turned and closed on the beat-up yellow Frigidaire on its side. At first it looked like a wad of old clothes, but as they got closer the pile of clothes was breathing. A thin black man in his twenties cowered between the refrigerator and a lawn chair. His head was pushed to the ground and his arms covered it.

When a Miami cop nudged him with his foot, the man started to scream, 'Don't shoot, don't shoot. I give up.'

A hand yanked him up to his feet. He was shaking and sweating with fear and stiff as a plank from head to toe, his wide, bright eyes shining out from under a bushy afro.

The sergeant grabbed him by the collar. 'Why'd you shoot at us?'

'Don't know, don't know. Just got carried away.' Spittle gathered on his lips as he chattered.

'Where's your rifle?'

He pointed with a shaking hand toward the refrigerator. One of the cops kicked it hard with a booted foot, moving it a few inches, exposing the butt of an old, cheap lever-action rifle stuffed behind the motor in the back.

The sergeant tightened his grip. 'Why aren't you dead?'

The man shook his head. 'Look,' he said, holding open his unbuttoned shirt and displaying a pattern of holes that looked like a connect-the-dots picture of a strawberry.

The sergeant said, 'You're too fuckin' skinny, that's all.' He turned to the cops. 'Let's go, and take this asshole with us.'

Tasker looked out over the city and saw smoke from four different fires. In the distance he could hear more gunfire erupting. This wasn't fun anymore.

LOUIS KERPAL shook as he handed the satchel over while staring directly at the gun. 'Please don't hurt me.'

Cole Hodges snatched the bag and looked inside, seeing the CCR T-shirt and patch as well as the cash. 'This is the satchel one of the parishioners bought for the reverend in Mexico. I knew what was in here by the way you held it. You see, Mr. Kerpal, I can read people, and you know what I saw in you every time we met?'

Kerpal shook his head.

'I saw greed.' Hodges moved toward the walkway leading to the street, using the .38 to motion Kerpal back to the front door. 'Greed is the root of almost all problems. As a bank manager, you should be a better example for the kids in the community.'

Kerpal started to whimper, sweat gushing off his forehead.

'You have broken a special bond between banker and customer. I don't think I can continue to do business with this bank. And I'm not comfortable with you finding out about my discretionary fund.'

Kerpal, shaking uncontrollably now, said, 'I won't tell anybody.'

Hodges smiled and said, 'I know.'

six

COLE HODGES held the satchel tight against his dark pin-striped suit as he maneuvered his Lincoln through the rubble on Miami Avenue. The crowds had already moved on to more profitable areas. The few stores that sat on the avenue carried things like old clothes and used books. Nothing worth looting.

Cruising toward the CCR's office on Brickell Avenue, Hodges made his plans. He had to grab some papers, shit he'd been working on for a year or so, like a new birth certificate and a California driver's license in the name of Irving Smalls. He was going to be a financial adviser with a degree in business from the University of Mississippi, magna cum laude, 1973. The million five from the CCR would cushion him until he siphoned another million or so from clients in the Los Angeles area, then he'd return to Florida. After he retrieved his papers, he'd decide what needed to be done with the good Reverend Watson.

No traffic in downtown today, he thought. An occasional police cruiser screamed past on its way to the growing riot. Not much to do in the affluent east business district. Too far for rioters to walk. Hodges pulled into the front of the twenty-story building, taking his pick of all the vacant spots. He'd never seen that before, usually he'd have to drive up the garage for half a mile. He walked through the front door, casually nodding to the feeble old security guard at the console. The ancient moron would've probably called the cops about a black in the lobby if he hadn't recognized him.

The CCR office was open but empty. Reverend Fat-ass must've gone to his flock. Too bad, thought Hodges, it would've been a hoot to blast the pudgy little preacher. Hodges had put up with enough bullshit from the round little faggot to justify a bullet in the head. Oh well, time to pick up his personal papers, erase the main computer's hard drive in case anyone wanted to audit the organization, and complete some strategic shredding. Just to confuse things on his departure to sunny California.

Hodges moved from one giant oak desk to the matching one in the corner of the room, plucking out papers and folders he needed. As he was about to reformat the hard drive of the main computer, he heard the front door open. A second later, Reverend Al Watson peered from around the doorstop.

Watson said, 'Going somewhere, Cole?'

'Greener pastures, my friend, greener pastures.'

'Is it the right thing, leaving our community in its time of need?'

'Cut the shit, Al. I collected my retainer and closed the account at the Alpha National in Overtown. You're gonna have to work the congregation some more.'

Hodges hit the enter button on the computer and watched as the warning came on the screen that everything would be deleted if he continued. Hodges hit enter again and the processor went to work. He looked up at the reverend, then pulled out his .38 and pointed it at the center of the pudgy preacher's belly.

'Back in the other room, Al.'

Watson, unflustered, backed into the main room. 'Cole, you're making a big mistake.'

'Only mistake I've made, Al, is not figuring a way to have more time to enjoy this. I'm not your do-boy, nor do I work *for* you. I'm no damn worker bee. Can't tell you how many times I cringed hearing you tell people what a *valued employee* I was. Goddamn, Al, I was the brains behind this whole operation.'

'Cole, I'm afraid somebody has a rather inflated view of himself. You can't kill me.'

Hodges smiled. 'Why, 'cause I'll feel guilty about it?'

'No, because I'm expecting a news crew from Channel Eleven any second. They want the CCR to broadcast a message of peace.' Watson paused and nodded toward the satchel of cash on the desk Hodges was sitting on. 'You do own a share of that, but only half at best. The rest is mine.'

Hodges said, 'Then consider the other half my inheritance.' Just as Hodges started to squeeze the trigger, the other door in the lobby flew open and a short man waddling under the weight of a TV camera walked in backward, filming a young woman in a neat, striped business suit. Her striking dark eyes were hard to notice with that long straight nose that came to a point like a saber. Another man walked behind the reporter.

Hodges said, 'What the hell is all this?'

Watson didn't change his expression and started to explain, 'This is the crew I told you about.' He turned toward the reporter, who had just finished her intro. 'Hi, Olga, how're you holding up?'

She smiled, revealing artificially white teeth, and said, 'Fine, Reverend, just need you to make the CCR's statement or give me your take on the riot.'

'I'm flattered, Olga, but I really don't know what to make of it.' He smiled warmly and clapped a hand on Hodges's back. 'But Cole here speaks for the entire organization. He needs some credit for his work. After all, he is my most valued employee. Talk to him about profiting in this time of tragedy and how wrong it is to loot, then I'll speak in a little bit.' He patted Hodges again and backed away from the desk, grabbing the satchel as he moved away. 'Isn't that right, Cole, none of us gets enough credit,' Watson said, backing toward the door.

Hodges started to protest when Watson said, 'See you after your interview, Cole,' as he closed the door.

Hodges made a quick phone call before his interview. No way was he gonna let the good reverend pull this off.

TASKER STOOD BEHIND the field force in the middle of Northwest Third Street in the section of Miami known as Overtown. Next to him were two more FDLE agents with MP-5s and one with an M-14 rifle. The FDLE agents' job was to protect the Miami cops from sniper fire. That kept most of their attention on the rooftops of the three- and four-story buildings that dominated this dilapidated part of the city. The crowd on the curb milled around, not willing to commit itself to action. A couple of blocks down the street, a group of about two hundred locals started raising hell with the other field force – throwing bottles and surging up and back. The physics of a riot were unique to each situation. The soccer hooligans of Europe often settled down quickly as the alcohol wore off, but a riot with righteous outrage at its root could grow on itself. Even if arrests were made that could incite the crowd further.

Since talking with Sutter about the past riots, Tasker viewed this one differently. He now saw there were people who just happened to live here and not everyone was causing trouble. In fact, it seemed as if just a few were really trying to stir things up. The people who lived in the neighborhood were going to suffer more than anyone else. Their houses could burn, kids get terrified and businesses be destroyed.

Tasker stood, amazed that things could be so hectic down the road and relatively calm here. He shifted the weight of his tactical vest, which held magazines of nine-millimeter as well as .223 rounds for his AR-15. The sweat that had been pouring out of him since the sniper on the roof shot up the SOT van now soaked his socks and waistband. His eyes burned from the sweat and his head pounded under his heavy ballistic helmet.

A middle-aged black man carefully crossed the street near the FDLE agents. He nodded politely to the heavily armed men, saying, 'Hello, officers. Be careful out here, these folks is crazy.' The heels of his shoes flapped on the ground because he wore old tennis shoes like slippers, crushing the backs with his feet. His lips covered one front tooth until he spoke.

Tasker smiled and nodded back, slowly turning as the man crossed behind them to the crowded side of the street. As the man's foot hit the curb, he turned and joined with some of the crowd screaming, 'Fuck you, cops, you goin' down tonight.'

Tasker laughed; so much for community respect. In the last hour, the taunts had turned from simple calls for justice and short rap verses to specific, personal insults. They liked to pick at his light hair and youthful face, calling him 'vanilla cracker' and 'creamy Oreo filling.' Tasker figured he'd been called worse.

A fat woman in really stretched pants and a Martin Luther King T-shirt, fifteen feet from Tasker, yelled, 'Hey, cracker, you gonna be sweatin' a long time. Can't dodge rocks all night. We gettin' us some cop's ass tonight!'

The agent next to Tasker said, 'You'd empty the whole clip of that AR-15 trying to stop her.'

Tasker nodded and tilted his head back to answer him with the clear face shield down. 'Vinnie, you should keep your shield down.'

'It's too hot and it fogs up. Besides, they're just loudmouths.'

He gripped the stock of the MP-5 as the flashlight under the barrel swept the rooftops looking for threats.

'Better hot than a bottle across your face.'

Vinnie touched a button on the short machine gun's trigger guard, causing the beam of the flashlight to narrow on a man leaning on the balcony of an apartment across the street. Satisfied he was no threat, Vinnie opened the beam again and continued his sweep. 'Like I said, Billy, just a bunch of loudmouths.'

Before Tasker could answer, a rock sailed into the middle of the agents from down the street. Then more debris came from the crowd.

Vinnie yanked down his face shield as a bottle shattered across it. He tilted his head back, saying, 'Like I said, Billy, a bunch of *dangerous* loudmouths.'

Tasker raised the rifle to his shoulder, sighting in on a bottle sailing through the air. 'I wish,' he muttered. All four agents moved from side to side, avoiding rocks and bottles. The cops in front of them, using their big shields to cover themselves, had no trouble. Two cops using their nightsticks like baseball bats were hitting rocks back in the direction they came from.

No one could see who was throwing shit because of the crowds right in front of them. The main body was in front of the field force with a string of people lining the sidewalks past Tasker and the other FDLE agents. It was getting hard to keep an eye on the rooftops with the crowd next to them, and still dodge the rocks.

A muscular guy in his twenties increased the intensity of his taunts as the rocks and bottles subsided. During a lull in the shelling, he screamed, standing on his toes as he leaned into it, 'You fucking cops are gonna pay. Yeah, that's right, you guys dressed in black. Too many of us, we'll run right over you.' Then he'd repeat a variation of the threat like a broken record, never resting.

Tasker saw Vinnie casually turn and lower his MP-5, closing the beam of the flashlight until he illuminated the man in the crowd; then, without looking at the man, Vinnie brought the light beam to a small dot on the man's forehead, between his eyes.

The man's mouth snapped shut in mid-sentence and he stepped back into the crowd, disappearing completely.

Vinnie laughed, 'The shot that's never fired.'

*

DARK CLOUDS ROLLED across the moon again, teasing the tired cops with a downpour. At least it would break up the crowd for a while. But like the earlier clouds, these brushed by to the west, sprinkling the lawns in Hialeah and the Redlands to the south, but only booming and casting the occasional flash of lightning over Overtown and Liberty City.

TASKER TWISTED his neck, trying to stay loose. It had been almost three hours since they'd moved into position, an hour since Vinnie had scared the screamer back into the crowd. The radio traffic coming through Tasker's earpiece from the other field forces told a similar tale: sporadic rocks and bottles while the big groups got more aggressive, moving in packs toward the cops, then in another direction. The police tactics, mostly dodging rocks and abuse and acting individually, changed to military tactics, moving as a group, using the whole field force as a threat. Cops are used to fending off threats alone; it isn't natural to be in a group. Tasker realized that it looked like two armies clashing. Although the whole conflict sent a good scare into Tasker, he noticed some of the other team members looked like they were having a ball.

A Miami captain walked over to the agents. 'Hey, guys, we got a problem.' The tall man in a tailored uniform pointed across a field. 'Some of the rioters broke off and took over our community policing office over in the strip mall.'

Tasker couldn't believe someone would refer to the dilapidated string of two stores and a police office as a 'strip mall.'

'Need you fellas to pump some gas in it. We're gonna retake it. Have to for psychological reasons. Can't let them think we're backing down. It'll embolden the crowd. Happened the last riot and can't happen again.'

Vinnie was already surveying the situation, dropping his MP-5, letting it hang around his shoulder by its strap. He pulled a 37-millimeter gas gun from his rear pack. 'No problem, Captain,' Vinnie said.

The captain turned to his field force and yelled, 'Gas,' causing half the cops to drop to one knee and pull their black gas masks from pouches. It was a drill practiced over and over: half covered while half put on their masks. The FDLE agents did the same thing, switching until everyone was protected.

Just the sight of the masks scared most of the crowd back a block or two, people fading into any open doorway they could find. The force moved toward the small police office, then parted so the FDLE agents could move up. Vinnie stepped up and lofted the gas gun, elevating the barrel to lob a round through the front of the office. Tasker could see people moving around inside the office as Vinnie fired the gas gun with a loud 'whoop' sound, not like a rifle. Then he unsnapped the barrel like a shotgun and dumped the empty round on the ground, quickly replacing it with another CS gas round. He raised the gun and sent a second round into the office. The gas started rising as people streamed from the small building.

Tasker shouted, 'Hey, Vinnie, shouldn't we have warned the other field force?'

'Oops,' Vinnie said, scrambling for his radio. He shouted into the radio, 'Hutch, we deployed gas downwind of you; you might need to suit up.'

Tasker heard a 'No shit' and a cough come back over the radio.

Tasker watched as the cops moved forward, forcing the crowd away from the building out onto the run-down baseball diamond. After twenty minutes of a decent wind caused by the threatening storm, Tasker and his group removed their masks. The cloud of gas had blown over a few blocks and dissipated. The crowd was still feisty, and after taking another minute to shake off the effects of the tear gas, they started to surge toward the other field force at the far end of the ball field. Tasker saw a gas grenade launched from the other field force, then another and another. Two landed in the middle of the crowd, scattering people; the third came close to Tasker's team. A radio crackled, 'Hey, Vinnie, we just launched some gas. Sorry.' Payback was a bitch.

Just then the clouds opened, first with a mist then a torrent, scattering the crowd better than any tear gas ever could.

THE REVEREND Al Watson felt giddy. That was the only word to describe the emotion he was experiencing driving south away from his former office. He patted the satchel of cash at his side and giggled. Not only had he bluffed his way out of a dangerous spot, he had Cole Hodges's share of the cash and had put that uppity shyster in his place. Maybe God did favor him. He'd spouted that Baptist bullshit for so long maybe God was just showing his appreciation.

At the red light between Tiger Tail and Bird Road, Watson looked in the rearview mirror to check his tight hair. There was no doubt he was one of the beautiful people, and now he was a rich beautiful person. He deserved it. He smiled at himself in the mirror and noticed a car behind him. On a second look, he realized the car had no driver. As he looked out the windshield, he caught a glimpse of a large black revolver pointed at his head from the side window. He heard a tap on the window and slowly reached down and touched the power window button.

'May I help you, friend?' Watson asked, with a noticeable shake in his voice. He was too scared to stomp on the gas.

'Yes, Reverend. I need your satchel.'

The heavy white man looked familiar. 'Do I know you, friend?' asked Watson, never looking directly at the barrel of the gun.

'Tom Dooley, FBI, and I'm gonna need your cash.'

Watson's voice cracked. 'Can we work this out, friend?'

'No,' Dooley said.

Watson didn't even hear the gunfire, everything just went blank.

seven

BILL TASKER'S BODY felt dull, that was the only way to describe it. He'd been on continuous duty for nearly sixty-five hours, and if that line of thunderstorms hadn't moved over the city he'd still be watching the rooftops for Miami PD. Now, in front of the Miami FDLE office, Tasker and the remaining members of the special operations team were breaking down their equipment and preparing for one long weekend. Someone had already cracked a case of Icehouse and started exaggerating the exploits of the team. Tasker focused on ensuring no tear gas residue remained on his gear bag or clothes. His eyes still watered a little, but his sinuses would be clear for at least a month. He had no idea his head could produce that much snot. If the general public found out the hidden benefits of tear gas, cops would never be able to buy it cheap again. Luckily, the two field forces gassing each other had also managed to gas some of the rioters so no one had taken advantage of the coughing, hacking cops. It was still embarrassing. The rain had been the biggest factor in breaking up the crowds, no matter what some of the team members were saying now.

Other FDLE agents were arriving from their various assignments throughout the city. Most had been able to nap for a few hours and grab some decent food, making them more active and talkative than the special ops team members, who'd had no respite. Tasker ignored the new arrivals until he heard the soft voice of Tina Wiggins behind him. He twisted to see her standing, like a model just off the cover of *Glamour*.

'There he is,' she said to an older agent standing with her. 'He's cute in black.'

The male agent said, 'How'd it go? We heard Steve Pape got hit. How is he?'

Tasker, turning to stand and face them, said, 'Clean wound through the arm. Lost some blood, but he'll be okay. He'll be braggin' about the scar and telling people he stormed the crowd alone in no time.'

'Did you get the bastard who shot him?'

'Yeah, just some crazed crackhead with a lever-action hunting rifle.'

The man smiled. 'How many times you guys plug him?'

Tasker shrugged. 'None. Not for lack of effort. The cops and us did forty-six thousand bucks' damage with return fire to the building he was hiding on.'

Tina cut in, 'I wouldn't worry about it. There was a lot worse damage on Miami Avenue and out Twentieth.'

Tasker said, 'Like what?'

'Six big fires gutted a couple of apartment buildings, about fifty stores were looted, forty houses were destroyed and a bank in Overtown was hit pretty good.'

'How many dead?'

'So far only three. A lot of injuries, one little girl was hit with a stray bullet but she'll live. Six cops, including Steve, were hurt. Overall, the city weathered it pretty well.'

Her dark, perfect lips had a hypnotic effect on Tasker. He gazed at the ends of her straight white teeth, framed by those lips, and lost track of where he was. It was through this fog he heard her.

'Bill? Bill, you okay?' She reached up and shook his shoulder.

'Yeah, yeah, just tired.' His eyes focused. 'Which bank got hit?'

Tina said, 'I think Alpha National of Overtown. They killed the manager and rummaged through a half dozen safe-deposit boxes.'

Tasker thought about his desire to surveil the bank before the riot. Too bad he wasn't there with the team when it happened. Things never worked out perfectly.

Tina continued, 'We heard one of the boxes that got hit belonged to the CCR's treasurer, Cole Hodges.' Her eyes lit up. 'Lots of cash there, I bet.'

Tasker looked at her. 'How do you know it had cash?'

'Everyone knows the CCR probably has ten boxes hidden all over Miami.' She looked off toward the city to the east. 'Just one would be nice.'

*

TINA STAYED and helped Tasker put up the last of his gear, unloading his AR-15, brushing off dust and tear gas from his vest, chatting with him about her first riot experience. Her brown eyes seemed to wrap around him and squeeze tight.

'This wasn't so bad. Since I spent most of my time watching the riots from the top of a condo, it was more like a TV show than an actual disaster.'

Tasker said, 'I would have been happy to trade for your intel duty.'

'You SWAT guys like that kind of tactical stuff.'

'I used to like tactical stuff more. Now I do it because it has to be done. I prefer more cooperative crooks, the kind that surrender or confess. Maybe I'm lazy.'

'I just thought you were easygoing.'

'I've heard that I'm too easygoing.'

She smiled, appraising him as she said, 'I wouldn't worry about it. I see a lot of the guys from the south handle things the easy way, just like the former New York cops here come down hard on everyone. It's a cultural thing.'

'You think?'

'Sure. South Florida is one of those few places where half the cops are from up north and the other half natives. You can really see the mix. In New York, it's standard to jump into someone's business; down here we let things develop. I wouldn't worry too much about it.'

He nodded, almost telling her about what being laid-back had done to him. He knew she'd heard all the stories and rumors about the incident, but he wanted her to hear the truth from him, and decided that now was not the time. Instead he changed the subject.

'Got any plans for your four days of comp leave?'

'My sister and I are going to go diving.'

'I didn't know you had a sister down here. Thought your family lived in central Florida.'

'They do, except Jeanie goes to FIU.'

'What's she studying?'

'She wants to be a teacher. But right now she's a dancer at Pure Platinum and doesn't want to give up the money.'

Tasker stared at her in silence. Was she pulling his chain? Had he not understood?

Tina said, 'That's right. She strips at Pure Platinum. You're the only one at FDLE I ever told. Hope you can keep a secret.'

'Yeah, I ... I can.'

She kissed him on the lips. 'Good, so can I.'

TOM DOOLEY chuckled every time one of his fellow ace FBI special agents walked past his desk. The clueless bastards had no idea his entire lower file drawer was stuffed with money. He'd hidden the Reverend Watson's satchelful of cash the last place anyone would ever look for it: the Miami office of the Federal Bureau of Investigation. All the years of being ignored by the other agents made this all the sweeter. In a few days, he'd figure what to do with the cash and then slide out on retirement. No one would ever notice the spending money he'd have. He could virtually disappear. Only need a PO box for his government check.

He sat at his desk in the bay that was his permanent assignment. There were eight other agents with desks in the open office that was actually a big opening in the main hallway. He had dividers on either side of his desk and a small, issued file cabinet to the right. On the wall were four of his citations for bravery and three photos of his sons. One was of his soccer team, with Dooley as the dutiful coach standing to the side of the youngsters. Dooley liked to gaze up at that photo all the time. Coaching those kids was something he was proud of, that didn't remind him of his darker ambitions. He left the photo on this wall no matter where he worked.

His supervisor had sent him to the robbery task force because some of the other agents had bitched about him. It kept him out of sight. But now he liked hanging out in his regular office. He'd heard that the Bureau was looking into the robbery of the Overtown bank. Originally they'd thought it was looters, but something had clued them in to a more specific crime. Dooley knew that if he stayed at his desk long enough he'd pick up some scoop and get an idea what was going on.

It had taken a few hours, but finally Dooley heard two of the younger guys talk about the bank. The lead agent was some kind of Mideasterner, or maybe even an Oriental, named Slayda Nmir but he liked to be called 'Mac.' Who could figure? The slim, dark, neatly groomed thirty-year-old looked more like a hairstylist than a Fed, and he'd clearly never cared for Dooley, but that didn't stop Dooley from barreling into a conversation with him.

'Hey, Mac. What's doing?' Dooley asked, sliding up to the desk the man was working at.

Mac looked up through rimless oval glasses. 'Got the robbery at the Alpha National in Overtown.'

'Yeah? Rioters loot it?'

'Don't think so. Looks like one robber, and he killed the manager.'

'No shit. Any leads?'

'A few.'

'What about the security cameras?'

'Have you ever seen the banks over there? The only cameras are focused on the tellers, and they only work once in a while.'

'The robber get much?'

Nmir looked Dooley over before he answered. 'Only a half-dozen safe-deposit boxes were popped. One belonged to Cole Hodges and Al Watson. Watson's gone missing. A witness said he's seen a cop hanging around the bank so we're looking into that, too.'

'A cop? How'd he know it was a cop?' Dooley swallowed hard, as a wave of adrenaline swept through him. Had he fucked up this bad?

Nmir hesitated, then said, 'He's a crackhead. Remembers a white Buick but says all cops look alike to him. The cop said he'd hurt him if he didn't move on.' His dark eyes stayed on Dooley, unnerving him.

Dooley had been around too long to panic. He knew more about being calm in the face of catastrophe than this dark-gened, curry-eating, perfume-wearing little son of a whore would ever know. Was he looking at Dooley with suspicion? Dooley doubted it. His mind raced as he considered his options. He took a breath as he saw a chance. An idea that could only have come from God slipped into his head. It was so perfect he had to move without going over it in his head. He could buy some time and put the suspicion off him with just a casual comment.

He said, 'I know a cop who was mighty interested in that particular bank.'

Mac said, 'Come on, Dooley, I don't have time for any of your games.'

'No kidding. A cop on my task force seemed obsessed with that bank. He even wanted to do his own surveillances there. Even after I canceled the idea.'

'Who is this guy?'

'An FDLE agent named Tasker, Bill Tasker. And he's even got a Buick the Bureau gave him for the task force.'

'Is he reasonable? I mean, you think I could talk to him about this just to clear things up?'

'He seems okay, but who can tell here in Miami? Everyone is running some kind of game.'

Mac said, 'Thanks, Dooley, I'll look into this. Maybe it'll lead somewhere.'

'Anytime, sport.' Dooley smiled, thinking, It'll lead somewhere, I guarantee it.

SITTING BEHIND the wheel of his Lincoln Continental, Cole Hodges saw the fat, red-faced FBI man stroll casually out of the plain three-story building in North Miami. He wrapped his big hand around the grip of his Rossi .38 and slowly put the car in drive.

Cole Hodges wasn't just mad, he hated this son of a bitch. Thinking he was smarter than everyone else. Not realizing that Cole was a much better crook than he was. Hodges wasn't even that upset that he didn't get to put one in Reverend Al's face, but what did piss him off, he was furious because someone else had what was his. Years ago in prison, Hodges had learned that you had to keep what was rightfully yours or everyone would start taking from you. Hodges lived by that creed and often used it to take from others, but he had never let anyone steal from him. Hodges remembered Dooley from their one meeting. He didn't seem like a common FBI man. Tougher and cruder than most, with a tendency to tie a long string of curse words together like he didn't even know he was doing it. Hodges was sure he'd give the guy something to curse about soon.

Hodges eased the car forward, waiting for the fat man to roll up in that cheesy white Buick. It would be sweet watching the FBI man's brain spurt onto the headrest from a hollow point into his nose. He opened the cylinder and spun it to see that all six rounds were seated properly, then clicked it shut.

'C'mon, meat. Got a surprise for you,' he said out loud to the empty car. 'You're not half as slick as you think you are.' Hodges couldn't believe that Dooley thought he was the only one interested in the cash. How could the FBI agent think that Hodges wouldn't keep someone on the reverend? As the reverend had walked out the door with the cash, Hodges had called his assistant and all-around fuck-up, Ebbi Kyle, who had seen the FBI man drive off behind the reverend's car. At the time, the pencil thin, part-time crack addict had thought it was an official FBI arrest and backed off. Ebbi never questioned anything. After Hodges took care of this problem, he'd be having a serious talk with Ebbi, too. That little shit had to get his act together.

Hodges saw Dooley's car finally exit the lot and head out toward the 826 expressway. As soon as the Buick was past him, Hodges would roll up and pop the man and take what was his.

The car rolled by and Hodges turned onto the street smooth as glass. You don't have to be a cop to follow people. Hodges laughed, this motherfucker's been followed twice in four days and still doesn't have a clue. Hodges watched to make sure, but the middle-aged man with the thinning hair kept looking forward, his hand nervously shifting on the wheel.

As Dooley stopped his car at the light onto the 826 heading east, the only other car caught an arrow west. It was time. Hodges slowly eased to the left of the Buick, rolling down his electric window with his left hand as he held the steering wheel and the gun with his right. The FBI man still hadn't turned to look. Hodges figured he'd beep to get Dooley's attention.

Hodges raised the pistol and started to tap the horn when it hit him like a sledgehammer: What if the man didn't have the cash in the car? How would Hodges ever find it if he killed Dooley first and asked questions later? He dropped the gun and looked straight ahead to not draw any attention to himself. He'd have to follow this ass around until he was certain he had the cash. Ebbi should've taken care of this. Now Hodges would handle it himself. One way or another, he'd make this FBI man wish he'd never heard of Cole Hodges.

eight

B ILL TASKER spent the ride into the robbery task force office going over in his head what he would tell Dooley about the need to go after serious robbery groups. In the days since the riots, things around the city had returned to the normal boiling point with the friction between the different ethnic groups just below the surface and the Miami police right in the middle. The local police forces had thousands of cops, more than thirty of them working primarily in robbery. The general street corner and convenience store robberies were worked by these units. No one was looking at the organized groups that actually planned robberies. The kind of guys they made movies about or who were profiled on the History Channel. This was the frustration of the cops on the robbery task force. The crooks actually causing the biggest problems got the least attention. That had been Tasker's goal the night the clerk killed the robber: recruit the robber as a confidential informant to help investigate other robbers he knew. Work up the ladder until they had an important robbery group ready to take down. It was the same story in all areas of law enforcement: narcotics, burglary, any crime where organized groups tend to make the biggest splash. Those ideas of working up the ladder had died on the floor of the Quick Stop when the clerk was faster on the draw than the bad guy. But as the police get more involved with informants, and efforts to penetrate criminal organizations become more intense, the potential for corruption among the cops grew, too. Tasker knew that all too well. An investigator might cut a corner or two to allow his snitch to stay on the street where he could make a case. Sometimes, especially in drug cases, a cop might see the carloads of easy money to be made and forget the oath he took when he became a cop. Tasker didn't work that way, no matter what people in West Palm said about him.

The whole trip from Kendall to the North Miami office, Tasker had built these facts into an argument with which to confront the FBI member of the task force and back up his demand for more important robbery cases. Dooley would have to see the logic in this argument. He knew the two local cops, Bema and Sutter, would jump right on board. They'd been screaming for the same thing, virtually electing Tasker as their spokesman.

Inside the building, he found their squad bay empty except for the mousy secretary the FBI provided to work on this task force, the telemarketing task force next door and the stolen car task force down the hall. The three squads also shared a crime intelligence analyst. Tasker's desk was clean because they hadn't worked anything since the convenience store clerk killed their only suspect.

After a few minutes, Tasker heard the continuous banter of Bema and Sutter as they came down the hall.

Bema finished a statement, 'And that's why there will be a Cuban president of the United States in the next twenty years.'

Sutter grumbled, 'Not if I can still aim a gun.'

Tasker stood, saying, 'Glad to see everything is back to normal.'

Bema smiled. 'Mr. SWAT. Ready to get back to work?'

Sutter said, 'On what?'

Tasker said, 'We'll work that out today. Let's pin Dooley down on some major investigations.'

Sutter said, 'We can't really look at the Overtown bank. It got hit during the riot.'

Tasker said, 'I heard. Who's working that?'

'We haven't seen Dooley, but I saw FBI guys on the news going through the bank. No one even tried to get into the vault. Just some boxes.'

Tasker said, 'Maybe the Bureau will want us to work some surveillance on the case. The FBI agents hate working nights.'

Bema cut in, 'The ones I seen hate working days, too.'

All three men laughed out loud at the expense of their missing partner.

Tasker cut out of the task force office about two o'clock with the intention of heading over to the FBI office a few miles west, near I-

95. He'd practiced what he was going to say to Dooley for so long that he had to try today. He figured the FBI man was roosting at his own office until the task force started to kick up again.

As he set his notebook on the roof of his Buick and fumbled with the keys, a thin, well-groomed young guy approached him. 'Bill Tasker?' asked the man.

Tasker took a second to look him over, always aware how long it would take him to reach for his Beretta in his belly pack. The guy didn't look like a threat, dressed in a nice suit and a World Wildlife Fund tie with a panda on it. 'I am, and who are you?'

'My name is Slayda Nmir.' He pulled an ID out of his back pocket. 'I'm a special agent with the FBI.'

'I'm sorry, what was your first name again?'

'Slayda."

Well, Sl-Slay-Slad.' Tasker didn't want to insult the guy.

'Call me Mac. Everyone does.'

Tasker paused to look at him more closely. 'Okay, Mac. I was just on my way over to the FBI office.'

'What for?'

'Looking for my fellow task force member, Tom Dooley.' Tasker paused and looked the young man over again. 'What can I do for you, Mac?'

'You know about the Overtown bank being robbed on Thursday?'

'I heard.' Tasker couldn't keep his eyes from shifting around him. What was up? The hair on his neck was standing on end.

'Know any of the details?'

'Nope.'

'The manager, Louis Kerpal, was shot and killed, and six safe-deposit boxes were opened. Three of the box owners said there wasn't anything but important papers in them. One box still had the jewelry the owner left in it. One owner was a Santoro, you know a Santeria priest, who's been dead for about a year. He was killed by a guy he put a curse on after cutting off his two index fingers.' Mac paused and appraised Tasker, like he might have something to say.

Tasker said, 'This is interesting, but why are you telling me?'

'I'm telling you because the last box most likely had something of value. Probably cash.'

'Uh-huh.' Tasker was waiting for the punch line.

'That belonged to the Committee for Community Relief. The outfit run by the Reverend Alvin Watson. Ring a bell?'

'I've heard of Watson and the CCR, but I still don't see what that has to do with me' Tasker's stomach tightened and he couldn't figure out why.

'Didn't you push hard for a surveillance of the Overtown bank right before the riot?'

'Yeah, we had some intel that it might be hit.'

Mac made a note on a steno pad, then asked, 'Where'd the intel come from?'

Tasker shrugged. 'I dunno, word on the street, that sort of thing.'

Mac nodded, made another note. 'Have you done any surveillance on it?'

'No, why?'

'Is this your only assigned vehicle?' Mac patted the Buick Century but didn't take his eyes off Tasker.

'Yeah, it is …' Then it hit Tasker like a brick. This guy was asking if he was involved in a robbery and murder. When you're used to questioning others, it isn't easy to realize when you're the suspect.

Mac kept rolling. 'Can you account for the time between the announcement of the verdict last Thursday and the time you reported to the Miami PD parking lot?'

'Yeah, well, I got gas and traffic was really rough.' Tasker stopped. His knees felt like rubber bands. 'Wait a minute. You actually checked to see when I reported to duty? You think I hit the bank? This is bullshit!'

'It may be, but I have to look at all angles here. Witnesses place you at the U.S attorney's office about one-thirty, and the FDLE radio log shows you at the Miami PD around five-thirty. That's plenty of time to cut over to Overtown and grab some spending money.'

Tasker looked at the smug agent and said, 'You ever been a real cop?'

This simple comment is known in all of law enforcement to be the harshest and most subtle cut you can use against an FBI agent. The inference being that all the accountants and teachers the FBI hires and molds in its own image don't have any street experience or common sense.

Mac looked like he'd been kicked. 'No, but I've been with the Bureau four years now. What's that got to do with anything?'

'I'm just curious how you jumped to this wild conclusion that I robbed that bank.' He felt his face flush and resisted the urge to just walk away.

'Did I say you robbed it?'

'Then why these questions?'

'It's called an investigation, and I have to do it to find out who took the cash.' Nmir's slim face showed no tension, like he was chatting with a neighbor.

'Then I'm not a suspect?'

'I didn't say that either.'

'Let's stop for one second and figure out how we got here. Why are you even looking at me?'

'A witness put a cop in a white Buick in front of the bank. I heard you were interested in the bank for the task force, you have a pretty big gap in your day last Thursday, and the manager was killed with a thirty-eight, a cop's kind of gun. Now, wouldn't you talk to someone with those kind of strikes against them?'

'Yes, I would, after I examined the source of the information. Like who was the witness.'

Mac looked hard at Tasker, like he was letting him in on a secret. 'Okay, I'll level with you. The witness is a crack dealer who works that corner, but everything else points to you like a big neon sign. I'm trying to give you a break. If you come clean right now, you could get one hell of a deal.'

Tasker's hand darted up and grabbed Nmir's lapel. The smaller man grabbed Tasker's twisting hand but had little effect. Tasker pulled the calm FBI agent close so their noses almost touched, and said, 'What kind of moron uses shitty information like that to accuse a working cop of a crime?'

Nmir answered slowly, 'The kind of moron who's seen your personnel jacket and knows what you've done in the past.'

Tasker felt a shock run through his body and released the other man.

Mac straightened his tie and said, 'Convince me I'm wrong, then. Just talk to me, Tasker.'

'You're way off.' Tasker grabbed a deep breath. 'Sounds like Tom Dooley may have given you some of your info. He didn't like the idea of us locals directing where we look for robbers. He was at the U.S. attorney's office, too. Am I right?'

Mac hesitated. 'He's a lazy loudmouth, but he is an FBI special agent. He has a duty.'

Tasker took another breath. 'I deny the charges and deny any of Dooley's assertions. Now what?'

'I have more work to do. Your administration will probably suspend you, pending the outcome of my investigation.'

'That's where you're wrong. I don't work for the Feds. I work for a decent law enforcement agency. They'll see this crock and tell you to pound sand. No way they'll suspend me.'

With that, Slayda Nmir nodded and backed away. Tasker watched him pull out of the lot. He'd thought no one cared about his past anymore. How many times could a bad decision ruin your life?

nine

'I'M SUSPENDED,' Tasker said, looking deep into Tina Wiggins's dark eyes. 'I cannot fucking believe this.'

Tina asked, 'What'd the boss say?'

'He's gotta follow protocol. The Feebs sent him a letter classifying me as a target. The director was cool about it. Said he knew it was a bunch of shit, but he had to put me on leave until it's cleared up.'

'Paid or unpaid?'

'Paid leave. That's what I mean, the director is supportive, only quietly. Shit, I never thought it'd go this far.'

An older Cuban agent sitting in the squad bay patted him on the back as he walked past. 'Don't sweat it, Tiger. Even if you were guilty I never seen the FBI ever indict someone on shit like this. A good cop can always outsmart them.'

'Jesus, I don't need to outsmart them, I didn't do anything.' His eyes bulged, looking at the older man.

'Okay, Billy, but good luck anyway. It's not like last time. No one thinks you done this. I'll be watching to make sure they don' try an' fuck you, no?'

Tasker and Tina watched him shuffle into the hallway. Tasker was too stunned to do anything but sit and feel the pulse of the office.

Tina said, 'Bill, you okay?'

He blinked hard a couple of times. 'I guess so. What about you? You can't be seen with me for a while, either.'

'Says who?'

'The director.'

'He can't tell you how to live your life.'

Tasker hardly heard her as he tried to consider his options. If he stayed within his comfort zone he would just sit back and let things happen. He did that once and it never solved anything. He'd have to clear this up fast and completely. His daughters and ex-wife couldn't face the media storm again.

'You're right!' Tasker said, springing to his feet and stepping toward her. 'They can't tell me what to do with my private life.' He held her shoulders, feeling an odd sensation surge through him. 'Policy says I have to check in at eight every morning and check out at five, but that's just over the phone, and the director shouldn't give a damn what I do in between or at night.'

Tina stepped back. 'Billy, this is not like you.'

'Good.'

'Are you sure about this?'

'It's the new me.'

'But what are you going to do?'

'Just like we do every day: develop some leads, then follow them up.'

'What do you have to develop?'

'For starters, I need to find out for sure how I even got mentioned. Then I'll pay a visit to the Eighth Street Boyz and see what I can squeeze out of them.'

'Why them?'

'That's who our intel said was going to hit the bank.'

'The Eighth Street Boyz are a tough group. Maybe I should come with you.'

'No, I can't get you involved. In case everything goes to hell, you need to be clear.'

Tina looked at him. 'But what if they have the money?'

'What do you mean? If they have it, I'm off the hook.'

'I mean, they're not gonna let you just waltz out of their clubhouse with a big box of cash.'

'Trust me, I'll work something out.' He felt as if his blood were on fire and his brain buzzed with possibilities. Then he came back to reality. 'Tina, I doubt the director wants you to be anywhere around me.'

She waved her hand, dismissing his concern. 'Oh. That's here in the office. No one can dictate *my* personal life. I can see you later. Like maybe at your house.'

'Really?'

'Sure. How 'bout eight?' She smiled at Tasker, almost blinding him with those perfect teeth. 'Bill?'

'Yeah?'

'You don't have the cash, do you?' Before he could answer, she held up a hand. 'I'm not saying anything except that Watson is a crook and he shouldn't get it back.'

'Doesn't matter. I don't know anything about any cash or safe-deposit box or even much about the CCR.'

She looked at him as deeply as he was looking at her. 'You could tell me and be safe knowing I'd never tell anyone.'

'Thanks, but I don't need the help in this particular situation.' Tasker thought he saw disappointment flash across her face, but he couldn't be sure.

TOM DOOLEY sat at his official desk within the actual Federal Bureau of Investigation offices in North Miami. He avoided the task force office down the street because he figured the members of the task force still there would hear he dropped a dime on Tasker. People were starting to talk about the FDLE agent who ripped off the Reverend Al. Nothing on the news yet, but the rumors were circulating. It was rare that one of those hotshot state guys ever got in trouble, so everyone wanted to believe it. In truth, Dooley had felt a little guilty setting Tasker up. He seemed like a nice enough kid and didn't give Dooley the shit the locals constantly threw at him. In fact, Dooley had thought he was a little on the spineless side until Tasker jumped out of the freezer during the robbery. He had balls. Dooley just hoped he didn't have enough brains to get out from under the Bureau's spotlight.

Dooley hadn't even known that Tasker had been in shit before. He seemed like such a Boy Scout. He'd heard through the grape-vine that Tasker had been mixed up with some crooked local cop in Palm Beach County but they never charged him. That just made him the most perfect patsy since Lee Harvey Oswald.

Dooley spent most of his day trying to figure out what he was going to do with the cash and where he was going to live. He didn't think anyone suspected his involvement, but sometimes he had the feeling someone was following him. He'd even pulled a couple of countersurveillance moves yesterday afternoon in case someone was behind him. Just a feeling. It would pass. The agent looking at the bank robbery, the fucking dot-head, or whatever he was, Slayda 'Mac' Nmir, seemed to have a pretty good focus on Tasker. The little bugger was industrious if nothing else.

He'd already managed to get Tasker suspended and was working on further leads a few desks away from Dooley at that very moment.

Whenever the young agent spoke on the phone or to another agent about the case, Dooley kept an ear open to pick up what he could. As long as they went after Tasker, he didn't see a problem. As he browsed through a brochure on the opportunities for Americans in Costa Rica, Dooley heard Mac, talking to an assistant U.S. attorney on the phone about his big fucking case. The one side of the conversation he heard didn't make him happy.

Mac kept nodding like the U.S. attorney could see him, repeating 'Uh-huh, uh-huh.' Then he said, 'No, just the witness and that gap of time no one can account for him. Nothing solid.' After a pause, he continued, 'That's right, he was never charged. In fact, the FDLE internal process cleared him in that whole thing, but something fishy went on.' He wrote down something, then said, 'No, he's suspended but the bank records don't show any odd spending, nothing out of the ordinary.' He closed by saying, 'I will. If something comes up, you'll be the first to know.' He hung up with a long sigh.

Dooley leaned back in his chair. 'Tough day, Mic?'

'That's Mac, Dooley.'

'Oh, you're Scottish, not Irish, I keep forgetting.'

Mac didn't reply, throwing a dirty look down to Dooley.

Dooley smiled, thinking, You fucking new guys think you're smarter than us seasoned vets. He unlocked the lower drawer to his small steel file cabinet and peeked at the satchel lying on the bottom, then chuckled.

'What's so funny, Dooley?' asked Mac.

'Nothing you'd understand, sonny.' Dooley sat, going over an idea he'd had bumping around in his head for a few hours now. He was always moving one step ahead of others, but now he needed to move way ahead. He could do something. Maybe plant evidence that Mac wouldn't find for a few days. Maybe make it so he's out of town in case anyone ever suspected what he'd done. Dooley opened the drawer again. There was a lot of cash in that damn satchel. Maybe it was time to move it anyway. Dooley gathered it up and got ready to leave for the day. It might be a good investment to give some of the money away. Sorta like the people who donated it had envisioned in the first place.

TASKER PRACTICED the breathing exercises he'd learned in the months following his near mental collapse before exile to Miami. The therapist had made it seem so simple: breathe properly and your problems go away. What a crock. Breathe properly and you have to keep living and therefore your problems get worse. Those were the negative thoughts the therapist had warned him about. Now, in his car it took deep breathing just to take the traffic northbound on I-95 until he could cut down Miami Gardens to the task force office. Before he could start his own investigation, he needed to know where some of it had come from. More accurately, he needed to know why Dooley had said anything at all. He knew the FBI agent had passed on information, but he didn't know what Dooley hoped to gain. It couldn't be interagency rivalries; at least he didn't think it could.

At the FBI task force building, Tasker zipped his Cherokee into a spot one row back from the building. He sat and looked at what used to be his office. Quiet today, the car theft guys probably out on one of their mammoth surveillances and his guys spread out over the city. He stared at the front door, his throat dry and breathing shallow. Should he really be doing shit like this? Would people accuse him of interfering with the investigation and trying to cover his tracks? This didn't seem like a good idea.

He wiped his face with his bare hand, then started to throw the Jeep into reverse when he saw Dooley pull up in his issued Buick. The fat man didn't hesitate to pop out of the car with his hands full and start to waddle toward the front door.

Tasker froze, quietly hoping the FBI man wouldn't notice him. Too late, he paused, mid-stride, looked down at the leather bag in his right hand and then changed direction to head straight for Tasker.

'What's doin'?' asked the heavyset man as Tasker lowered his window. Then, with a different look, he cocked his head. 'You off suspension?'

'No, thanks to you,' Tasker snapped.

'What's that supposed to mean?'

'I know you pushed Mac Nmir toward me. Was he so weak on leads you guys had to make something up?'

Dooley bent down and set the heavy leather bag between his legs. 'You're way off there, cowboy. I told the investigating agent of the FBI that I heard you and others show a lot of interest in that particular bank. Nothing personal, but I have a responsibility to report things that may be pertinent to a bank robbery.'

Tasker took a second to gather his thoughts and assess his former partner. Dooley was doing his fair share of sweating from the heat as he bent down to pick up the bag again. Filling his lungs with air, Tasker said, 'You know our interest was in the Eighth Street Boyz robbing the bank, not the actual bank.'

Dooley nodded. 'I know, I know. That little sand nigger has gone overboard on this whole thing. It'll blow over soon enough. I wouldn't worry about it.'

'I gotta worry about it. It's my life.'

Dooley turned like he'd said all he was going to say. 'You need to relax. Go home, have a beer and grill a steak.'

'I wish I could, Tom. But I don't think like that and I haven't used my grill in a month. But I know what I *am* going to do and I don't give a shit what the Federal Bureau of Investigation thinks about it.'

Dooley shook his head. 'Sounds like you're going to do your own little investigation. I doubt you should get involved. Let little Mac handle it.' He started toward the building, his right arm weighed down by the leather bag, and said over his shoulder, 'Good luck, kid. In whatever you do.'

Tasker wished he had a pistol as he watched Dooley disappear into the building,

AFTER A FEW MINUTES of cooling down and a quick box of Kentucky Fried Chicken to fill him up, Tasker was on Seventh Avenue headed south looking for the clubhouse of Miami's most famous street gang, the Eighth Street Boyz. They were famous for being around so long, almost fifteen years, and being tough. They were responsible for at least twelve murders and thousands of beatings. Things had changed when their leaders found they liked being on TV and hired a media relations team smart enough to turn their image around, at least within the confines of Liberty City and Overtown. In the past two years, they had tried to show young people other ways of becoming a success than dealing crack. Unfortunately, most of the Miami cops believed that alternative included organizing theft rings and jumping on the occasional big hit, like the Alpha National Bank of Overtown.

Tasker took a right on Tenth Street, hardly noticing the stares of the young African-Americans on the corner who obviously couldn't figure out what a white guy not in a police car would be doing in this neighborhood. He looked for the converted bar that now stood as the headquarters for the Eighth Street Boyz, even though it was on Tenth Street. He wondered if they really couldn't have found something on Eighth and kept everyone from making jokes about it. He had heard that they kept the name because the Cubans didn't like them taking the name of their community's most famous street. Even though this was NW Eighth Street and the Cuban population and business district centered around SW Eighth, more popularly known as Calle Ocho.

Tasker pulled right up front and, without hesitating, slid out of his car and up to the front door of the mainly windowless, partially painted, low-roofed building where he hoped to find some answers. Now he wished he had a gun. Since he'd turned in his Beretta when he'd been suspended, he'd had no choice unless he wanted to carry his personal Remington hunting rifle, but that would be a little obvious even in Miami. It didn't matter, not even gang members wanted to risk hurting a cop. He took only a few seconds to build his nerve, then pushed through the unlocked swinging door.

A black man in his early thirties gave Tasker a tired look. Never changing his hands as they wiped down a glass from behind a small bar, the man asked, 'You a cop?'

'What do you think?' Tasker took a moment to glance around the room. It was just the two of them and he could tell from the spartan surroundings that no one was hiding behind any furniture. A broken-down sofa sat on one wall, a couple of tables with chairs were set around an elaborate pool table.

The bartender continued to assess Tasker, then said, 'Well, Officer, in that case, unless you have a warrant, reviewed by an authorized state attorney, signed by a sitting member of the Miami-Dade County or circuit bench and presented to me immediately, you better get your cracker ass out of here.'

'Whoa, whoa, hold on, Clarence Darrow. I just want to talk. I'm not here to hassle anyone.'

'Talk about what?'

'The Alpha National Bank in Overtown.' He kept his stare on the man.

'In case you haven't looked around, this is Liberty City. You gotta cross I-95 before you reach the area known as Overtown.'

'I thought Liberty City started up by Sixty-second Street.'

'Liberty City is a state of mind. It starts and ends where we want it to.'

'Then where's Overtown?'

'Stop playing games, man.'

'No games. I'm just interested in the Alpha National in Overtown.'

'Why would you ask us about something in the ghetto?'

'Why did the FBI say they were asking?'

The bartender screwed up his face. 'The who?'

'The FBI. Didn't they come by and ask any questions?'

'When?'

Now Tasker was confused. 'I don't know. In the last few days?'

'I haven't seen no Feds, and the Boyz would've told me if anyone was by. I think you got the wrong place.'

Tasker looked at the calm man. He thought, *Un-fucking-believable.* Then he asked out loud, 'No one's been by?'

'Are you deaf? I told you no. Now why are you asking about an Overtown bank?'

Tasker felt his confidence slip away, but pushed himself. 'The Alpha National Bank in Overtown lost some cash during the riot.'

The bartender set down the glass. 'You think we're stupid enough to waste our time on some low-life Overtown bank?'

'You're stupid enough to have your clubhouse on Tenth Street when you're named the Eighth Street Boyz.'

'Listen up, cracker. If we hit a bank, we'd hit the white man's bank. And even if we did, why would I tell you?'

Tasker nodded. 'That's a good question.'

'How 'bout a good answer?'

'I know some of you are trying to be role models. This story gets out, a lot of kids could be disappointed. You help me out and I guarantee I keep it quiet.' It was a long shot, but all he had right now.

The bartender looked like he was considering it, then he smiled, looking right at Tasker.

Tasker felt someone else in the room and jerked his head around to see four more men around him. Another younger man, maybe twenty, stayed by the door and slid a bolt that locked the swinging door closed.

The bartender said, 'Two things, cracker. We may have thought about that bank, but we found out Cole Hodges does business there and we're not about to fuck with him.'

Tasker swallowed and said, 'What's the other thing?'

'We ain't got time for suspended cracker cops.'

Before Tasker could say anything, he felt a couple of sets of hands seize him by the shoulders and arms.

COLE HODGES had decided to take other measures after two days of watching the fat son of a bitch. His plan now was to follow Dooley from the FBI office and, when the opportunity presented itself, knock that cop asshole over the head and find out where he'd hidden the damn cash. Hodges felt this type of action was a little beneath him, but he couldn't get ahold of Ebbi Kyle, so he'd have to do it himself.

Hodges saw Dooley's white Buick Century heading toward the front of the lot and got ready to follow him. He could see how the FBI lost everyone on surveillance, with the damn Cubans switching lanes and old Jews from the Beach driving along at twenty miles an hour, it was hard trying to stay with someone and not be too conspicuous.

Dooley drove like a bat out of hell until he hit US 1, then slowed, heading into Aventura. Hodges lost him turning into the giant mall, then saw him with a briefcase walking into the T.G.I. Friday's. Hodges scrambled for a parking spot, cutting off an elderly woman trying to maneuver her Cadillac into the spot. He checked his revolver and did a quickstep toward the restaurant.

Slipping in the front door, he still hadn't decided how he'd handle this. He spotted Dooley at a booth way in the back. He could slide in next to him, explain things. Who knows, maybe they could come to an agreement. He could threaten him. Most of the neat, clean FBI agents didn't stand up well to threats. Hodges didn't have that sense about Dooley. This guy was tough or at least seasoned. Hodges made his way down the crowded bar, heading right for Dooley's booth. He had his hand in his coat pocket wrapped around the revolver. He was within ten feet of the booth when he realized there was someone with the FBI man.

Hodges made a sharp turn on the ball of his foot and mingled with the after-work crowd having a drink with the other yuppies living in the trendy area. Hodges slowly worked his way around to see who Dooley was talking to. He saw a soft feminine leg all the way up to a short black skirt. Mid-length dark hair hung across her face. She was young, around thirty. Then Hodges saw her face. That long, sharp nose and all-business attitude.

'How did that bitch hook up with him?' he mumbled loud enough to draw some stares from patrons around him. He definitely had to hold off on his plan for now. Not with her hanging around. He released the revolver, looked at the young lawyer type next to him, grabbed an empty mug and said, 'Hit me, my friend. It seems I've been stood up.'

ten

TASKER FINISHED dabbing on peroxide and stuck another Band-Aid on his knuckle, then checked the mirror one last time. He looked like a lousy pro boxer. His black eye had faded but now he had cuts around his left eye and a split lip. His questioning of the Eighth Street Boyz hadn't gone as he had planned, but on the bright side, their beating of him hadn't gone as they had planned. Tasker had gotten ahold of one of the old metal chairs in the bar, and after a few hard swings had managed to get out the door alive.

Tasker didn't want anyone to know he was looking into the case, but he was pretty confident the Boyz wouldn't file any kind of complaint. That meant he was still under the radar and had some time.

He limped – damn that short Boyz who had kicked him low – back to Tina in the living room. He had already explained his reasons for going to the Eighth Street Boyz Tenth Street clubhouse but she was still pissed he'd do something that foolhardy. Then he told her how Dooley had ratted on him. She seemed to believe him on his actions and on his innocence.

Mentally, Tasker didn't feel as bad as the other time he'd been suspended. The big difference this time was Tina Wiggins nestling under his arm as they quietly watched the news before having dinner then going to a movie on what could officially be called their first date. He savored the curve of her tan shoulder as it found a place along his side; both of them splayed on the couch, the Channel Eleven news anchor itemizing the destruction of the riot. Mentioning the FDLE special operations agent who was recovering from a bullet wound in the arm.

They watched quietly until, without notice, Bill Tasker's face appeared behind the news anchor. The announcer started, 'And now the story of a cop who may have used the riot as a shield for his own crime. Here's Olga Vasquez with the story.'

Tasker sprang to his feet, almost knocking Tina to the floor. 'What's this bullshit?'

Tina shushed him. 'Let's listen.'

A thin, attractive Latin woman with a long, pointed nose, wearing a short red skirt, standing in front of the Miami FDLE office, started the report.

'Rick, tonight officials from the Florida Department of Law Enforcement are not talking about one of their own who is currently under investigation by the FBI for the robbery of an Overtown bank and the murder of its manager.'

Tasker squirmed through the details, but was relieved no one from FDLE would come on camera. The FBI spokesman confirmed an investigation, but that was it. He breathed a little easier until the end of the report.

The young reporter continued, 'Special Agent Tasker has only one significant incident in his personnel file, which involved the death of another agent but, officials said, was not related to the current allegations.'

'I think I'm gonna be sick,' said Tasker.

The reporter continued, 'Although FDLE has refused comment, a source within the FBI has indicated that an indictment and arrest are imminent and that evidence exists suggesting that Special Agent Tasker had planned the robbery for weeks prior to the riot.'

The phone rang, jolting Tasker out of his trance. 'Hello,' he answered sharply. After a pause, he asked, 'How'd you get this number?' Then, 'No, I have no comment.' Tasker slammed down the phone as the TV report concluded.

Tina asked, 'Who was that?'

'*Miami Herald.*'

'Relax, baby. They never get it right. It'll all blow over.'

Tasker sighed. 'Why me?'

'Billy?'

'Yeah?'

'Can you help me?'

Tasker remained monotone, asking, 'How?'

'Need a loan, that's all. I'm used to a certain lifestyle.' She smiled, obviously trying to diffuse things.

'So am I, and it doesn't include sodomy from some lifer at Marion.'

Tina laughed, then said, 'Let's go out to eat instead of eating here.'

'I already started cooking. Why do you want to leave?'

'I don't want to be seen here.' She giggled at his stare. 'And your spaghetti sauce smells like it burned.'

TOM DOOLEY SAT in his Buick three houses down the street from Tasker's town house and settled in for his chance. He was pleased, no, proud, of his execution of a well-laid plan. Talking to that news babe Olga was just about the sharpest thing he'd ever done. She was so into being a 'journalist,' even working for that shitty station, she'd never give up her source in the FBI. Now that she'd reported Tasker's story, the Bureau would do whatever was necessary to bury him. The pressure on Slayda 'Mac' Nmir would already be enormous. The fucking cock-sucking, ass-kissing special agent in charge probably blew a gasket when he heard that story. Now they had to make the case or drop the allegation, and the FBI didn't like to admit it was ever wrong.

Dooley chuckled at the whole situation as he patted the satchel on the seat next to him. He'd decided to find a new place to hide the cash after he put the nail in Tasker's coffin. Dooley reached in and pulled out several stacks of cash wrapped in *Miami Herald* newspaper with a rubber band holding it all securely. He opened the ends and counted the five separate bundles. He was holding about sixty grand. Each bundle had different denominations and varied in thickness. He tossed in the two biggest bundles, leaving about ten large in his lap.

Dooley turned his attention back to the house just in time to see Tasker and a knockout babe with long brown hair hop into a Jeep Cherokee and zip down the street. This was his chance. His heart skipped up to a steady, fast rhythm as he realized he still had a few holes in his brilliant plan. Where should he hide the cash? It had to look natural, like a little stash in case of trouble. He had to make it hard for Tasker to find before the FBI came to look for it. He had to get into the house without leaving any trace or suspicion that the house had been entered. Fuck! He hadn't thought through this plan to the end.

His eyes searched the street in both directions. All clear. Taking the cash, he slipped out of the small car, careful not to slam the door. He quick-stepped past a couple of nice but small houses, and a BMW parked in front, looking all around, feeling his head rotate like something out of *The Exorcist*. In a few seconds, he was past the first door into the town house and to the covered patio of Tasker's unit. The courtyard was screened with a view of several other town homes, each with four units.

Dooley stopped, breathing hard, his blood pounding in his ears, looking around the screened room. He tried the front door, then the sliding glass door. 'Didn't fucking think so,' he said to himself quietly. He could try the windows, but that would open him up to view from the neighbors and look damn suspicious. What could he do?

Then he saw it. The perfect spot. The guy was already eating tonight, and with any luck Tasker would eat tomorrow's dinner in stir. The gas grill on the porch was perfect. He thought, Okay, Tommy Boy, just toss the cash in there and get the info to the FBI somehow. He opened the lid to the grill.

COLE HODGES had decided he really didn't need the heat from killing an FBI agent but he did want this fucker to pay. After following the fat bum all the way out here to Kendall, curiosity had kept Hodges from taking action. He had to know what this motherfucker was up to.

First, the guy had had dinner with the news reporter, then cruised to a house in South Miami, probably his own, and now he was doing some kind of surveillance in Kendall. No way it was official. Hodges had never heard of an FBI agent working alone. This guy Dooley had to be working some kind of scam.

Sitting way down the street, Hodges could see Dooley move inside the car, then, after a Jeep pulled out, the fat man hopped out and fast-walked to a house. Hodges went ahead and started up the street in his gold Lincoln. He looked for any sign of Dooley and then, when he pulled next to Dooley's vehicle, he leaned over and took a look inside. He froze. The satchel was sitting on the front passenger seat all by itself. It couldn't be, he thought. What had he done to make God love him so much?

Hodges jumped out of the car and bounded to the Buick. Locked, but Hodges had defended car thieves before and whipped out a buck knife with a four-inch blade. With a quick thrust under the lock and a few twists, the door popped open and he grabbed the satchel. He scanned the surrounding houses quickly to see if anyone had noticed, then looked to see if Dooley was hightailing it back to his car. All clear. Hodges gave the rest of the car a quick once-over and then locked the door and closed it. The gash where he had used the knife was clearly visible.

Back in his car, he checked the satchel again and decided most of the cash was still there. Hodges said out loud, 'Thank you, Mr. FBI.' It would've been a chore to track down the good reverend after he left that day. That's why he'd had Ebbi Kyle try to follow him. He hoped Dooley had dealt with Al Watson the way he deserved. Now the question was: Should he drive away and let the FBI man wonder what had happened, or should he get some satisfaction and let the man know he'd taken back what was his? The smart move was to leave.

As he sat there, the question answered itself as Dooley came lumbering out to the road. Hodges saw his head snap and his pace pick up as Hodges slowly pressed the accelerator, his electric window whirring down, a grin spreading over his face as he saw the recognition in Dooley's eyes.

Hodges said, 'That's right. I got it now. 'Preciate you picking it up for me. Now you don't tell on me and I won't tell on you.'

Hodges hit the gas as Dooley broke into an all out run for the Buick. Hodges cackled, knowing he'd be halfway to Liberty City before the dumbass got that little-piece-of-shit car rolling. He made a quick calculation on how long it would take him to leave town and how hidden he could stay. It didn't really matter because Dooley was obviously working alone and was an FBI agent, not a Miami cop. He'd never find Hodges unless Hodges wanted to be found. The CCR attorney sped up and turned onto the main road and good times.

eleven

B ILL TASKER lay across his bed, still dressed in his shirt
from the night before, with the sheets twisted in a ball next
to him. The TV, showing the morning newscast, had the volume
turned down. A crack of sunlight penetrated the heavy curtain
drawn across the sliding glass door. Sweat soaked the sheets
and hung in the air. The sound of a Weedwacker strummed
through the closed doors and mixed with the central air unit
laboring against the South Florida morning sun. His head had
a beat of constant pain, reminding him not to question a street
gang alone again.

Tasker rolled over and saw 8:05 on his alarm clock. 'Oh shit,'
he yelped, springing upright. Then, remembering he had no job
to go to, he relaxed, flopped back down on the wet sheets.

He didn't even have to check in by phone. The director had
told him it was bullshit, and it was okay as long as he wasn't
getting into any trouble. Tasker figured getting beaten wasn't
really trouble, it was more like punishment. Staring up at the
ceiling, he cursed the fact that he hadn't slept two hours the
whole night, and it wasn't because of Tina. She had made a polite
exit around eleven, saying he shouldn't aggravate his injuries. She
was a fun date, but, man, she could spend. He'd gone through
a couple hundred bucks between dinner and drinks. That was
cash he should've been saving in case he was suspended without
pay. Right now his bosses were backing him, but after the news
report the night before he didn't know how long that support
would last.

As he thought about the news report, he noticed the same
reporter on his silent TV. Finding the remote in the tangle of
sheets, he clicked up the sound. Instantly he realized it was a
repeat of the same story.

'Great,' Tasker sighed, surveying the wreckage of his bed. 'I can't live like this,' he said, shaking his head. He realized he could be buried by these charges if he didn't take action. He just wanted to lay out his actions to a reasonable person so they'd see he had nothing to do with the robbery. Who should he talk to? His bosses? They were already on his side. The FBI? They were the ones after him. Dooley? He'd obviously told the Bureau he thought Tasker had knocked over the bank. He had to do something and do it fast to straighten out this giant misunderstanding. He'd learned in West Palm that just letting things ride wasn't the answer. He'd waited out that mess and it had ruined his life.

He spent an hour cleaning up his town house as he ran through his arguments in his head. Then he said out loud, 'I've been interested in all types of robberies, not just banks.' His big argument was an alibi. He could account for all his time the day of the robbery. The problem was that no one had seen him. Traffic had been at a stand-still. It didn't matter – unless he spoke up, he was screwed. He had considered a lawyer but never had had any luck with them. He figured an attorney wasn't needed until he got charged. He had nothing to hide. How many times had he heard crooks say that?

He needed to talk to Tina. Picking up his portable phone, he strolled out onto his patio. The air was clean but warm. He tried her cell but got no answer. He tried her direct line at work but got put through to the operator. He heard a female voice say, 'Florida Department of Law Enforcement, may I help you?' He clicked the off button and slammed the phone onto the lid of the grill.

'C'mon. I need a break.' He took in a deep breath and realized he hadn't eaten yet and it was after ten. Maybe that was the problem, he was hungry. He needed food to get his brain working. He needed a clear investigative goal. Pancakes sounded pretty good, with bacon, but it was a little late. Maybe a sandwich? He looked at the grill. He hadn't used it since his daughters had visited a month ago. A hamburger would hit the spot.

He opened the patio gate to the front and grabbed the *Miami Herald* sitting by his front door. Heading inside with the paper under his arm, he looked for the grill lighter. When he tossed the paper on the table, he saw one line of a smaller front-page article that made him freeze: *FDLE Agent Suspected*. He opened the paper and confirmed his worst fears. Just like last time, it was becoming a media frenzy.

'Fuckin' Sandersen!' he said out loud, as he threw the paper down. His eyes fell on the only thing that showed from the patio: the grill.

TOM DOOLEY spent the morning in a panic. He'd locked himself in his den and told his wife to leave him the hell alone. He had to think. How had that fucking son-of-a-bitch collard-eating jig figured out where he was and that he had the money? Where had he gone? What was he going to do now? He didn't like the feeling of not having all the answers. He'd spent his whole life knowing the score, and being left in the dark went against his nature.

He jumped at a knock on the door and bounded to it, if only to scream at his wife for bothering him after he'd told her to stay away. As he was about to explode, the sight of his youngest boy stopped him. At thirteen, Andy was as slight as his mother was broad.

'Sorry, Dad, I need to ask you something,' the boy said, almost quaking in his huge, baggy bathing suit and saggy tank top. His Adam's apple bobbed as he stared at his father.

Dooley caught himself. This kid didn't have a mean bone in his body, even if he was a mama's boy. Dooley relaxed his grimace and spoke softly. 'Whatchu need, Andy?'

'I'm going to the movies and Mom said to see if you had any cash.'

Dooley grunted a short laugh. 'I'm a little short right now, son.' He dug in his pocket and looked at his money clip. He peeled off two tens. 'How's that?'

The boy smiled. 'Great. Thanks, Dad.'

'No problem, pal. Hope to have more later.' Watching the teenager bounce down the hall, clutching the money tightly, he smiled, but only for a second.

Dooley closed the door, refocusing on his problem. Maybe he should go back to Tasker's house and retrieve the money from the grill. Ten grand was better than nothing. The thought of settling for a fraction of the one and a half million turned his stomach sour. He'd never have another clean chance at that much again.

Then he seized on a bigger problem: That fucking asshole,

Cole Hodges, knew everything. He was a witness who, if he wanted to, could cause all kinds of shit. No matter what Dooley did about the cash, he couldn't leave Hodges around to blab. He just didn't have the contacts to find the scumbag. The FBI never had a lot of informants on the streets because the agents relied on local cops helping when they were looking for someone. It never mattered who found a fugitive, because the Bureau's media machine made sure they got the credit. Why not treat this like any other investigation and bring in a local? Dooley knew enough cops that he figured he could get one he could trust to find Hodges and the money. But who?

Dooley sat down, concentrating on his mental Rolodex. He kept coming back to two cops. The two he most often worked with: Derrick Sutter and Rick Bema. Why not use the robbery task force to find a fucking robber? But which one?

He leaned back, breathing deeply, picturing each man in his mind. He'd had problems with Sutter. He never really trusted those people and Sutter had more attitude than most. The Miami cop seemed to be friendly with Tasker and might not want to screw the guy, even for a pile of cash. That left Bema.

The Dade County detective would have the contacts, still lived at home and was always bitching about money. He was a definite possibility and if it didn't work out, Dooley could always kill him, too.

TASKER GLANCED at his watch and realized he'd been at his kitchen table for thirty minutes. If he had a gas oven, maybe he could solve his problem now. He blinked his eyes and an image of his daughters popped into his head. He had to do something. But what was his next step? He believed the Eighth Street Boyz when they said they didn't do it. The beating they'd laid on him seemed pretty sincere. He still couldn't believe the FBI hadn't even gone by their clubhouse and asked a few questions. The Eighth Street Boyz were the reason he'd first asked about surveillance on the bank. Were the Feds that focused on him? Mac Nmir didn't impress him as such a bulldog that he'd ignore any other leads. Tasker figured it was up to him.

If he were running the investigation, he'd obviously talk to the people at the bank. Since the Bureau would surely have been there, he'd have to be careful. He took a few minutes to clean up and dress, even put on a tie so he might be mistaken for a Fed. He backed out the Jeep and slowly started toward I-95. He wasn't sure where he was going, but in Dade County, I-95 and the 826 would take you just about anywhere. He headed north toward the bank, realizing that if he got caught he could be charged with witness tampering or obstruction. It wasn't like the movies, where it was romantic to clear your name. Here in Miami he could aggravate any problems he had. The FBI's inattentiveness had pushed him to take some chances. If he didn't find out who'd taken the cash, then he might find that, as a convenient target, he would end up taking the blame.

The Alpha National Bank of Miami, Overtown branch, was the product of a lawsuit claiming the bank ignored the less fortunate neighborhoods. Obviously the Overtown branch held little in common with the main office downtown. The eight-car parking lot was empty as Tasker pulled in his Jeep. He quick-stepped right inside the small, dinged, peeling door. The tellers looked up, almost startled that a white man had walked in the door. A younger white woman in a professional suit motioned to him from behind the single desk in the corner marked 'Loan Department.'

Tasker turned toward her, welcoming her smile and blue eyes. She stood up, almost as tall as him, and offered her hand. He had to concentrate to look in her eyes.

'Lilly Dane, may I help you?' she asked, her eyes running up and down Tasker like a scanner.

He flashed his backup badge, since he didn't have an ID anymore, and said, 'I just need to follow up on some of the things we asked about the robbery.'

'When did you ask?' She seemed confused.

'Last week. After the manager was shot.' He tried to sound bored. His stomach rumbled as he pushed on. He'd never had to impersonate a cop before.

She nodded and said, 'Oh, you mean Mr. Nmir with the FBI.'

He paused, then committed. 'Exactly.'

She lowered her voice and said, 'Let's talk in the back where it's a little more private.' She led him toward the counter then through the rear door. She stopped in a narrow hallway and motioned him past. He could barely squeeze by, noticing her amusement at his discomfort. Once alone in the small office, she turned quickly, bumping into Tasker. 'Now, what did you need to know?'

'I was just going over information leading up to the robbery.' Tasker was surprised she hadn't asked him for more identification or why he was following up anything.

'I told Agent Nmir all I knew, which wasn't much.'

'Can you go over it?'

Now she paused and looked at him, but he wasn't sure if it was apprehension or something more personal. Then she said, 'I didn't know Louie Kerpal outside of work, but he seemed like a nice guy. I asked him if he wanted me to wait with him the day of the riot. He was so particular about protocol, he sent me on my way so he could call the main office and lock up.'

'Was that the last contact you had with him?'

She nodded.

'Anything else you think I should know?'

She thought about it and said, 'I went through which boxes were opened with Agent Nmir and then gave him the supporting documents.' Her hand dropped to Tasker's knee. 'I had no idea the FBI employed such attractive men.'

He shifted in his hard wooden chair. 'Which boxes were opened?'

She snatched her hand back and dropped to a professional tone again. 'Several, but the only one that looked like it was missing anything was the one rented by Cole Hodges.'

'*Looked* like it was missing stuff?'

'We haven't been able to reach Mr. Hodges to confirm there was anything there.'

Tasker nodded and considered this.

The bank manager added, 'Louie always got excited Thursdays when Mr. Hodges made deposits.'

'Why was that?'

She shrugged. 'I guess he was just proud of a well-known client. He also liked to open the box vault for someone not storing drugs.'

Tasker ignored the comment and asked, 'What do you think was in the box?'

She leveled her eyes at him and simply said, 'Cash.'

LEAVING THE BANK, Tasker took a few minutes to look at the surroundings. He walked out onto the sidewalk and looked back at the bank. A small black man in a dirty T-shirt that bore a Confederate flag with a red circle and slash over it stared at Tasker.

The man said, 'What are you doing here?'

Tasker ignored him.

The man came toward him. 'Cops disturb the natural flow of the neighborhood.'

Tasker looked at him. 'What makes you think I'm a cop?'

'You all look the same.'

'What's your name?'

The man looked surprised, then said, 'Everybody calls me Spill.'

'Well, Spill, you're wrong, I'm no cop.'

'Then what are you?'

'An actor.'

'No shit, you're an actor? Prove it.'

Tasker slowly started toward his car. 'Spill, I'm acting like you don't stink. I'm acting like you're not bothering me. And now I'm going to act like I miss talking to you when I drive away.'

Tasker saw the messy street bum stare at his Cherokee as he headed west toward the interstate.

TWO HOURS AFTER the idea of using Bema popped in his head, Dooley concentrated on the road while listening to his task force partner.

'What's this all about, Tom?' Rick Bema asked from the passenger seat of Dooley's Buick.

'I got a proposition for you, *amigo*, and we need to speak in private.'

'Private is in the car, not the fucking Everglades.' Bema twisted to face him as Dooley pulled the car over on the side of a deserted access road next to a deep-water canal in the industrial section of Miami. As isolated as you could be without taking an hour drive west.

Dooley said, 'This is fine, we're all alone.' He sighed like he'd been exercising and turned to face the younger man. Dooley's hand rested on the butt of his revolver tucked inside his coat pocket. 'Now, Rick, I have an opportunity to make some money, and I thought you might be interested.'

Bema cut his eyes up and down the portly FBI man. 'Yeah?' he said slowly.

'Could you use, say, a hundred grand?'

'Yeah,' he said with more authority.

'What would you do for that kind of cash?'

'What needs to be done?'

'Find someone and keep your mouth shut.'

'Who?'

'Cole Hodges.'

Bema took a second, 'That crook, why?'

Dooley explained how Hodges had taken the cash from the bank, and skipped most of the following details. He waited for the big question and it came.

'Did Billy Tasker have anything to do with it?'

'Nope.'

'Then who set him up?'

Dooley tightened his grip on the pistol. 'Me.'

Then Bema surprised him. 'If Hodges took over a million, why is my share only a hundred large?'

Dooley smiled. 'All right, *amigo*, how 'bout twenty percent?'

'Why not fifty-fifty?'

'Because I brought this deal to you. I'm already involved.'

'Yeah, and lost the money, so I want fifty percent.'

Dooley said, 'Thirty.'

Bema: 'Forty-five.'

Dooley: 'Forty, and you help me throw the blame onto Tasker.'

Bema paused. 'What do I have to do?'

'Make a phone call.'

'How much money are we talking about?' asked Bema.

Dooley did some fast calculations in his head and said, 'Around six hundred and change. Think about it, Rick, all that money, tax-free. You can *buy* a fucking girlfriend with that kind of jack. Trust me, *amigo*, it's easier that way.'

Bema hesitated. Dooley thought that the Cuban son-of-a-bitch bastard turd was about to back out, so he fingered the trigger of his hidden pistol. He'd force the guy out of the car first, then pop him so he'd be easy to drop in the water. Bema still stared at him.

Without warning, the young detective simply said, 'Where's a phone?'

*

AS THE SUN began to set and the temperature to drop to just under ninety, Bill Tasker finished writing down all his thoughts on the case against him and making a list of lawyers he'd call tomorrow. His lack of progress in the case convinced him he might need some legal help. His trip to the bank showed him that he could still do some police work. Finding out about Cole Hodges was the first lead that interested him as a cop. In every case, at least big cases, something happens that changes things, that breaks it open. Maybe this was that spark. Tasker's instincts said that Hodges was more involved than a possible victim. That was the advantage he had over the FBI: He had a real cop's instincts and that couldn't be underestimated. After the Oklahoma City bombing, it was a state trooper, following his instincts, who had caught Timothy McVeigh, and the FBI almost screwed up the case by withholding documents just before the bomber's execution.

Tasker looked around the first floor of his three-bedroom town house. At least it was clean. He sighed and let his gaze flop toward the patio. It was still a mess and he was hungry. Time for his earlier idea of a hamburger while he straightened up. He slowly leaned forward to slide off the couch as he wondered how he'd gotten so tired doing so little during the day. He wandered onto the patio to the grill and, squatting down, checked the propane gas canister. Feeling like it had some juice left, he turned it on and hit the automatic ignition on the off chance that the worthless thing would work. Instead, all he heard was a hollow click. He stood up, cursing, and padded back into the house to find the lighter and see what he could throw together to grill.

As he rummaged through the refrigerator, he heard a sharp knock on the front door. He thought about ignoring it, then it turned to a banging, much louder this time. He slammed the refrigerator door, annoyed someone would invade his sulking time.

Almost to the door, he answered another set of knocks, 'Coming, coming, what's the problem?' Pulling open the door, he stood silent for a moment, then blurted, 'What's this all about?'

Tina Wiggins stood, smiling, her arms filled with groceries. 'Thought you might like a home cooked meal. Sorry I didn't call.' She looked at the staring Tasker. 'Did you have plans?'

Tasker blinked hard a couple of times. 'No, no, come on in.'

He stepped back as she came through the door and seemed to take over the room.

'Sorry about the banging. My hands were full and I had to kick the door to make any noise.'

Tasker didn't care if she'd driven a car through the patio, he was glad she was here. 'Whatcha got?'

She said, 'Steak for the grill.'

'Great, I was just getting ready to fire it up.'

Without warning she leaned across the breakfast bar, reached a slim hand around his neck and laid a deep, serious kiss on him. It seemed to suck the air out of his lungs and made the blood rush to his head. She let go like it was a wrestling hold and he took a step back.

'Wow,' was all he said.

'I'm sure I can come up with more of that later.' She smiled and focused her eyes on him like lasers.

Another knock broke his pleasant daze.

'Who's that?' asked Tina.

'Probably someone with ribs,' Tasker said, moving with deliberateness through the living room. When he opened the door, he was surprised again. Slayda 'Mac' Nmir stood in the doorway with three other men, all dressed in casual clothes but looking deadly serious.

Tasker said, 'What now?'

Mac held up a legal-looking document. 'Warrant for your house.'

Tasker's eyes bulged. 'You got paper? For this house? On what PC?' He knew that probable cause for a warrant, commonly known as 'PC,' could be slim, but there had to be something.

'Anonymous tip that you stashed some of the cash here.'

'Now that's thin.'

Mac shrugged. 'That's what I have.'

Tasker raised his hands. 'Okay, you got me.'

Surprise flashed across Mac's face. 'Huh?'

'In the kitchen, on top of the fridge.' Tasker bowed his head. 'C'mon, I'll show you.'

Mac motioned for the other FBI men to stay put and followed Tasker into the kitchen. As they walked through the house, Tasker stopped and raised a hand toward a speechless Tina.

Tasker said, 'Tina, this is Mac. Mac, Tina.'

Mac asked, 'And who is this?'

Tasker hesitated. 'My ...' He looked at Tina. 'My friend. Another FDLE agent.' He looked at Tina. 'Be right back.'

Mac hurried to follow Tasker into the kitchen. Tasker reached on top of the beige Amana side by side and grabbed a large round coffee can.

Tasker said, 'Here it is,' handing it to the FBI agent.

Mac eyed him carefully as he slowly twisted off the lid. He reached in and pulled out a small wad of cash. 'What's this?'

'All the hidden cash in this house. That's correct, I'm Mister Big all right.'

Mac didn't crack a smile. 'I wouldn't joke. C'mon, Tasker. I've been really good to you. I don't want a spectacle, but I gotta do my job.'

Tasker sighed. 'Gimme a break, Mac, an anonymous tipster? That's the oldest trick in the book. I've got nothing to hide. I'm just waiting for you guys to clear me' He was pissed, but something about the young FBI man made Tasker ease up. The guy seemed okay. 'Tom Dooley could have had as much to do with that robbery as me.'

'No way, he may be an idiot but he's FBI.'

'That's crazy. I'm a cop, too, and you're still hassling me.'

'But you're not Bureau.'

'You guys do know that shit is annoying, don't you? Like you're better than everyone else.' Tasker fixed his eyes on Mac. 'What about Cole Hodges?'

Mac froze, then said, 'How'd you get that name?'

Tasker gave no response, wanting to see if he could spook someone else for a change.

Mac paused then said, 'Mr. Hodges has been unavailable.'

'Unavailable?'

'As in missing.'

'Maybe that's a lead you could pursue.'

Mac stiffened. 'I won't divulge the workings of this investigation or the FBI.' He locked his gaze onto Tasker and continued. 'Now, Mr. Tasker, how do you know about Cole Hodges?'

'I asked around. You know I can look into things, too.'

'If you talked to any witnesses, I can look into new charges.'

'You mean the Eighth Street Boyz? Someone had to look at them. You guys never even talked to them.'

'Why? They didn't do it.'

'You're that convinced it was me?'

'Let's look around and see.' Mac composed himself and lowered his voice. 'We do have this tip. It'll only take a few minutes.'

'A two-year-old could've come up with the tipster trick to get a warrant for a fishing trip for evidence.'

Mac said, 'The tipster said it was in your grill. Let's take a look.' He stood, staring Tasker down. Tasker shrugged and padded out of the kitchen, past Tina, who hadn't moved, and then through the sliding doors, with Mac right behind. Mac held up one finger to the other agents, who were still milling around out front.

Still feeling calm and in control, Tasker thought this might end the whole inquiry. As they approached the grill, Tasker held out his hands like the girls on *The Price Is Right*, saying, 'And here it is. A two-year-old GrillMaster, with separate propane tank.'

Mac rolled his eyes, stepped past Tasker and lifted the lid. All activity froze. Sitting on the grill itself were four bundles of cash all crammed to one side.

Tasker swallowed hard. 'Wait one damn second. I don't know what the hell is going on, but …' As he started to go on, Mac turned to look at him. Bile backed up in his throat and cut off his air. He gasped but couldn't speak for a few seconds.

'I wouldn't say anything, Tasker,' Mac said. He motioned for the others to come in and then sprang to action himself. 'Turn around, Tasker,' he said, helping the shocked man to spin, patting him down as he did it. Mac turned to the nearest FBI man. 'Steve, check that couch, inside and out.' As the man moved, Mac said to the other two FBI agents, 'Clear these rooms and the upstairs.' They darted into an open doorway.

The first agent, Steve, said, 'The couch is clean.'

Mac turned Tasker back around. 'I'm not going to put you in cuffs. You can sit here on the couch. We shouldn't be too long.' He looked up at Tina. 'You can leave or we'll search you, and you have to stay on the couch, too.'

Tina looked from Mac to Tasker, trying to decide what to do.

Tasker hesitated, then said, 'You should go.'

She grabbed her purse and started toward the door.

'Hang on,' Mac said. 'We need to have a look in your purse before you go.' He crossed the room and had the purse before she could argue. He pried it from her hand and did a quick peek inside.

Tina finally regained her composure, looking at Mac and the other FBI man. She ran her hands down her tight tank top, then lifted her short tennis skirt, exposing her panties. 'You think I might have the cash secreted on my body, too?'

Mac said, 'Sorry, but we have to be sure.'

She stepped toward the door. The hurt look on her face told Tasker that she thought he'd lied to her. She held back a parting comment and slipped out, slamming the door as she left.

Tasker stared at the two FBI men, who were joined by the others.

The oldest agent said, 'All clear, Mac.'

Tasker remained silent as they started the search. The screech of Tina's tires lingered in his ears.

twelve

TOM DOOLEY GRUMBLED silently about the working conditions he allowed himself to accept. He sat in the passenger seat of an eight-year-old, rusted-out, yellow Camaro, fingering the trigger of his .38 as the residents of Liberty City walked past, barely noticing the only white face around. The car itself smelled musty and the window on his side rolled down only halfway. This, added to the fact that he was suddenly poor again, caused his stomach to growl with acid and his morning coffee.

He caught a glimpse of Rick Bema still talking with a tall, young black kid wearing an Oakland Raiders windbreaker over a Miami Heat T-shirt. Bema seemed pretty casual with the guy, talking with his hands like all Cubans, then after a few minutes handed him some cash. The muscular Dade County detective bounded across the four-lane highway and slipped back into his Camaro.

Bema said, 'He don' know where Hodges would be, but he know his right-hand man. A guy named Ebbi Kyle. He say that Kyle might be over at the Liberty City branch of the CCR.'

Dooley nodded. 'How much you pay him?'

'Fifty.'

'You guys always overpay snitches. I'd have given him a smack in the noggin and sent him on his way.'

'And you still wouldn't have a chance to find Hodges and our money.'

Dooley smiled, catching the subtle changes in his partner's speech. He used 'our money' now and seemed plenty interested in finding Hodges. Bema also understood the importance of keeping the pressure on Tasker so no one started looking at them.

'You know anything about this Kyle character?' asked Dooley.

'Just a description: black, skinny, with green eyes. They call him "Pitcher" on the street.'

' 'Cause he played baseball?'

'Naw, man, street names aren't always that obvious.'

'Then why's he called Pitcher?'

'My man says we'll know when we see him. Suppose to be some kind of reformed crack addict the CCR helped and now he runs the branch office.'

Bema cranked the old car and shot out into traffic in search of the office west of the interstate in Liberty City.

DOOLEY SANK LOW in the seat, half out of embarrassment and half out of not wanting anyone to be able to identify him later. Not many white people traveled the smaller avenues of Miami's Liberty City or Overtown. This old rust bucket didn't attract any attention, but a white guy did. Dooley figured enough people had seen white Buicks that he didn't need to add another piece to the puzzle for Mac Nmir or anyone else working on the bank robbery.

Bema tapped his fingers to the beat of some rap shit as the car rumbled and rattled down Seventh Avenue.

Dooley said, 'I thought you'd listen to Latin music.'

'I like all music.' He twisted the volume until the bass shook the cheap plastic door handles. 'One day I'll have a Corvette with a real sound system. And leather seats with a sunroof. Move out on my own. What d'ya think, Tommy, pretty sweet, no?'

'Yeah, Rick, sweet.' But for now he was still in a shitty Camaro, so he ducked lower.

The branch office for the Committee for Community Relief sat in the middle of a five-store strip mall on NW Sixty-second Street, across from the Scott housing project. Someone had painted 'CCR' in white across the front window. Dooley noticed that all the stores were actually different community service groups. He figured no one else wanted an office with nothing but glass in the front to protect their valuables.

Bema circled the building, then parked in the rear. Every space was open, making Dooley wonder if anyone was inside the beat-up little office. They counted three doors in and knocked at the unmarked metal back door. Dooley instinctively swiveled his head, checking for anyone hanging around. All clear.

Bema knocked a little harder this time. The dead bolt turned and Dooley heard a male voice.

'Why don't you use the front?' A thin, light-skinned black guy stopped mid-sentence when he saw the two men. Instantly, Dooley understood the guy's street name. He had ears like the handle of a water pitcher. They stood out three inches. The man's light green eyes appraised them as he asked, 'Who're you?'

Bema flashed his badge and shoved the man inside. Dooley followed him in, closing the door behind him. The back room was empty except for a desk and one chair. A doorway with no door led out to the open front room with no furniture.

Bema kept backing up Hodges's gofer until he bumped the chair and flopped down in a heap. His eyes were wide and bright as he looked from Dooley to Bema, then back.

'What's up?'

'You Ebbi Kyle?' asked Dooley.

'Maybe.'

Dooley sighed. 'You may think there's more than one jig with green eyes runnin' around, but I guarantee you're the only one with ears like that. Now I'll ask only once more: Are you Ebbi Kyle?'

He nodded his head, keeping his attention only on Dooley now. He said, 'I ain't done nothing wrong. You can't hold me.'

Dooley said, 'What gave you the impression you're under arrest?' He smiled and looked around the bare office. 'Tell me, Ebbi, what kind of work you do around here?'

'Whatever the CCR needs.'

'You mean whatever Cole Hodges needs.'

'He my boss, yeah, I do things for him.'

'Where is he now?'

Ebbi looked at Dooley and hesitated, before shrugging.

Dooley ran his hand down his face and said, 'I told you that you're not under arrest – I didn't say that you could refuse to answer my questions.'

Ebbi said, 'I got rights and one of 'em is to shut up.'

Bema cut in. 'Tom, I think he needs to understand that this is not official so we don' have to follow any laws.'

Dooley nodded, and without hesitation grabbed Ebbi by both ears and slammed his head into the desk. Dooley cackled and said, 'Those things are magnificent.'

Ebbi looked up, shaking his head and wiping blood from his nose.

Dooley went on. 'I got rights, too. I got the right not to listen to your shit.' He stomped hard on Ebbi's left foot, the old sneaker doing little to absorb the blow. Ebbi sucked in breath hard.

Dooley said, 'I got the right to know where that fucking creep Cole Hodges is.' He slapped Ebbi with a backhand. Dooley pulled out a knife.

Bema said, 'Not here, we don't want a track back to Hodges. Let's take him.'

Without acknowledging his partner, Dooley scooped up the dazed man and hustled out the door. They crammed him in the backseat of the Camaro and sped off with no one noticing a thing.

BILL TASKER SAT silently in his living room. He'd placed himself on the edge of the couch about eleven that morning and hadn't moved three inches in the last three hours. The house didn't look too bad, considering what had happened. The FBI were the most polite cops he'd ever heard of. They even put the plates back in the cabinets properly. They'd gone through every drawer in the whole house and replaced everything just as carefully. Tasker could remember search warrants he had executed where they'd sawed through desks and drilled walls looking for cocaine or drug money. Thank God for little favors like neat cops.

Tasker's phone had been quiet that morning, clearly a testament to Tina's ability to keep her mouth shut. He was afraid of an unending stream of questions but so far no one seemed to know about the FBI raid. That left only a few questions for Tasker to ponder: What would Mac Nmir do now? Indict him? Make a probable cause arrest? Now Tasker knew that this was no misunderstanding. Someone had clearly set him up. He couldn't believe people really thought he was a murdering bank robber or that anyone would fall for cash planted in his grill, but then again he was learning new things about the FBI every day. This guy Mac Nmir even seemed pretty smart, but you can't teach common sense, and Tasker suspected they didn't even try at the FBI academy.

The big questions facing him now were: Who would set

him up, and why? He thought about all the guys he'd locked up over the years and there were a couple of possibilities. The cash probably hadn't been planted until after the news story, so anyone might have seen it. The whole thing might have been a misunderstanding until someone had taken it a step further and planted the money.

This CCR attorney, Cole Hodges, certainly had a stake in the cash. But why would he steal it if he had access to it anytime he wanted? Why would he frame a cop he'd never even met?

Tom Dooley also figured in the scheme, but it seemed to Tasker that all Dooley had done was tell his side of the surveillance-on-the-bank argument. He probably hadn't even meant anything by it, just said he knew Tasker was interested in the bank. He'd actually seemed sorry that day outside the task force. He also didn't seem smart enough to carry out a plan like this.

Tasker had to attack this problem. Clearly no one in an official capacity would help. He was stumped, and as a result had been quite content to sit on the edge of his couch half the day. He jumped at the sound of the phone, hesitating even to answer it. Finally on the fifth ring, he snatched up the portable.

'Hello.'

'Billy, are you okay?' asked a soft female voice.

He paused for a second, making certain it was who he thought it was. He mumbled, 'Yeah, I'm okay. How about you?'

'An FBI man came around asking all kinds of questions.'

Tasker recognized his ex-wife's voice now. Calling her by the wrong name was one of many mistakes he'd made in their seven years of marriage. He cleared his head and asked, 'What FBI man, Donna?'

'He had a funny name and a nickname that didn't suit him. A dark, cute guy, but I can't remember his name.'

'Slayda Nmir? Mac?'

'That's him. What's it all about?'

'Didn't he tell you?' Tasker asked, suddenly understanding how far this thing had spread.

'He said you took some money from a bank.'

'What did you say?'

'I told him you wouldn't take any money.'

'Good, 'cause I didn't.'

Donna said, 'I also said you wouldn't take any responsibility, or initiative or control. Basically, I said you're not a taker.'

'Thanks, I think.'

'This sounds worse than the whole Jack Sandersen thing. At least the FBI wasn't involved in that.'

'That's the problem. The FBI wants someone in jail and they don't care who. In West Palm, the state attorney really looked at the evidence and moved pretty quick.'

'Billy, you'd tell me if you were involved, wouldn't you?'

'You were never sure about me the last time.'

'Not at the time, but now I see it was a mistake to implicate you. What about this time?'

'This is just a mistake, pure and simple. It's got nothing to do with Jack Sandersen or anything else. The FBI just jumped to conclusions and someone is helping them jump.'

'What's that mean?'

'Nothing.' He didn't want people thinking he was paranoid as well as a criminal.

'The FBI agent, Slayda, says you're "evasive." '

'What'd you say to that?'

'I told him "vague" was a better word.'

'Great. With you on my side, Donna, I'm sure I'll come through this pretty well.'

Donna took a breath. 'C'mon, Bill, you have to know that this is a shock.'

'Is this the first you've heard of it? You didn't see it on the news up there?'

'It was on the news? Like last time?'

'Not really, just Channel Eleven and the *Herald*. But they reported that I'm a suspect. I got relieved of duty, too.'

'Without pay?' The panic in her voice leaped across the phone line.

'Don't worry, I won't miss any payments.' He paused to let her say that wasn't her concern, but she remained silent. 'How're the girls?'

'Good. They miss you.'

'I want to see them soon.'

There was silence on the line for so long Tasker forgot he was talking on the phone until, out of left field, Donna asked, 'Are you seeing anyone?'

Tasker hesitated and then said, 'Not anymore.'

Donna replied, 'That's too bad, 'cause you deserve someone special.'

Tasker took a deep breath and said, 'You're right, I do.'

DOOLEY KEPT FACING the terrified man in the backseat during the ten-minute ride to the Miami River. Ebbi Kyle had hardly said a word once he realized this was not an official visit by two friendly law enforcement agents. Dooley didn't like to hurt people. It gave him no thrill at all. But he had to find Cole Hodges as well as his money, and he didn't care what he had to do to make that happen.

'Where are we headed, Rick?' Dooley asked, turning his head to see some of the freighters pulled up the river.

'Trust me, I know a place where no one will ever notice us and our friend,' Bema said, pulling the car down a rough, narrow road. He stopped next to a stand of Australian pines. The closest ship was still a couple of blocks away and it didn't look like anyone wandered this way too often.

Dooley worked to stand up from the low car, then reached in and hauled out Ebbi by his short, kinky hair. He dragged the young man to an old folding chair wedged in next to the trees and shoved him down.

Ebbi took a second, then looked up at the two men standing over him. No one said a word.

Dooley appreciated the quiet moment in his day, listening to the breeze blow through the thick pine trees overhead. No real traffic noise made it back here. He looked at Ebbi and said, 'So, you startin' to understand the nature of this interview?'

Ebbi nodded.

'Gettin' back to the subject, where is your boss, Cole Hodges?'

Ebbi said, 'I tol' you, man, I don't know.'

Dooley made a big show out of pulling out a Schrade Cliphanger knife and opened it with one hand. The cheap but sharp blade clicked into place and caused Ebbi Kyle to let out a short yelp. Then Dooley said, 'Tell me what I want to know or I'll make your birth certificate a worthless document.'

Ebbi said, 'Look, I don't know. I swear on my mama I don't know where Mr. Hodges is. He don't check with me every day.'

Dooley didn't acknowledge the response. He reached over and grabbed Ebbi's legendary right ear with his left hand and then brought the knife down in a long arc, slicing most of the top of the ear off. Dooley inspected his prize for a moment, then tossed it the ten feet into the swirling river. Within about two seconds, something swam up and grabbed the bloody ear, splashing as it disappeared below the surface.

Ebbi didn't know what to scream about – the pain or seeing his ear used as bait. Before he could say anything, Dooley brought the blade across Ebbi's chest, opening his shirt and causing a line of blood to appear, then leak down his front.

Ebbi gasped again.

Bema calmly said, 'You best tell the man what he wants. White guys can't handle knives, he's liable to cut you too bad for you to speak.'

Ebbi's green eyes looked like Fireking saucers. He touched his chest, checking his hand for blood, then his ear. 'Dear Lordy, Lordy, Lordy, what are you doin' this fo'? I been clean goin' on three years now. I ain't done nothing wrong.'

Dooley said, 'Yeah, you have, you haven't told me where Cole Hodges is.'

Ebbi, panting now, said, 'He'll kill me fo' sure.'

Dooley swung the knife again, severing the other ear cleanly. 'And I won't?'

Ebbi didn't have enough hands to stem the blood. 'He stay over on Ninth Street, sometimes. He got the big condo on the Beach, too.'

Dooley said, 'He's not at the condo, we been there. What do you think we are, idiots?' He reached down and took Ebbi by the chin, focusing him away from his wounds. 'Now, where's this place on Ninth?'

'It's an apartment we used for CCR workers who needed a place temporarily. Ain't been nobody in it for a few months. Mr. Hodges, he tol' me to call him there if there was any problems.'

Dooley said, 'Oh, this is a problem, Ebbi, this is a big fucking problem.'

thirteen

RICK BEMA had been skeptical of this whole plan, but it sure seemed to be coming together now. He still felt bad about ratting out Tasker to the FBI, but figured those assholes would never be able to make a case anyhow. That'd give him and Dooley plenty of leeway to spend their cash. Not that he'd quit his county job, he just wouldn't hustle for overtime anymore.

Now, with Dooley next to him, rattling on about how rich they were going to be, Bema felt pretty good. He had already told himself he had nothing to do with killing the little green-eyed crackhead with no ears. At most, he'd helped Dooley wrap some chain around his thin legs before they dumped him in the river. Bema wondered what had grabbed Ebbi's ear when it had hit the water. He'd heard rumors that the river had piranha in it from all the rich South American kids flushing their exotic fish. Sorta like the alligators in the New York sewers. Maybe the piranha would eliminate any evidence of their interview with Hodges's assistant. Bema didn't know if the piranha stories were true or not, he just knew he hadn't been in the water in the past two years.

They parked down the street from Hodges's hideaway. The Lincoln the CCR attorney had been driving was in a spot behind the two-story building. Bema felt good about the whole situation.

Dooley, looking up at the apartment through a pair of binoculars, said, 'What do you think?'

Bema replied, 'We check the apartment. Nothing to lose. He not there, we leave without trace, no? Someone is there, we question them. He there, jack-fucking-pot, man.'

'I agree,' Dooley said, shifting his bulk to squeeze out of the cramped Camaro. 'I'm gonna nail that asswipe to the wall.'

Bema didn't say anything to cut into the man's macho time. He just nodded and followed Dooley through a back door that led directly to the stairway to the two upstairs apartments.

The door on the right had the letter C and the name Jackson under it. On the left was D, with no name. Dooley leaned his head against the door, listened for about thirty seconds. He looked up and shrugged his shoulders.

Bema whispered, 'What's that mean?'

Dooley replied, 'I hear shit, but I can't tell if it's coming from inside.'

'You're too old to hear people in an apartment?' Bema shoved past him. 'Let me try.' He placed his ear on the door for five seconds and, without notice to Dooley, stepped back and kicked the door hard. It only shifted, cracking along an inner seam. Bema threw his shoulder into it and forced the door the rest of the way, splitting it along the seam.

The two men entered the three-room apartment quickly, scanning the living room with their pistols drawn and in front of them.

Bema pointed to the TV that was on a news channel. 'That's what I heard.'

Before Dooley could answer, a nude black man with a small pot-belly but some decent shoulders, drying his head with the towel draped over his face, wandered out of the bathroom into the hallway connecting all the rooms in the apartment.

Dooley swung his pistol wide and struck the man hard through the towel, knocking him off his feet. He thumped against two walls before settling on the cheap, thin, green carpet. The tan towel immediately stained red. As the man sat up slightly, Dooley laid into him again, striking him three times with his pistol before Bema intervened.

Bema stood between Dooley and the bloody figure on the ground. 'What're you, man, crazy?'

Dooley panted without answering.

Bema continued. 'Maybe we should at least make sure it's our man, no?' He leaned down and jerked away the bloody towel. As soon as he realized it actually was Hodges, Dooley pushed forward and savagely kicked him in the ribs twice before Bema could stop him.

'Whoa, whoa, big man. We need to talk to him.'

Dooley, wild-eyed and red-faced, screamed, 'We need to teach this fucking son-of-a-banana-eating-monkey a lesson in respect.' He kicked Hodges in the head, this time knocking him out cold. Dooley leaned over the motionless man. 'You know the grief you caused me? I oughta fucking carve you up right here, right now.'

Bema eased him back, noting the white foam at the corner of the FBI agent's mouth. Bema knew this guy was close to the edge and that he had to speak carefully.

Bema spoke calmly. 'Now, Tom, we need to step back.' He carefully pushed the heavier FBI man back a few steps. 'We need him awake and talking, Tom. We gotta find the cash, that's our only goal, you understand?'

Dooley nodded absently, still staring at the body on the floor. His breathing moved from panting to longer, heavier breaths.

Bema continued. 'Now, you're way too close to this whole thing here. You're gonna kill our only chance to get the cash back.' He paused to assess his effect on Dooley. 'Why don' you pull the car around while I have a friendly chat with the man here?'

'No, no fucking way.'

'Now, Tom, give me a shot. Then if he don' say nothin', I'll hustle him down to you and we visit the river again. You can do anything you want.'

Dooley stared at him, then back at Hodges, who was starting to stir.

Bema saw his interest in Hodges and spoke up again. 'C'mon, Tom, it may feel good now, but the cash will feel good for a long, long time, no?'

Dooley took in a deep breath and slowly, barely, nodded.

Bema patted his shoulder. 'Good, good man. Now get us the car.'

Dooley nodded and shuffled toward the main room, throwing one more kick into Hodges's leg as he passed. He looked back when he reached the door and said, 'But if he don't talk, he's all mine.'

'I promise.'

Bema watched the door close behind Dooley. If he had rehearsed it with that psycho, it couldn't have gone better. He knew Hodges had heard most of it. He let it sink in, then said,

'Hear that, counselor? You can tell me where the cash is or deal with that nut down by the river. Your choice.'

Hodges sat up, then leaned against the wall, using his fingers to check the blood on his head and ear. He took a deep breath and looked up at Bema. 'Go on, I'm listening.'

'It's simple. We want the cash. Tell me where it is and we're outta here. Hold out and I guarantee that crazy son of a bitch will ruin your whole week. No?'

'I see your point, young man, but I am not in possession of the money. Money, I might add, that belongs to the CCR.'

'And you are going to return it to them?'

'Yes, you see I *am* the CCR, or at least a big part of it.'

'You can cut the shit and tell me where it is.'

'Listen, Mr....? I'm sorry, I didn't catch your name.' He slowly started to stand.

'My name is Mr. Impolite,' Bema said, punching him in the stomach, doubling him back down to his knees. 'And if you don' tell me where the cash is, you're gonna meet Mr. Fucking Rude down in the car. Now where is the satchel?'

Hodges sucked in some air but didn't answer.

Bema drew his small automatic and said, 'Okay, just come on and we'll see if you're more talkative after Dooley carves you up some.'

Hodges stood again, holding out his hand to slow down Bema. 'Okay, okay, it's in the freezer.'

'What? You think I'm stupid? Man, what do I look like? A Puerto Rican?'

'No, my friend, I'm saving us both some trouble. The satchel is stuffed in the freezer of that old Amana in there.' He pointed toward the tiny walk-in kitchen.

Bema eyed him cautiously as he backed toward the kitchen, keeping his gun pointed at Hodges. He motioned for him to follow. Once they were both in the small kitchen, Bema said, 'Open it.' He pointed toward the refrigerator with his pistol.

Hodges moved slowly and opened the small upper door of the old refrigerator. He reached inside and pulled at a cloth satchel until it broke free of some frost. He held it up for Bema's inspection.

Bema said, 'No shit.' As he stepped toward the bag, Hodges threw it toward him and then lunged at the surprised cop. They both crashed back into the wall, Bema's gun clattering to the floor. Hodges turned, searching for the weapon, and made a wild grab for it as Bema took a toaster in his right hand and slammed it down on Hodges's head.

Hodges fell, dead still, to the floor. Bema paused, looked to make sure the injured man couldn't get to the gun, then slammed the toaster onto his head two more times. He tossed the bloody toaster onto the counter, reached down and retrieved his gun, then took the satchel. He froze when he looked inside. The pile of cash stunned him. It must've weighed fifteen or twenty pounds. And big bills, too. He couldn't believe it.

He closed the satchel and tossed it toward the front door. Bema looked around the kitchen, barely noticing the lump of flesh on the floor, and took a long twist of paper towels from a roll on the counter. He ran the wad of towels under the faucet and proceeded to wipe the toaster, refrigerator and counter. He didn't need some bright Miami cop to tie this to him. Not when he was on the verge of becoming wealthy.

Bema wanted to whistle as he finished his sweep and headed for the door. Now all he had to do was decide if Dooley was worth keeping around.

TASKER FIGURED it could be worse. He sat behind the wheel of his Cherokee on a sunny South Florida day on his way to meet Tina at the Dadeland Mall, but first he wanted to see if he could find anything out about Cole Hodges.

Heading out Sixty-second Street near the Scott housing project, Tasker pulled the Jeep into the dirt lot of a small office in front of a series of basketball courts. A hand-painted sign read 'Community Center.' Tasker stopped at the open door to wait for the older black man sitting behind the desk to notice him. Tasker cleared his throat.

The man looked up from the paperwork on his desk. A smile spread across his face. 'Billy, should you be out and about?'

'Probably not, Deac.' He shook his old friend Deac Kowal's hand. 'Just needed to see a friendly face.'

'Well, you came to the right place. Have a seat.'

'As long as it won't hurt your image to be seen talking to me.'

'Billy, I don't worry about FBI foolishness. I know you're not involved with that bank job.'

Tasker relaxed. 'Deac, I need some info and thought you'd be a good guy to ask.'

'Shoot.'

'Before the riots, you said you once tried to take over the CCR but the Reverend Watson had Cole Hodges go after you.'

Deac nodded. 'Yeah, thought we could do some good, so we tried to use some of the money the CCR raised to actually redevelop the community. Didn't get too far.'

'Where's the CCR's office?'

'The business office where Hodges and Watson work is over near the bay on Brickell Avenue. They got four or five little branch offices around town. One of them in the next block. Just an empty shell, really. Nothing gets done there.'

'Can you tell me anything about Hodges or Watson?'

'I heard they're both in the wind. No one has seen either of them since the riot. I think Watson skipped town.'

'What about Hodges?'

'He always kept a lower profile. He may be around, but no one knows it. No one would miss that scum. He gives snakes a bad name.'

'Crooked?'

'He's a lawyer, isn't he?' He paused. 'If you're asking if I've ever heard he committed a crime, I'd have to say no, except ...'

'What?'

'It was said he skimmed the cash the CCR took in.'

'I heard that already.' Tasker moved on. 'Do you know where he came from?'

'No, I don't know him personally and never cared to. Sometimes it's better to avoid certain people. Know what I mean?'

Tasker nodded. 'I hear you.'

AN HOUR LATER, still thinking about his meeting with Deac Kowal, Tasker glanced around the open spaces of the Dadeland Mall in Kendall. The mall had once been a marvel of size and convenience, but had been eclipsed by the ever-growing new malls popping up all over South Florida. He felt uneasy being out in the open, as if someone was trying to kill him. In a way, someone was trying to take away his life, and the whole thing set him on edge.

Tina's call had surprised him for two reasons: first, that she'd called after leaving his place the way she had the night before last, and second, that the call was short and cryptic, telling him to meet her in the food court of the mall now. He'd needed an excuse to leave the house anyway, so he now found himself waiting for Tina.

Looking around, he remembered his mom dragging him to the Palm Beach Mall when he was a kid. At the time it'd seemed like the biggest place in the world. By comparison, it now looked like a convenience store. Thinking about those torturous trips to the mall, Tasker had to stop and buy his mom a neck massager from the As Seen on TV kiosk. She said things like a massager were more to drown out his dad than to relieve stress, but he decided it worked either way. Retirement had agreed with them and he didn't want any word of this to leak up to them in North Carolina. Not after his dad's reaction the last time he'd been in trouble.

He was always amazed at the mass of people that flowed through these giant indoor malls. The Miami area was twice as interesting because no two people looked like they came from the same country. The Jamaicans and Islanders moved casually from store to store; the Cubans bustled, in a hurry like everything they did; and the South Americans pushed past people, oblivious to others' needs. It used to upset Tasker, but a friend had explained that it was a cultural thing and not a manners issue. He didn't know why, but that made him feel better about having some Colombian cut in line or bump into him without ever acknowledging him.

He didn't see Tina coming until she seemed to materialize right next to him, sitting on the edge of a wishing well fountain.

'Billy, you okay? You look like you haven't slept since the raid.'

'I haven't.'

'That's not a good sign.' Her eyes met his, then ran up and down his body like she was assessing a suspect.

Tasker said, 'Don't worry, I'm not thinking about eating my gun.' He paused, then added, 'Yet.'

She looked around the food court, then leaned in close to him. Her brown hair swept across his arm. She rattled his bag. 'What's this? Something for me?' Her face lit up a little.

'Massager.'

'Really.' She cocked one eyebrow.

'Neck massager.'

She looked at him.

'For my mom.'

She smiled. 'Good answer.'

They sat on a nearby bench and Tasker asked, 'What was with the cryptic phone call?'

'I didn't know if they'd tapped your lines and I saw surveillance at your house. That's why I didn't just come over.'

'Surveillance at my house?'

'Yeah, looked like younger FBI guys, but I wasn't sure.'

Tasker was skeptical. 'A title three on my phone and surveillance. I think you're watching too much TV. The FBI doesn't work quick enough to get a tap this fast, and I haven't seen anyone around the house.'

'That's my read on it and you can't be too careful.' She cocked her head. 'Been anywhere you don't want them to know about?'

'Yeah, all over. The Eighth Street Boyz, the bank, and this morning I saw my buddy Deac Kowal.'

'The black guy with the city?'

'He's retired now. But he told me the CCR's attorney, Cole Hodges, is definitely a crook. He's a lead I'm trying to follow up.'

'Why would he take his own cash?'

'It wouldn't have been his, it would've been the Committee for Community Relief's.'

'But he could still get to the box.'

'I haven't worked it all out yet.' Then Tasker looked at her and said, 'I came here, what's so important?'

Tina took a moment, then said, 'I'm sorry I ran off the other night, but the whole thing just freaked me out. I don't care what you did, I'm just disappointed you didn't feel like you could tell me.'

'There's nothing to tell, Tina. I've been set up and now I'm just trying to figure it all out.'

She stared at him silently as he thought, Why not? It sounds crazy enough to be a movie plot. In real life, no one ever gets framed, but now I have to convince people someone is setting me up. He felt like a moron. No one would believe him, not even his girlfriend.

Tina said, 'We'll work something out. Do you have a lawyer yet?'

'I'm looking.'

'Can I help with something?' She gave him a deadly earnest look.

'Not yet. I don't want you implicated in any way.'

'If it involves moving a couple million dollars, you can go ahead and implicate me.'

That comment stayed with him the rest of the evening.

SLAYDA 'MAC' NMIR leaned back into the Gap store across from the Dadeland Mall's food court. He watched Tasker and the female FDLE agent, Tina Wiggins, talk for about ten minutes before she hugged him and headed toward the south exit. Mac, who prided himself on his cool professionalism, had to take a second to savor the action of her long legs grinding against each other where they met her trim but shapely upper body. He took a breath and refocused on Tasker, who was still sitting next to the wishing well, just staring into space.

Mac had to admit that the guy sure seemed lazy to be some kind of master criminal. When he wasn't sulking around his apartment, he lay on his couch for long stretches, apparently trying to sleep. When he did leave the house, surveillance had managed to lose him every time within a few blocks. Mac was curious how Tasker knew so much about Cole Hodges and why he'd talked to the Eighth Street Boyz. Mac puzzled trying to figure out the state cop. He always thought crooked cops didn't pout when they were discovered. They set about pushing the blame on someone else or tried to run. This guy seemed real torn up that anyone would even question his integrity. If it weren't for his past, Mac would have figured he couldn't be involved in a bank robbery. Just when Mac would start to think the guy was innocent, something would pop up to incriminate him. His interest in the bank for surveillance. Who would ever think someone was going to rob a run-down piece-of-shit bank like that? The crack dealer who saw Tasker's car in the area. His disappearance before the riots. Someone should have remembered seeing him during that time. The gas pump records computer at the state pumps hadn't been activated because of the state of emergency, so he might have been one of the thirty-two cars to gas up in the four hours prior to the verdict. And most damning was the cash they'd found in his grill at his town house. Mac had to admit he'd never have gone for a search warrant if his boss hadn't told him to make something stick after the news story came out on Channel Eleven. Everyone thought it was Mac who had leaked the story. Although he loved seeing his work in public, he'd never even met the young reporter who'd broken it. That Olga Vasquez, who he'd heard had fucked half the agents over at the DEA. Now the office was awash with inspectors trying to figure out who'd let out confidential information.

Now, as he watched Tasker and reviewed the acts in his head, he had his doubts again. The grill was outside, after all, and easy enough for someone to plant the cash in, but there was always something else. Something no one could plant and was part of Tasker's permanent record: the shit he got into up in West Palm Beach with the crooked cop on the force. He'd paid a price, with the transfer and his wife leaving him, but still if the reports were accurate, he didn't always do what people expected. He had his own kind of edge. All Mac could do was keep watching and see what turned up.

fourteen

TASKER HAD BEEN on I-95 northbound for almost an hour and a half before reaching the Forest Hill Boulevard exit to West Palm Beach. He didn't mind the drive. Getting out of Dade County felt like someone lifting a curse off him, and the anticipation of seeing the girls kept his mind on happier things. He'd almost cried when his ex-wife called him out of the blue and said he could see the girls as long as they didn't stay down at his town house. She was just worried about the effect of news stories or seeing another FBI man question their dad. She had seemed pleasant, even supportive, when she had called the night before.

The trip gave him a chance to think about something other than who had set him up and how he could straighten out this mess. An attorney he'd retained had told him to sit tight and he'd figure out what the Feds had on him. The thing that bothered Tasker was that the attorney talked as if he were guilty and they would just try to get away with it, instead of believing he had nothing to do with any of this dirty business. Tasker figured the guy had been in Dade too long and was used to representing real crooks.

Tasker also spent the drive thinking about Tina Wiggins, who'd been good about calling and even risking the occasional visit to see how he was doing. He had the feeling that, even though she wouldn't admit it, she thought he'd robbed the bank and had the cash stashed safely somewhere. She was a hard one to get a fix on, but he sure didn't mind trying to figure her out.

As he turned into the neighborhood he'd lived in for three years before banishment to Miami, he noticed the cleaner, almost renewed look to the houses, with fresh paint and new shrubs. He saw his girls in the driveway more than six houses away and let a broad grin break out across his face. It didn't even dim when he noticed his ex-wife, Donna, leaning in the front door frame, her blond hair in a loose braid, tight belly peeking beneath a short T-shirt. He almost didn't recognize her at first and couldn't figure it out until he realized it was because she was smiling.

IT HAD BEEN the best day he'd spent with his kids and former wife since the divorce. Things had been light and easy and the girls giggled nonstop from the first minute he tossed them in the air, through lunch and a long session on the trampoline, which almost cost Tasker his chicken sandwich.

Playing the girls' favorite game, super-bounce, Tasker had caught Donna out of the corner of his eye.

'What are you grinning about?' he asked.

She talked through her smile in that quiet cracker drawl that she could turn into a laser when provoked. 'Just nice to see you and the girls together.'

'And not feel like killing me?'

'Yeah, that, too.' The easy shrug with the smile could stop any man.

He bounced Emily, the younger, to the side, then flopped onto his butt. Scooting to the edge of the trampoline and next to Donna, he said, 'Why now?'

'Don't know. Maybe knowing you're in trouble and knowing you're basically a good guy who doesn't deserve all that's happened to you.'

'Thanks, Donna. You didn't deserve what happened to me either.'

She gave him a weak smile this time, then said, 'What's gonna happen? I mean, they're not saying this was an accident or poor judgment, like the Jack Sandersen incident. They're calling you a crook.'

'I know. And they're way off the mark. The problem is ...'

'What?'

'There's a couple of problems and I should be able to work them out.'

'That sounds like the man I married,' Donna said, reaching a hand behind his neck and planting a long, deep kiss right on his mouth.

I could get used to this, he thought.

*

TASKER'S RIDE BACK seemed like a dream. He'd almost forgotten that someone was trying to ruin his life. Now he felt like he had a reason to fight back. He turned into Kendall, feeling almost good. Coming up his street, he was surprised to see Tina Wiggins's FDLE-issued Monte Carlo in front of his town house. He found her spread out on a lounge chair on his patio, shirt lifted to her midriff and jean shorts rolled high on her perfect, long legs, soaking up the sun.

She said, 'Sorry, didn't think you'd mind if I made myself comfortable while I waited.'

'Not at all.' He fumbled with the keys so badly he barely managed to open the door, feeling her smirk behind him as he tried to concentrate. He said without turning his head, 'What brings you out this bright afternoon?'

'Maybe I was lonely. Needed some companionship.'

'Yeah? That mean you're convinced I'm not a bank robber?'

She smiled, following him into the house. 'Means I don't care. Honest cop with a good job. Rich bank robber. Both have their advantages.'

He looked at her bright face framed in that light brown hair and couldn't tell whether she was serious or jerking him around. Her look now said something else. This time he was the one who kissed her, only briefly thinking about his kiss with Donna less than two hours earlier. Tina showed no surprise, as she pulled him to her and their lips met. Her hands fell to his butt and squeezed as their kiss became deeper and more involved. He pulled her with him and they tumbled together, still kissing, onto the couch in his living room. He almost thought he'd black out, the feeling was so intense, then Tina pushed away.

'What's wrong?'

She said, 'Not one thing,' then pulled her white polo shirt over her head, displaying two round breasts pushing out along the edges of her white bra. The color difference between the bra and her bronze skin was striking. Tasker felt light-headed but maintained. Why couldn't he have more days like this? Vaguely, he was aware of the sound of a phone somewhere, almost like it was muffled. Then he was startled to reality by Tina's voice.

'You gonna answer that?'

'Let the machine catch it.' He pulled her to him and kissed her again.

The machine in the kitchen clicked on after the fourth ring and he was prepared not to listen to it, but Tina hesitated as the message started. He cringed when he heard the voice and fought the urge to spring up and kill the machine.

On the machine, Donna was chattering on about what a good afternoon she'd had and that she'd never thought about reconciliation until this afternoon. She ended with, 'If we'd spent a little more time like we did this afternoon and less time judging each other, things would have been a lot different. Maybe it's not too late.'

Tina had now backed away from him and listened intently as he tried to come up with an explanation. Before the machine had clicked off, she had her shirt back on.

Tasker said, 'Tina, wait a second.'

'Billy, there's nothing to explain. I don't own you. I just thought we had something different. Don't you see you can trust me? You don't have to hide things from me.'

She was up and out the door before he could speak. Looking up at heaven, he said, 'One thing, just let one thing work out for me and I'll be a happy man.'

TOM DOOLEY SAT at his desk in the robbery task force, acting like he was working when, in fact, he just liked being at his desk because no one bothered him there. The solitude and being near the cash kept him calm. To avoid an ugly situation with Bema after they'd stolen the cash back from Cole Hodges, he'd agreed to store the money in one of the office's temporary evidence lockers. It was safe inside a small, locked cubbyhole and it couldn't be opened unless you had both keys to it. This way, with Dooley holding one key and Bema the other, neither could access the cash alone. Like having control of a nuclear missile silo. Dooley thought this arrangement was better than splitting the money because it kept Bema from spending it, and now Dooley had more time to figure how to screw the young Metro-Dade detective out of the cash.

The office had been pretty quiet since the riots, with only Derrick Sutter ever giving him a dirty look, as much because he didn't like him as because Dooley had ratted out a fellow law enforcer. For all Dooley knew, the Miami cop had his mind on the cash and was pissed someone else had taken it. Dooley was starting to see that this town was full of crooks.

Dooley had migrated back to the task force office, too, because he didn't want that hotshot Mac Nmir noticing him too much now. He'd accomplished what he needed to and now Nmir was on only one scent: Bill Tasker. He'd let the little dark agent keep digging and maybe make a decent case against the FDLE agent.

As Dooley finished some calculations on how long he could live on different amounts of cash, he glanced out the window at the front of the squad bay and almost stopped breathing. As he stood to walk toward the window, he faintly heard Derrick Sutter say, 'Damn, would you look at that shit.'

Dooley was speechless. Staring out the window at the parking lot, right in front of the building, he saw Rick Bema, a twenty-seven-year-old thirty-nine-thousand-dollar-a-year still-living-at-home cop, getting out of a brand-new fire-engine-red Corvette convertible. The detective had on a new tailored suit and paused by the car to chat with some of the guys from the stolen car task force, who looked at the car with envy both personal and professional. What had this stupid son-of-a-bitch shit-eating faggot done?

Dooley waited in the office, trying to act uninterested until Bema walked in.

Bema said, 'Hey, guys, ask me what's new?'

Sutter said, 'The car and the suit.'

Bema smiled. 'Correct both times.'

Dooley, controlling himself, said, 'What gives, Rick? Why the new stuff?'

'Well, Tom, when I moved into my new place over on South Beach, I decided I needed a new car and look. Know what I mean? A new image.'

'Yeah, new image.' Dooley smiled and said in a lower tone, 'Rick, could I see you back in the conference room a minute?'

ONCE IN THE ROOM, Dooley paced a few moments before confronting his partner in crime.

'What were you thinking, Rick?'

'What d'you mean?'

'You know what I fucking mean. The car, the apartment. Jesus, Rick, we're supposed to be keeping a low profile.'

Bema gave him a surprised look and dug out a key hooked to a small green square. 'The money is safe. I used my own savings for this. Even *you* can't tell me how to spend my own money.'

'You wouldn't have spent it, you cheap bastard, if you didn't know you were about to have a windfall. You gotta use your head or we're gonna get nabbed.'

'You gonna mind your own fucking business, my friend, or I'll have a little chat with Agent Nmir. What you think 'bout that?'

Dooley bit his tongue, watching the young cop tuck the key back into his left front pocket. His head snapped up as Sutter peeked in the door.

Sutter said, 'What's this, a private meeting? Comin' up with a case you don't need me for?'

Dooley said, 'This don't concern you.'

Sutter completely ignored him and said to Bema, 'Nice wheels, Rick.'

'Thank you, my friend.' He turned to Dooley and said, 'Now, that's a man who appreciates the finer things.'

Sutter went on. 'You move out of your folks', too?'

'I did.'

'What about meals? I know you Cuban boys are awful particular about your food.'

'I moved out, that's all. I still visit my mama for breakfast and dinner. She miss me otherwise.'

Dooley couldn't stand it anymore. 'You fuckin' guys can talk about Rick's puberty, but I got work to do.'

Sutter said, 'Like what? Blaming Bill Tasker for shit he didn't do?'

Dooley froze. He turned to eye the Miami detective. He couldn't get a read on the lean, muscular black man. 'What's that supposed to mean?'

Sutter smirked. 'It means that he's the only straight guy around here and I think I'm the only one around here not getting rich and I may start to resent it.' Without warning, he spun on his heel and headed out the door.

Dooley watched him disappear around the corner, then looked at the grinning Rick Bema. He thought, Is everyone on the make?

*

TASKER'S HEART RATE was steadily increasing as he nego-
tiated traffic on US 1, headed toward the ramp for northbound
I-95 in Kendall. The smaller residential town had somehow
kept its quiet appeal through the explosive growth of Miami.
When he was suspended, he'd been told not to go to the FDLE
office, but no one had told him to stay away from the task
force office. He still had some things in his desk and he had to
prove to himself he could see his old partners without his legs
shaking.

After his twenty-minute ride north, he headed east on Miami
Garden Drive and into the parking lot of the business plaza
that housed the FBI-sponsored task forces: robbery, telemarketing and stolen cars. Sliding into a spot next to a beautiful red
convertible Corvette, Tasker's heart was racing as he slowly made
his way toward the front door. Just inside the entrance, he almost
ran head-on into Tom Dooley. They both froze, assessing each
other silently for a minute.

Dooley looked at him, clearly not as friendly as he'd been
during their last conversation. Dooley said, 'What brings you up
here again? I figured you'd been indicted by now.'

'Thought you were in my corner.'

'Shit, I thought you were innocent until they found that cash
at your apartment. So I'll help in the investigation if they ask me,
but young Mac Nmir made the case hisself.'

Tasker clenched his fist. 'He had a little help with the
evidence.'

Dooley took a second and said, 'How do you figure?'

'The cash they found in my grill came from someone.'

'Like anyone'll ever believe that bullshit. Tasker, this is Miami,
not Hollywood.'

Tasker raised his fist and Dooley threw both hands up to block
the punch. As soon as he saw the opening, Tasker threw his knee
into Dooley's hip. The heavy man took a step back and lowered
his hands. Tasker popped him right in the face. As he grabbed the
older FBI man, Tasker felt a hand on his shoulder and turned.

Rick Bema said, 'Hold on, Billy. If everyone hit him who
wanted to, he'd never be out of the hospital.'

Tasker relaxed his grip and backed away.

Dooley spit out some blood. 'Shit, the day this ass-licking
faggot can kick my ass is the day I retire.'

Without saying a word, Tasker popped him in the face again, then walked inside.

ACROSS THE STREET from the task force, FBI Special Agent Slayda 'Mac' Nmir lowered his binoculars and made some notes. Maybe Tasker had some balls after all. Hitting that guy didn't mean you were a bad person, just one that was around Dooley. Nmir couldn't count the number of times he'd wanted to do that himself. He'd been following Tasker in his Bureau Ford Taurus for an hour when he'd stopped at the task force. That surprised him, but not as much as the Metro-Dade cop Rick Bema stopping the fight, then polishing a new Corvette in the lot. Maybe he'd been hasty in his initial assessment of the case. Tasker could have partners. He had to line up an interview with Bema just as soon as possible and without any warning.

IN THE CORNER of the plaza's parking lot, behind the wheel of a new stolen Ford F-150 pickup truck, Cole Hodges adjusted the bandage around his head. The Jackson Memorial emergency room physician had made him look like a goddamn Pakistani convenience store clerk. The beating that Cuban cop had laid on him was bad enough, but right now he didn't have ten dollars to his name. He was pissed off, had a headache and was ready to handle his business. Now.

fifteen

IN THE TASK FORCE BATHROOM, Tasker rinsed the
blood off his knuckles, wishing he'd used his elbow instead.
It felt right to slug that tub of lard but he didn't know what
repercussions it might have with the FBI investigation. He
looked at his face in the mildewed mirror, realizing how much
this mess had taken out of him. He let out a little cry, thanking
God no one else was in the two-stall, two-urinal rest room. He
opened the small head-level window to let some air circulate
and then splashed some cool water over his face. As he dried
off, the door behind him swung open and a smiling Derrick
Sutter appeared.

Sutter said, 'Well, well, if it ain't John Dillinger.'

Tasker didn't know how to take that, so he kept staring at him
in the mirror.

'Relax, Bill, I'm just joking. Shit, the FBI jerk-offs are the only
ones who believe any of that bullshit. Besides, after what I just
saw through the window, you're more of a Gerry Cooney. The
great white hope.' The thin black detective smiled.

'I shouldn't have hit him.'

'Why not? Most times I wonder why I didn't smack him
sometime during the day' He smiled as he eyed Tasker. 'Shit, I
had your kind of money, I'd never come back to this dump.'

Tasker jerked his head up.

Sutter held out his hands. 'Calm down, slugger. I was joking
again. Don't hit me, too.' He paused for effect, then said, 'Really,
no one thinks you did it.'

Tasker let out his breath and smiled. 'You think?'

'Maybe a few. Mainly 'cause they like the idea of a crooked
FDLE agent. You guys don't usually get hooked up. You do the
hooking up and lots of locals get jealous.'

'I'm only gonna say this once: I had nothing to do with any of the things they're trying to lay on me now.'

Sutter smiled again. 'I believe you, I believe you. That still doesn't answer a big question.'

'What's that?' asked Tasker.

'Where's the CCR's cash?'

'Why do you care?'

'Bill, I always care when there's more than a million dollars in cash floating around my city and no one knows where it is.' He paused, eyeing Tasker. 'You got any ideas?'

'You know, for everyone saying I'm innocent, a lot of people think I know where the cash is.'

Sutter kept him in a sideways glance. 'That doesn't answer my question.'

Tasker paused and said, 'I got some weak ideas, why?'

'Because I got some good ideas.' Sutter smiled. 'You go first.'

Tasker paused, assessing the sharp-featured black detective. Was this just another guy on the take? Something told Tasker no. They were in a ten-by-ten bathroom with one window. It was as good as the cone of silence.

Tasker started slowly. 'I been looking around.'

Sutter broke into a grin, his gold-rimmed front tooth shining. 'I can see by the scab on your eyebrow you're the one the Eighth Street Boyz thumped.'

'You heard?'

'Everyone heard.'

'I also went by the bank and talked to the new manager.'

'And?'

'This CCR attorney, Cole Hodges, keeps popping up all over the place.'

Sutter's eyebrows rose. 'Really?'

'Yeah. What do you know about him?'

'Not much. He's a bigwig and I know a lot of cops are scared of him and I never knew why.'

'Can you see if you can find out? I mean, discreetly?'

'What's in it for me?'

Tasker looked at him. 'No cash, if that's what you mean.'

'I was hoping for ...'

Tasker waited for him to finish, then decided not to push it and said, 'What about your ideas?'

'This is nothing official, mind you, but I've been keeping my eyes open, too.'

'And?'

'And I didn't even get my ass kicked.' His eyes glowed.

'Funny.'

Sutter nodded. 'You're the only one I wouldn't suspect if someone from this task force kilt that bank manager and stole that money.' Occasionally, Sutter's Miami roots overtook his college English classes.

Someone from the hallway tried to push into the tiny bathroom.

Sutter held the door and said, 'Occupied, come back in five minutes.'

A voice said, 'There's more than one stall.'

Sutter said through the door, 'Trust me, there is some shit flying in here you don't want to see.'

Tasker held his anxiety to push Sutter to his point. Finally, he said, 'Okay, I'm hooked. Keep going.'

'It's obvious a lot of the information that nailed you came from Tom Dooley in the first place. Now that may be innocent info passed on by a concerned law officer, but then again we're talking about Tom Dooley.'

'Yeah?'

'Anyways, he hasn't been around much at all since the riot and he don't give me the time of day. It may be because he knows I think he's a rat, but it may be that he's been busy on other things.' Sutter opened the door and peered down both hallways, then closed it again, leaning on it to keep it tightly shut. 'Then, last week he and Rick Bema become real buddy-buddy. Have lunch together, working on something just between the two of them.'

'So?' asked Tasker.

'Today the Prince of Calle Ocho showed up in a new Corvette.'

'That's his?'

'You saw it, then.'

Tasker nodded. 'Anything else?'

'Saved the best for last.'

'What's that?'

Sutter took a second, obviously savoring the power he held

in this conversation. 'The two of them, Dooley and Bema, have something in temporary evidence.'

'So?'

'We haven't worked a case in weeks and those two haven't done anything for longer than that. They got something personal up there.'

'How do you know?'

'They check it once a day. They keep the keys separate so they have to be together. I noticed it the other day and watched them every day till today.'

Tasker had to think on that one. He could pass it on, but there really wasn't anything to look at yet. Just a suspicion on his part. Mac Nmir would be the only one who would be able to check on it effectively, and he'd never believe an FBI agent would be capable of something like that.

Tasker said, 'You come up with anything else?'

'Not yet, but I'm working on it.'

'Thanks, Derrick. Might be some help later on. You with me?'

'If that help involves grabbing a million bucks, you can count on me.'

Tasker just looked at the Miami cop, realizing he wasn't kidding this time.

TOM DOOLEY waited for Tasker to get what he needed out of his desk and leave in his Jeep before worrying about tracking down Bema and chewing his ass out some more for flashing their new-found wealth. The dumb shit just didn't seem to get it. This was a long-term plan to retire, not blow the cash quick and have everyone asking questions. Before he was too hard on Bema, he had to figure out what to do with Tasker. The son-of-a-bitch cunt shithead seemed to have a little more guts than Dooley had given him credit for, and he'd said he was about to mount a defense. What would happen if Dooley were able to short-circuit that defense? Make it some kind of accident. This would be the last killing and maybe the most important one. If Tasker died with these questions unresolved, people would assume he robbed the bank, and the whole investigation would end up closed by exceptional circumstance. Dooley grinned at the idea as he trotted from office to office, trying to find his partner.

He found Bema by his Corvette, of course, wiping down the trunk where a bird had dropped on it.

Dooley said, '*¡Hola, amigo!* How's it goin'?'

Bema kept rubbing, barely looking up.

'What's wrong?' asked Dooley.

'I still pissed you treat me like a little kid today. I not stupid. I know how to spend my own money.'

'Never said you were stupid, Rick. I just disagree on spending money right now while things are still hot.'

'That's fine, but you're not the boss.'

'No, but I'm majority owner of the cash, remember?'

'That's another thing. I was the one who got the info on Hodges and I'm the one who got the cash back. I think we should be equal partners.'

'You can think all you want, but we already have an agreement.'

Bema let the rag slip out of his hand as he turned to face Dooley full on. 'I been thinking about a lot of things, *amigo*. And I been thinking I don' need you at all. I could talk to Mister FBI Special Agent Mac Nmir and in about three minutes have him off Bill Tasker's back and on yours and never get implicated myself.'

'Sorry, *amigo*, but you're overestimating your intelligence by about three thousand percent.'

'Maybe so, but I still got the key to the evidence.'

'So what?'

'I also know something you don'.'

'What don' I know,' Dooley said, mocking the Cuban's accent.

'I know your fellow FBI agent Mr. Mac Nmir followed Billy Tasker here.'

Dooley looked at him. 'So?'

'So, I noticed that Billy drive off and Mr. Mac Nmir is still sitting in his government car across the street, watching the task force. Why would he stay if Tasker left?'

Accent or not, that caught Dooley's attention. He instinctively raised his eyes and, without even trying, saw the young FBI man in his G-car in the lot across Miami Gardens Drive. What did that clown want? He turned his attention back to Rick Bema.

Bema continued. 'Know that an equal partner would never

consider walking across the street and talking to him. But a junior partner might.'

'Rick, you ain't gonna tell no one nothing, so cut the act.'

'No, by telling Nmir, I could get you off my back and still have the fee I already took from the bag. You'd be the only one implicated. And a decent guy like Bill Tasker is off the hook. This option is looking better and better.' The muscle-bound detective smiled.

'What fee?'

'The forty grand I took when it was still frozen. You don't see nothing, do you?'

'So I'd say we're pretty equal anyway.'

'No,' he said, without humor or accent. 'Now we split what's left or I drop a dime on your ass.'

'You're bluffing,' Dooley said, believing it.

'Don't push me.'

'Push you? I fucking dare you. He's right across the street. Go spill your guts. But when you back down, remember our deal and remember who the junior partner is.'

Bema looked shocked on his bluff being called. He turned without a word and stomped to the edge of the parking lot, then looked across the six-lane avenue toward Nmir's brown Taurus. He paused like he wanted Dooley to say something or call after him, but the FBI man just stared. He felt like reaching for his pistol and ending Bema's threat right then and there, but there were too many witnesses and it would be tough to explain.

Bema, still at the edge of the parking lot, took a step through the short, sparse ficus hedge and now stood on the empty side-walk as cars buzzed past at fifty miles an hour. Dooley could see Nmir over Bema's shoulder. Nmir acted like he didn't notice the detective coming toward him, but it was obvious he saw Bema waiting to cross the street. Dooley knew this game. In a second or two, Bema would turn and give Dooley a chance to back down, and right now Dooley figured it would work.

Dooley wasn't used to this uncomfortable feeling of panic. Even if this stupid spic was just fooling around, it had to look suspicious to Nmir. If he called out now, Bema would know he had the upper hand and who knows where his stupid demands would end; but if he came back on his own, everything would be all right. He watched as Bema turned, like he expected Dooley to concede. The smirk on his face said it all; he knew he was in charge and Dooley would have to kiss his ass. That made Dooley remain still and silent. The guy was bluffing, he had to be.

Bema waited for one car to pass and took a step into the road. He paused, waiting for other traffic, and slowly continued his trek toward Slayda 'Mac' Nmir.

Dooley felt the fear rise in his throat. He could see Nmir opening his door to greet Bema, who was still not to the middle of the road.

Then it happened. Maybe the first thing to truly shock the twenty-six-year FBI veteran in a long, long time. He stood open-mouthed as a big black pickup truck raced from out of nowhere, striking Bema square on and sending him back across the two lanes he'd just crossed and onto the curb in a heap of blood and strips of Joseph Abboud suit. Dooley could hear the sickening thud of Bema's body as it slid across the sidewalk and into the same gap in the bushes that he had cut through to cross the street in the first place. Blood from his massive head wound seeped onto the sidewalk and toward the hedge as the blood from his mangled legs filled the gutter near the street. Traffic slowed as several cars stopped and the drivers ran over to help the fallen pedestrian.

Dooley stared, not breathing. This was incredible. He caught a glimpse of the driver. Some kind of Middle Easterner in a turban or something and real dark-skinned. Dooley remained motionless until he saw Mac trying to cross the traffic and come toward him. That snapped Dooley out of it and he shot over to Bema's lifeless body. He figured he had about ten seconds till Nmir made it across, and the drivers coming to assist were still a few feet away. Dooley leaned over the body like he was checking the pulse or something, and quickly ran his hand through Bema's pockets until he felt the plastic square that held the evidence key. Fucking perfect. As he reached into Bema's pocket, he realized the inside was already soaked with blood. He slipped the key into his own pocket just as Mac approached. He had the money, no partners, and Mac Nmir as a witness to the accident. Somewhere he must have done something to make God happy.

Mac finally made it across the street, running toward Dooley and the body. 'Is he dead?' the young FBI agent asked, clearly stressed by the accident, pushing through the two drivers who had stopped.

Dooley couldn't help the sarcasm. 'No, nitwit, he's napping.'

'Jesus, Dooley, what happened? Why was he coming to see me? Did you see who hit him? Is there anything we can do? Did you call nine-one-one?'

Dooley cut him off. 'Calm down, Nmir. He's dead. The fucking truck must've been going fifty when it hit him.' He looked at the spreading pool of blood and suddenly doubted Mac's ability to solve any type of case. If he couldn't figure out Bema was dead, he wasn't the sharpest knife in the drawer.

Mac was panting now. 'I know, I know, I saw it was a black guy.'

That was when it struck Dooley. It was Cole Hodges with his head bandaged. Bema had fucked it up and hadn't killed him like he said. No wonder no one had discovered the body or reported the smell. That was just one more problem he'd have to handle, but right now he was in control.

sixteen

TASKER SAT on his patio with a bottle of Icehouse in his hand and two empties next to him on the ground. He'd spent the afternoon contemplating what Derrick Sutter had told him. The problem now was what to do with the information. Should he try to explain it to Mac Nmir and let the FBI handle it? They hadn't gotten much else right, why would this be any different? Should he look into it himself? On suspension and suspected of the crime could cause him problems if he got caught. Tasker just didn't know who he could trust. It seemed like anyone who even heard about the cash became instantly corrupted. He personally couldn't care less about it. He'd be happy if he just figured out his personal life.

Earlier, after talking with Donna, then punching Dooley, he'd gotten a glimpse of what his life used to be like. When he'd enjoyed the groove of an investigation and felt as if he had nerves of steel. He'd never been a tough guy, but nothing really scared him either. He'd always taken his fitness and tactical training very seriously. He had good judgment and never acted like a bully, treating people professionally and following the rules laid out by the agencies he'd worked for. It was that one time. The time he'd bent the rules and tried to show some leeway and fucked up. This time he hadn't screwed up. He didn't have anything to do with it. This time he was going to straighten it all out himself.

Now, with half a buzz on, his mind worked on his problems from different angles. Was the frame-up over or was there still another chapter? Things like that gnawed at him. As he started to write down some thoughts, he heard a car door slam nearby. The way things had been going, if he'd had a gun he might have reached for it, but when the patio door swung open and he saw Tina Wiggins he was glad he was just sitting there, a little drunk.

She gave him a slight smile, 'Hey.'

'Hey,' he answered, not bothering to rise.

'Sorry I ran out. Maybe I'm just a little insecure.'

'Sorry I didn't tell you I was going to see my family.'

She pulled up a lounger and sat next to him. 'You still have feelings for your ex, don't you?'

He hesitated, then figured he'd lived with enough lies the past four years. 'Yeah, I guess I do. But I have no idea where we're going. It was just an afternoon. Sorry.'

'Don't be. You have any idea how many guys would just lie? Most still living at home would hand me a line of shit. You're a special kind of guy. Sort've weird, but special.'

They both laughed and she kissed him again, leaning over him and lingering, letting her breasts lie across his chest. Then she said, 'You doin' okay?'

'Yeah, the same.'

'I mean with the car accident stuff.'

'What car accident?' He sat up as she pulled back to her seat.

'You haven't heard? It's been all over the news and I thought someone would have called you.'

He leaned forward. 'Tell me, what car accident?'

'The Metro cop from your task force, Bema, was a victim of a hit-and-run in front of the task force office about four this afternoon.'

'Is he alive?'

'DOA.'

He stared at her. 'Any suspects?'

'No suspects, lots of witnesses.'

'What time did it happen? I mean exactly.'

She shrugged. 'Four, I think.'

Tasker took a second and a gulp of air. 'I must've just left.'

This time, Tina showed her surprise. 'You were at the office today? Why?'

'I needed some papers, but I really wanted to see if anyone knew anything about my case.'

'Did you find anything out?' She leaned in close, her eyes wide.

He looked at her. Was it a good idea to risk her reputation, too? He needed help, but she wasn't involved and had a bright future. He started to shake his head, when she spoke.

'C'mon, when are you gonna trust me?'

'It's not that.'

'Then what?'

'I hate to involve you in this mess.'

She grabbed his face with both hands and turned his head toward her. 'Billy, I am involved. Now give it up. What'd you find out?'

'Derrick Sutter, the Miami cop, said he thought Tom Dooley and Rick Bema were acting strange and that they had something stored in a temporary evidence locker.'

'At the office?'

'Yeah.'

'And he thinks it's the cash?'

'Yeah, maybe. Shit, who knows? It's not enough to act on and it sounds kinda far-fetched anyway.'

'We gotta start someplace,' said Tina.

'I guess.' Tasker let his voice trail off.

'Billy, I know you don't like going head to head with people, but this is getting serious. Maybe it'd help if you talked to me about what happened when you were in West Palm. You said that was the root of your problem.'

'I said it was the start of my problems, and you have to know the story already.'

'Only the rumors, and they change every time I hear them.'

'It's not the right time.' Tasker felt anxious, like he needed to get rid of her, but he kept his seat.

'Then when?'

'After I straighten this mess out.'

'What if you can't?' Her eyes penetrated his.

'Then the prison psychologist at MCC will have plenty of time to help me.'

TASKER PULLED OFF I-95 near the Fort Lauderdale airport. He didn't like working in Broward County because the supervisor in the Broward FDLE office was an asshole. But this could be important.

He walked into the administrative building of Broward University early in the day, before the workers were tired and crabby and less likely to answer questions. He needed background on Hodges and this was the only lead the Florida Bar could provide, other than his office address. So here he was at the private university in Davie, right in the middle of Broward County, twenty-five miles north of Miami. The school sat near the Miami Dolphins training camp in an area where several minor schools shared facilities. In all the time Tasker had been in South Florida, he'd never been to this campus before. All he knew of Broward was that it was a school for rich kids and guys trying to earn a law degree on a part-time basis.

At the registrar's office he surveyed the front counter until he found the only clerk who didn't look like a Catholic school matron. He smiled as he came toward her, reading her name tag.

'Hello, Rachel, could you tell me how I'd go about finding out about one of your alumni?'

The twenty-five-year-old with sandy hair didn't look up, but said, 'What would you want to know?'

'Exactly when he graduated, who his professors were, that sort of thing.'

She continued to read something off her computer screen and said, 'That's not public record, sorry.'

Tasker gave her a second, then said, 'Rachel, this is important.' He held up his backup badge and hoped she wouldn't ask for ID.

She raised her head, looked at the badge, then up at Tasker and smiled. 'Cool. Who are you after?'

TEN MINUTES LATER, as he traversed the small campus to the law school, Tasker looked through the four sheets of paper Rachel had provided. The two biggest things Tasker had learned were that the Cole Hodges who had attended the school had been born on November 12, 1958, and that there was one professor still there from when Hodges had been in school in the mid-eighties. That date of birth put Hodges in his early forties, and Tasker knew that wasn't right. He hoped this old codger of a law professor would remember him.

Tasker ran down the corridor of small offices until he found one with the name Mulemann on the door. He knocked and opened the cheap door, as a scratchy voice said, 'Yes?'

Tasker looked around the incredibly cramped office, quickly noticing the poster saying 'Proud to be in the ACLU' and a book on the desk titled *Police Totalitarianism*. Tasker thought, Oh shit, and gathered his thoughts.

'I'm Bill Shelton with the Southern Poverty Law Center.' He watched the hunched old man quiver at the thought of a representative from the 'Southern ACLU' actually here talking to him. The PLC had actually done some good work against the Klan. Tasker didn't mind the role.

Mulemann ran a hand over his liver-spotted forehead to smooth out his remaining gray-wire hair. 'Oh yes, sir, what can I do for you?'

'First let me say, Professor, that I've heard a lot of good things about you.'

'Really, where?'

Tasker hesitated. 'You know, throughout the circuit. We always appreciate good lawyers with high ideals.'

The small man smiled with satisfaction. Tasker let him glow for a moment as he thought of his next tack.

'I don't want to bother you, Professor, but we are considering letting one of your former students do some work for us and we wanted an idea of his background. Could you help us in the most confidential way? No one will ever know we talked.'

'Of course, of course. Who is it?'

'Cole Hodges.'

The professor's small lips dropped into a frown.

'Do you remember him from the mid-eighties?'

'Oh, I remember him, I'm not a doddering old fool. He really doesn't acknowledge the university for getting him where he is today. In fact, he has been quite rude when I've approached him on behalf of the school.'

Tasker noted the hostility in the old man's voice. 'What was he like as a student?'

'Back then we only had two or three minorities in the program.'

'How many do you have now?'

'Two or three.' The old man cleared his throat and continued. 'Cole was a nice enough fella his first year.'

'Why just his first year?'

The professor sat silently, obviously trying to gather his words carefully. 'Something happened right at the start of his second year and he definitely slowed down. His studies suffered, his demeanor changed, and he withdrew from anyone remotely close to him.'

'Any ideas what happened?'

'Well, it was so dramatic that I went to the dean with it. That's why it's so clear in my memory. I was afraid he might have a drug problem. You know how the blacks can be. They keep their problems locked up and turn to drugs or alcohol.'

Tasker started to doubt this guy's sanity. Was he a racist member of the ACLU or just an average hypocrite?

The professor kept talking. 'Cole gained weight all of a sudden and became quite moody; that's why I suspected drugs. Later he evened out, and by graduation he seemed straight.'

'Did the dean help him?'

'No, the dean told me to drop the whole thing or we would look like we were picking on him because he was a minority.'

Tasker nodded to buy time, while he considered the ramifications of these facts.

The professor said, 'Does any of that help?'

Tasker smiled. 'I think so.'

seventeen

TOM DOOLEY SAT at his desk, playing with the matching evidence keys. What incredible luck. Bema is killed and Dooley had the cash all to himself again. The trick this time was to make sure Hodges didn't get his hands on it. That son-of-a-prick bastard had more tricks than Penn and Teller. Even after Bema was supposed to have killed him, he kept surprising Dooley. Logically, the money was safest right where it was in temporary evidence. It wasn't unusual for the cops from the two task forces to keep personal shit in the lockers. Cops being cops, there was always one of them hiding something from a wife or storing naked photos of a girlfriend in them. The problem was that the Bureau could do an unannounced audit of the lockers at any time. This policy was to discourage exactly the kind of behavior that kept half the lockers full at any given time.

DOOLEY HADN'T RUN straight to the money after Bema's accident for several reasons, not the least of which was that he had ended up with blood on his shoes and the cuffs of his pants. The warm, sticky sensation had made him squeamish and he figured it might look funny running to the locker while the paramedics worked on his partner in front of the office. He took the night to calm down, checking for Hodges the whole trip home and locking all the doors once he was there. His wife had heard about the accident and even gave him some distance, letting him play some Nintendo 64 with Andy, then watch the Panthers whip up on the Blackhawks. If every night were like that, he wouldn't be so desperate to leave.

That morning on his way in, he had considered his options, but they were all clouded by the fact that Tasker seemed to have figured out the game. Now the question was what to do about it. Let it be and see if Tasker could get someone to listen to him, or take action and shut the asshole down? If he did talk, and Nmir or some other enterprising agent looked hard enough, they might make the connection to the havoc of the past two weeks and Dooley. This was a question he'd have to consider for a good long time.

Now, at his desk, he let the keys fall back into one outline. The empty office added to his good mood, giving him the time and space to think, not only about his problems but about his plans as well. Some traveling – Boston for family, Atlantic City and Vegas to wash the first fifty grand or so of the cash, then Cancún. He had always liked the resort, and with the old lady at home and the extra money, he could make some serious time with all the Jewish broads from Long Island who loved to soak up the sun down there.

He finally decided he couldn't wait any longer and slowly wandered toward the evidence room, stopping in the copy room first, then the files room, chatting with the few people working. Once in the evidence area, he took a minute and then headed toward locker 16 in the upper right corner. As he was about to pull the keys from his front pants pocket, he heard a voice.

'You okay, Dooley?'

Dooley jumped and twisted to see Derrick Sutter in a nice blue suit, standing in the doorway. His dark skin tone almost matched the suit and made the collar of his white shirt seem to glow.

'Huh?' asked Dooley.

'Are you handling the Bema thing okay? It had to be rough at the scene.'

Dooley took his hands out of his pockets and smoothed his polo shirt over his big belly. 'Yeah, yeah, it was nasty.'

'Why didn't you take the day off?'

'Had some things to catch up on.' Dooley looked at Sutter again. 'Why are you all dressed up? You got court?'

'No, man. Bema's viewing is this evening. Aren't you going?'

'I'm not much for funerals.'

'Who is, but the man died on duty. Show some respect.'

'We'll see. I got to take care of ...' He just looked around, his mind a blank.

Then Sutter said, 'You got something in evidence?'

'No, why?'

'Just wonderin' what you're doing in here. And I thought I saw you and Bema take the keys to one of the lockers.'

Dooley hesitated, racing through the possible answers. 'We were thinking of grabbing some court records for background on a case and thought this would be a good place to store them, that's all.'

Sutter nodded. 'I'll be around for a while if you need anything.'

'Thanks, but I'm all set.' He watched Sutter strut away and then said under his breath, 'Pretty much set for life.'

BILL TASKER TURNED in his bed to look straight up at the ceiling. He wasn't sure what time it was, but the sun had cleared the sliding glass door and he felt as if he'd come out of one dream into another. He'd never spent a night with a woman so intensely. Tina seemed to appreciate every movement he made and wasn't shy about expressing it. After the first shock of realizing just how much difference a Wonderbra could make on the shape of a woman, he still thought she could pose for any magazine he would ever buy. Her legs, while visible in street clothes, were still a miracle of nature, and her firm butt and muscular back left no doubt about her feelings on gym memberships. Still, the most amazing thing to Tasker, who'd dated a few times since the end of his seven-year marriage, was that Tina Wiggins trimmed her pubic hair. Not just around the edges but in a tight and symmetrical pattern, and for no other reason but aesthetics. He'd never been with a woman who took the time to shape her pubic hair, and it still caused him to smile, hours after the fact.

He lounged in that dreamy half-sleep state, feeling the weight of the body next to him. For some reason she was on the outside of the covers, but at least she hadn't fled out the door at dawn. Shit, she did more running from his apartment than Carl Lewis. It was nice just to smell her near. Something was different. He couldn't put his finger on it, but he sensed a definite change in her. It had been an odd twenty-four hours, having spent time with Donna, his ex-wife, leading up to a serious kiss and some fond memories, then to make love to Tina after wanting her for over a year. Still it was funny that his thoughts kept drifting back to Donna. She had been a brand-new teacher of twenty-two when he'd met her while on a security detail at a sports bar. Her bright eyes and blond hair had been magnetic and hadn't lost their attraction in the twelve years since. She'd just seemed to have had enough of his sulking after he'd gotten in trouble, and didn't want to have anything to do with him. Until yesterday. Tasker lay there, kicking himself for being in bed with the girl of his dreams and thinking about the one that got away.

As he turned to face her, he ran his hand through her hair. It didn't feel right. Then he realized she smelled entirely different and her hair was thicker, stiffer. He opened his eyes and saw the blond hair fall across the pillow. Before he could lean up to look, that pretty face turned and came into view.

'Whoa!' he yelped, then contained himself, trying to decide if he was still asleep or not.

'Surprise,' Donna said.

Only then did he notice that she was fully clothed and lying on top of the covers.

'Hey. What? Ah, where? Um, was there?'

'The girls and I thought we'd brighten your day.'

He smiled, still trying to clear his head. 'The girls are here?'

'Watching *Rugrats* in the living room. I hope you don't mind.'

He shook his head, smiling. 'Mind, of course not.' His eyes darted around the room uncontrollably, looking for clues to Tina's whereabouts and evidence that could be used against him.

Donna asked, 'Anything wrong?'

'No, no,' he shot back immediately, then noticed the bathroom door closed. This could be a train wreck if he wasn't careful or lucky. Maybe a bus would pile through his bedroom wall right now, making the problem of his ex-wife finding his girlfriend seem minor by comparison.

He slid out of bed, wrapping a sheet around him as he did. 'Excuse me,' he said, backing toward the closed bathroom door. He turned, trying to shield the door with his body. His legs were a little shaky, but holding up well. He steadied himself and tried the knob to the bathroom. Unlocked. That was a good sign. He opened the door and darted in, taking a few seconds to realize Tina wasn't there. Where had she gone? Would she be back? He took a second to gather his thoughts, relieved himself, then brushed his teeth, emerging from the bathroom slightly more confident, and impatient to see his two daughters.

He said, 'You did surprise me. When'd you get here?'

Donna, sitting on the edge of the bed, smiling, said, 'Only five minutes ago.'

'How'd you get in?'

'We were going to knock, but the front door was unlocked. Really, Bill, you should be more careful.'

'You're right, there,' clapping his hands together and letting out a nervous laugh. 'Give me a second to get dressed and we'll join the girls.' He waited for her to leave.

She smiled. 'What's wrong, Bill? You grow something in the last four years?'

'What?' Then, realizing the reference, laughed. 'No, just more modest.'

'Too bad, because you still have a killer chest and arms. Only a few new scars.'

'Not nearly as many fights as a patrolman.' He fingered the longest scar running down his left shoulder. 'And this is from my rotator cuff surgery.' He waited, motionless.

She took the hint and sauntered out of the room. He took the time to throw on some shorts and a T-shirt, then checked the room for signs of Tina. It looked all clear except for the empty condom wrapper on the floor next to the bed. He didn't think she had noticed it.

After giving the bathroom another once-over, he calmly entered the living room, to be greeted by his two angels and another smile from his wife. He froze, thinking of her as his wife, and then corrected himself. Ex-wife. She had asked for the divorce when the media frenzy and his guilt had consumed their whole life. He'd been the cause, he never doubted that. The alcohol to deaden the pain. Then the alcohol-induced behavior. He couldn't deny that he'd become an absolutely different man, and now, looking back on it, a man he was ashamed of.

He greeted the girls in front of the TV. The older, Kelly, said, 'Ya know what we watched last night?'

He smiled. 'No, what?'

'Mom called it your show. The funny old police show.'

Tasker straightened. 'If you are referring to *Hill Street Blues*, it is not a funny old show, it is the basis of all police work done today.'

Kelly looked at him with wide eyes. 'Really?'

'No, not really, but it was a good show. Not like the stuff on today. I won't watch a cop show now.'

'Will you watch *Rugrats* with us?'

'I'd watch anything with you,' he said, tickling Kelly and flopping next to Emily.

Both girls giggled and their mother smiled broadly, pulling Tasker toward the kitchen to talk and let the girls watch their cartoon. 'Daddy will watch in a little bit.' She weathered the protests, then looked into Tasker's eyes when they got in the kitchen. Donna said, 'You look out of it. Anything I can do to help?'

'Nothing at all.' He smiled, but his eyes made a pass over the room just in case, and Donna caught it.

'What are you looking for?'

'Nothing. The place is kinda messy, that's all.'

She smiled and lifted her hand, displaying a dark red lipstick in a gold case. 'I know. This was lying on the couch and I didn't want the girls to make a mess.'

He froze like a deer caught in the headlights of a tractor trailer.

Then the impossible happened. Donna giggled. The girls were absorbed by a cartoon and his ex-wife was taking great pleasure in this torment.

'Bill, we've been apart almost four years. I didn't think you'd become a monk.' She moved closer to him. 'I know you've met girls. That doesn't bother me. It did when we were married, but not now.'

'Donna, that was the booze. I never meant to hurt you. Things got out of control.'

'And I left you. I remember the story. But that doesn't mean I stopped loving you. Things happen. Don't add to your guilt now.'

'I have met a few women, but not many.'

'Bill, you've got deep blue eyes and perfect teeth. If you weren't so quiet, you'd be a walking party. I understand, really I'm not mad.' Then she kissed him. Deep and hard and in front of the girls, watching from the living room.

It was like his life had just shifted into the fast lane. As he started to get swept up in the euphoria, he heard a knock on his door.

He unlocked his lips and said quietly, 'Don't move.' Kelly had beaten him to the door and had it open before he left the kitchen. He heard a man say, 'Is your daddy home?' and Kelly said, 'Sure.' Like she knew the man.

Tasker froze when he reached the entryway and saw his visitor: Slayda 'Mac' Nmir.

COLE HODGES SAT in the Denny's on south Dixie Highway almost to Homestead, twenty miles south of Miami. He picked at his fried catfish and studied the figures on a legal pad in front of him. It was obvious to him he couldn't resurface as Cole Hodges. Even if the FBI couldn't prove anything, it would only be a matter of time before they determined his true identity and he'd have to finish his twenty-year sentence for robbery as Luther Williams. He didn't care much for St. Louis or the damn Missouri State Prison. All this led him to spend a few minutes reviewing his current finances. He had sixty grand in a Charles Schwab account and eleven more in treasury bonds. Seventy-one thousand dollars wouldn't carry him too far. There was no question he needed to get his cash back from that asshole Dooley. It wouldn't be easy this time. The man would be on guard and ready for trouble. Hodges might have to be sneaky, because he sure as shit wouldn't be lucky enough to find it on a car seat again.

He pushed the plate away and adjusted the ball cap he was wearing to hide the bandage that still covered his tender scalp. At least he had handled that Cuban dog who'd smashed his skull with a damn toaster. That was another lucky break. Sitting in the parking lot when that asshole started across Miami Gardens Drive. Then the dipshit had waited on the side of the road like he was daring Hodges to make his move. The sound of that sack of shit bouncing off the grill of the truck was music. Sounded better than any B. B. King song ever recorded. Hodges had seen the new Corvette that son of a bitch had bought with his money. Money he'd earned in his time with the CCR. Now that was justice. Hodges wasn't as mad at Dooley, he just wanted his cash back. Anything else was just gravy.

eighteen

TASKER WAVED good-bye as Donna, holding back her tears, backed the Honda minivan out of the driveway. The girls looked grief-stricken, but Donna was right not to let them see Daddy talk to the nice FBI man.

Tasker turned in the doorway to face the calm Mac Nmir, sitting on the edge of the couch waiting for his chance to chat.

'This better be good,' Tasker said, with surprising power. 'I got an attorney now and you know that.'

'You're not in custody and don't have to talk to me. Tell me to leave and I'm gone.'

Tasker thought over the proposal.

Mac said, 'But then you'll never know why I came by.'

Tasker gave it another ten seconds, then said, 'Okay, talk, but it better be good.'

Mac began, nonplussed by the attitude. 'First, I'll say I have my doubts about your guilt.'

'Finally.'

'Let me finish. I didn't say I thought you were innocent, I'm just curious about a few things. But I have to warn you, I'm under big-time pressure to take what I have to the grand jury, and you know what they say about the federal grand jury.'

'A prosecutor could indict a ham sandwich if he wanted to.'

'Right. If I don't come up with anything else in the next few days, you're it. I go with what I have, which includes a couple of witnesses, no alibi and of course the cash we recovered from your grill. I'd say that's plenty.'

Tasker's legs lost their stability and he sat quickly in a chair near the dining table. It was hard to act calm in the face of that statement. 'Then why are you here?'

'Ask a few questions and give you a chance to refute my findings. Just man to man. No official court documents. No reports. Just us, talking.'

Now Tasker could only nod.

'I've been watching a few things, and I saw Rick Bema pull into the task force lot in a new Vette just before he was hit by the truck.'

Tasker stared at him silently, waiting to see where this was headed.

'Where'd he get the money for a Vette?'

Tasker shrugged. 'I wish I knew.'

Mac kept going. 'Why'd you go by the office yesterday?'

Tasker said, 'Left my checkbook and a couple of bills.'

'You see the truck that hit Bema?'

Tasker shook his head.

Mac, clearly getting frustrated, said, 'Look, I know you don't like the Bureau and don't think I'm a real cop, but I really just want to hear your side of things.'

'I don't know what to tell you. You're one of the few people I've never lied to. I don't know how the cash got in my grill. I didn't have anything to do with the bank robbery. I don't know what else to tell you.'

Nmir nodded and then asked, 'Why'd you hit Dooley yesterday?'

'Because he's an asshole.'

Nmir said, 'Now that, I believe.'

TASKER FELT SHITTY. He'd been ordered not to go to Rick Bema's funeral because he might come in contact with witnesses in his case. That meant two things: He was still a serious suspect in the bank robbery, and Mac Nmir hadn't told anyone he'd seen Tasker at the task force the day before, otherwise he'd have had his ass chewed for that, too. He couldn't complain, because FDLE had given no indication his pay was about to be cut off and his bosses had gone out of their way to say what a decent guy he was. All that gave him hope.

After his encounter with Mac Nmir, Tasker had to get out and do something, even if it was only working on his fitness. The way things were going now, he'd need all his strength to fight off the other inmates at MCC or wherever they intended to hold him till trial. He headed down toward the bay near downtown because of the ocean breeze and the beautiful women who were always strolling from one shop to another or over to Trader Vic's. Plus the causeways substituted for hills in the dead-flat South Florida landscape.

He parked his Jeep in the lot for Bayfront and trotted slowly toward the water. Quiet day without many tourists. After a few minutes, he picked up the pace into a nice trot and cruised north along the water. Separated from the traffic and running away from his problems, he tried not to focus on any of his current trials. As his Nike Air running shoes hit the ground, the sea breeze hit him in the face and he picked up his pace, his feet gliding over the cement sidewalk, sweat beading on his forehead.

TOM DOOLEY HAD hardly started his surveillance of Tasker in his wife's brown six-year-old Ford Taurus station wagon, which was as long as a boat and twice as hard to handle, when Mac Nmir showed up and the blond lady with the two kids left. Within two hours, Dooley found himself trailing a jogging Tasker along the water in Miami. The surveillance was easy but now he didn't have any plan. He was winging it, hoping something popped into his head. He didn't even want to think why Mac Nmir had gone to see Tasker alone. This was only half his problem; he still had Hodges, fresh from his hit-and-run of Bema, running around. As long as he had the money, Hodges wasn't much of a concern.

Dooley could park along the waterway and still see Tasker jogging up to four blocks away. It really didn't matter if he lost him, because Dooley knew where the Jeep was parked and no matter how good a runner this guy was, he still had to drive home. Dooley was content to watch and bide his time, with no real plan to follow. It would definitely be to his benefit if Tasker bought the farm before anyone started looking too closely at him, or his attorney had the opportunity to spill out any of the defense's theories. Dooley pulled back out into traffic on Bayshore when Tasker turned toward a small secondary causeway over to one of the residential islands in the bay

As he slowly maneuvered the clunky station wagon to close the gap, it came to him like a bolt of lightning. He'd take a page right out of Hodges's playbook. Just a nudge with the car on this quiet little bridge and Tasker would be fish food or roadkill.

Either way, that left only one obstacle for Dooley to deal with, and Hodges was hiding himself.

Dooley eased the road yacht a little faster and checked for other traffic or pedestrians. This could work out.

BILL TASKER, former marathon competitor, former husband, former West Palm Beach cop, pushed it up the incline of the short, empty bridge, heading for a small foot trail he remembered just to the right at the end of the bridge.

This was nice, he thought. No traffic, no hassles. He could hear one car come onto the bridge as he pressed on.

TOO EASY, that's all Dooley could call it, checking for witnesses, then, seeing it was all clear, hitting the gas. He barreled after Tasker, who was against the guardrail on the right side of the bridge with no sidewalk. The key was to minimize damage to the car and, if there was any, get it fixed up in Fort Lauderdale, where no one would think to trace it. Tasker was near the end of the bridge when Dooley came on him with the giant car.

With a few feet left on the bridge, Dooley gave up any doubts and gunned the Ford's eight-cylinder engine, closing the gap in seconds.

TASKER HEARD the car as he approached the end of the bridge and saw the foot trail breaking right. The two-lane bridge was wide enough for both pedestrian and vehicle traffic, so Tasker didn't even look over his shoulder when he heard the car coming up behind him. It sounded like the car was moving pretty fast, so he moved as close to the short guardrail as possible and picked up the pace so he could make it to the end of the bridge before the car.

As Tasker took the last two steps, on the bridge, he realized the driver was being a prick about it and hadn't moved to the other lane. These rich people could be very territorial about their community. This guy was obviously making a statement about joggers on his island.

Tasker took the last two steps, then, without even looking, took the big jump to the right and landed squarely on the foot trail. The car passed by, still on the fast side, to whichever estate it belonged. As he resumed a steady pace on the trail, Tasker thought, Rich people are a pain in the ass.

*

TOM DOOLEY WASTED little time dropping that tank of a car at his house in South Miami, so the old lady could do her shopping. The whole trip down to the house and then back in his Bureau issued Century, he fumed about his fuck-up. Not only had he managed to miss Tasker with the car, he'd dinged the old land yacht, first on the bridge, then on a sapling on the island as he came off the bridge and onto the side of the road. Both dents were small but still reminders of how out of control this whole fucking plan had gotten. Jesus, he went from a simple theft of cash from a safe-deposit box to all this shit: framing someone, planting stories in the media, planting the good reverend and Hodges's assistant, Ebbi Kyle, in the Miami River. Was it worth this much trouble? He could just wait out his time with the Bureau and try to live on that fifty-percent pension. After a moment, he realized he'd better stick with his plan to keep the money.

He pulled into the task force lot from Miami Gardens Drive and managed a spot two rows from the front door. He knew exactly what he intended to do: grab the money, leave it in an inconspicuous box, packed inside an old refrigerator he'd been too lazy to move out of the storage bay he'd rented two years ago. Once the boys had started accumulating things, there'd seemed to be less and less room for his stuff, so, rather than fight with the old lady about it, he'd just rented a storage area. After showing his badge and muscling in on the manager a little bit, he'd gotten it for twenty-five bucks a month for at least five years. No one even knew where it was. He should've thought of it sooner and avoided all the heartburn of the past few weeks.

Fast-walking past the offices, hardly noticing a soul, he did a quick once-over of the evidence area and plugged in both keys to the locker he'd secured with the late Rick Bema and twisted. He paused to admire his trophy, sitting crumpled in the locker. He reached in and pulled out the sack, instinctively looking back and forth. He reached in his baggy front pocket and pulled out a black plastic yard bag he'd borrowed from home and tossed the CCR's satchel in it. Perfect.

As he made his way to the front door, he froze at the sound of his name. Spinning on his heel he saw Derrick Sutter in another suit strutting toward him at a fast gait.

'Dooley, wait up.'

Dooley stopped without answering.

'Where you been?' asked Sutter.

'Who're you, my boss?'

'Nah. I figured you'd go to Bema's funeral, that's all.'

Dooley winced. 'Shit, when was that?'

Sutter stared at him. 'This morning, ten o'clock. Pretty good crowd there, but not you.'

'You're right. I shoulda gone, but I got backed up. Now I got other things to handle.' He headed back toward the front door, turning once to see Sutter eyeing him and the bag carefully.

AS DOOLEY REACHED his car, he tossed the bag in the front passenger seat and took a quick look across the street to make sure Mac Nmir wasn't watching the lot again; then as he was about to close his door, a young woman on foot asked Dooley a question.

Dooley's head snapped up and he had to concentrate on what the girl had said. To say she was stunning was like saying Ross Perot was crazy. She stood at least five-ten, with the most perfect, large boobs sticking out of a white cut-off T-shirt. Her midriff revealed a circular tattoo with a flaming ring around a tight belly button. The painted-on blue jean shorts just made it to her hips. Dooley took a deep breath and said, 'Excuse me?'

She smiled, revealing perfect white teeth. 'I was wondering where the Aventura Mall might be?'

Dooley returned her smile and casually moved out from his Buick to meet her in the next row of cars. 'That's easy, my dear. Just head east on this road to US One and head north less than a mile.'

She put her hand on his shoulder and leaned in close. 'I'm so sorry, I'm bad with the whole north, south, east and west thing. Can you just point out the way for me?'

Her touch and voice combined to give Dooley a pretty good woody. 'Sure,' he said, following her gentle pull to the edge of the lot so he could look down Miami Gardens Drive. He raised his hand. 'Drive down this road to US One. It's a big intersection and you can't go any further this way. Then turn left.' He pointed to the north. 'The mall will be on your right after a few blocks.'

The girl smiled again and gave him a half-hug, saying, 'Oh, thanks very much.'

'My pleasure,' Dooley said, watching her slowly saunter away. A work of art.

He walked back to the car, reflecting on how nice a package the girl was, and didn't realize until he was backing the car out of the spot that the bag of money was gone. He frantically checked under the seat and around the car. In his rearview mirror, he noticed Derrick Sutter pull out into traffic in his FBI issued Buick Century. This could get ugly.

*

nineteen

BILL TASKER had spent the evening on edge, waiting for Tina to show up. He had felt like a teenager after she'd called around six, asking if it was all right if she came by for a little while this evening. Three days ago, he'd have shouted for joy, but things were more complicated now. Donna had come on strong and even though she'd been scared off by Mac Nmir, she'd called that afternoon to make sure everything was still okay. It sounded like she was surprised Tasker had answered the phone and was not in jail. He hoped it didn't come to that.

He was excited Tina was coming over, no matter what feelings for his ex-wife were whipping around inside him. Donna knew he was seeing someone and tried to be open-minded about it, but that would change if she ever actually got a look at Tina. After Nmir's little intrusion that morning, there wasn't much risk of Donna just showing up unannounced. He scurried around making sure everything was in its place, especially the three-pack of condoms he'd bought on his way home from jogging at Bayfront.

He almost bounded to the door when he heard the chimes, then opened it casually. Her smile blinded him.

Tina said, 'How'd you spend your day?'

'Wondering what happened to you this morning.'

'Sorry, but you were asleep and I needed to run by my place before I met my sister for breakfast.'

'What time did you leave?'

'Not too early. Maybe eight.'

He did the math, trying to figure the odds that she had seen Donna and the girls pull up and was just playing it cool.

He finally said, 'Any problems with traffic or anything on the way to your sister's?'

'No, why?'

He didn't know why, he just wanted some kind of reaction. 'Because I had a visitor after you left.'

'Who?'

'Mac Nmir, the FBI agent investigating the bank job.'

'What'd he want?'

'He gave me another chance to explain my side of things.'

She brightened. 'Billy, that's great. I knew they'd see you were innocent.'

He held up a hand. 'Not so fast. He gave me the chance, but I couldn't come up with anything new.'

She stared at him. 'I know you didn't take the cash, Billy. He'll figure it out, too.'

Tasker just looked at the floor.

'You think he's locked on you because of the past?'

He nodded.

She led him to the couch and sat close to him. Real close. Her perfume filled his nostrils and the smooth skin of her arm felt warm against his neck as she gave him a hug.

She said, 'Isn't it about time you told me about it? I mean, exactly what happened in West Palm?'

He shrugged, trying to think of a reason not to tell her. Jesus, he'd told her everything else, even Derrick Sutter's secret hunches about the case and the cash, and that shit was much more sensitive than a four-year-old shooting incident.

She squeezed him again and said, 'C'mon, I'm listening.'

He nodded and took a deep breath. 'It's not really a long or complicated story.'

'Doesn't matter, I'm right here for the duration.'

He looked into her eyes, fighting the urge to decline the chance to tell his story and just go to bed, but instead started.

'You know I was a West Palm Beach cop before coming to FDLE.'

She nodded.

'I'd compromised with my dad, who wanted me to go into his dry-cleaning business. He had a store off Glades in Boca Raton and paid my way through Florida State thinking I'd just work for him, but it didn't last a year. I wanted to move away to try police work. Finally I decided to stay in the area and go to work for the West Palm Beach PD. I was in the area and I got to be a cop. It was the only thing I wanted to do.'

She agreed. 'I was the same. I think a lot of cops view it as a calling more than a job.'

'Exactly. Anyway, to keep the peace with my parents, I stayed in West Palm.'

'And that made it all right to be a cop?' She seemed captivated.

'No, but it lessened the disappointment. Plus everyone knows that West Palm Beach is one of the best departments in the state. Even my dad was proud when I came home in uniform the first time.' He looked into her eyes. 'So I have a few good years at West Palm and start thinking about bigger and better things. I know FDLE is a great outfit and can be pretty exciting, so I take the chance, and after all the interviews and all the background checks I get hired and, incredibly, assigned to the West Palm Beach field office.

'I had it all: great job, two beautiful little girls, and a wife who still spoke to me.' He stopped to catch his breath.

Tina said, 'I know your trouble had to do with another cop.'

'Yeah, Jack Sandersen. He'd been a vice cop with me at the PD and we'd been friends since I was a rookie. I guess I was with FDLE about three years at the time. Turns out there was a corruption investigation going on in the office against him. Pretty serious stuff – skimming money from dope dealers, shaking down prostitutes. They had a solid case against him, too. When it came time to arrest him, they sent me and a brand-new agent to make a low-key arrest while the case agent directed a search warrant at his ranch in Loxahatchee.'

'Like a horse ranch?'

'Typical little ranch for out in the western county. Three acres, one horse and a couple of dogs, but the house was first class, with a pool and Jacuzzi.' He stopped, deciding how to phrase the story. 'Anyway, the new guy, Tony Bitello – we called him "Bitchalot" because he was always bitchin' about something. Anyway, we met Jack at the front door and he was cooperative right from the start. Bitello came on a little strong because he was new, and that's how they did it in New York where he'd come from.'

'I've heard about him.'

Tasker nodded and kept going. 'We took Jack back to a rear bedroom while they conducted the search, and he seemed okay.

After a few minutes, when we were alone, he says to me, "Billy, I'm done. It's all true." '

Tina's eyes widened. 'What on earth did you say?'

'I tried to make sure he was calm. I didn't want a scene, and there was no way I was gonna cuff an old friend. Bitello was in the room but he was just milling around, complaining about being kept from the actual search.' Tasker swallowed hard before continuing. 'A few minutes later, Jack starts working on me about how bad it'll be for him on the inside and that he didn't have anyone he was close to. He kept on while Bitello wandered out into the main room and got shooed back to me. Finally, Jack gets to his point.'

Tina was hypnotized. 'What was his point?'

'He wanted a minute alone in his bathroom to get himself together. Now I know you never leave a prisoner alone on his turf, but part of me has to know he's going to try to commit suicide. But I'm not sure. It's just not registering with me.'

'My God.'

'I tell Bitello that I'm lettin' Jack take a leak and he starts to go in with him, but I block the way. He starts up with procedure and that it's a bad idea. I basically ignore him.'

'Wow, this isn't anything like I heard it.'

'You've heard the allegations after the search warrant and the official story that was designed to let me keep my job.'

'You have my attention.' Her eyes felt like an interrogation light.

'Well, partly because I'm an idiot and partly because I wasn't thinking about anything other than giving my friend some privacy, I let him go to the bathroom. After about a minute, with me and Bitello waiting on either side of the door—'

Tina interrupted. 'Was he suspicious?'

'Oh yeah, he told me clearly what a dumbass idea it was.'

'I'm sorry, keep going.'

'After a minute, there was no sound, so I opened the door, kinda expecting to see him hanging from a wrapped up shower curtain. Instead, Jack stood there with a Smith model 66 revolver and it was pointed at me. He had a stashed gun in the medicine cabinet and intended to escape. I backed up, but when Bitello saw the gun he went for his. I shouted for him to stop, but Sandersen blasted him from two feet away. I threw myself at him and twisted the gun back at him, and in the fight he got shot in the head. It was too late, Bitello was already dead and the other agents were pulling me off Jack Sandersen's body.'

'Billy, that doesn't sound even close to the story I heard.'

'It gets worse, much worse.' He ran his hands over his face and took a deep breath. 'So I get sent home, everyone thinking it's a good shoot. Not thinking about my stupid decision yet. Then they find some of my personal stuff during the search warrant. Things like my hunting rifle, diving gear, you know, all the stuff one buddy might loan another or leave at someone's house if they had a lot of room. Nothing to it at all. But it gets them thinking, and of course the internal affairs guys from Tallahassee have to investigate the shooting and death of an agent. They read into these things at Jack's house, and a day later, while going over his finances, see he bought both my daughters prepaid college tuitions. Now they see a conspiracy.'

'I understand your stuff there, but what about the tuitions for the girls?'

'I guess the shakedown business was good, so he bought gifts for friends. He never even told me.' He took another breath. 'So now the media gets ahold of it and runs with the story. They report a theory that Jack and I were partners in crime and I killed him to keep him from talking. The local newspaper, *The Palm Beach Post*, literally stalks my parents and wife while I vegetated at home. I almost thought it was funny, and figured it would blow over in a couple of days. I did nothing.

'It lasted a week, then two, and instead of easing up, the media bore down. I became a hermit, my wife and kids had to visit her family in New Smyrna Beach, and my dad ...' He stopped.

'What about your dad?'

'He had a coronary at his store with three reporters waiting outside. Two days later, I was cleared when they found no other connection between Jack and me and that he had bought thirty-five prepaid college tuitions for all his friends' kids.

'From there, things just went downhill. I won't go into details but the transfer, drinking and self-pity all added up to me being single, sorry and in the same shit again.'

'Billy, I had no idea.'

'Now you see why I can't just let this play out. Especially now that the media is so involved. I have to clear this thing up.'

After a couple of quiet hours on the couch, Tina stood and started to gather her things.

'You can't stay?'

'I'm sorry.'

He tried to figure out how not to sound like a lovesick puppy. 'How 'bout lunch tomorrow?'

'I'm meeting my sister.'

'Bring her along.'

She smiled. 'That'd be fun. Where?'

'I'm meeting Derrick Sutter over at Chili's on Eighty-eighth at noon. How 'bout that?'

'He's the guy who told you about the cash in temporary evidence?'

'Yeah, just a hunch.'

'We'll be there.'

Tasker felt different after talking about the Sandersen incident. Not better, just different. And watching Tina leave, he started looking forward to a Chili's turkey burger.

DOOLEY COULDN'T BELIEVE he'd lost the money a second time and to another fucking nigger. Sutter was smart and now he'd either negotiate or act. The best he could hope for from Sutter was a fifty-fifty split. The only reason Dooley figured he'd even get that was to keep his mouth shut. Whatever happened, it better happen soon, because he didn't have the stomach for much more of this shit.

Dooley sat at his desk in the robbery task force, knowing that sooner or later the city detective would show up. He checked temporary evidence to see if the guy was slick enough to hide the cash back there, but he hadn't checked out any lockers. Dooley just sat and stewed. Where had Sutter found that gorgeous woman to use as a decoy? Dooley wouldn't mind getting her in some type of settlement.

While he waited, he checked the chambers of the old .38 the Bureau had issued him. The model 13 Smith & Wesson was a relic from another time, but he had resisted the move to automatic pistols, partly because he liked the reliability of the revolver and partly to separate himself from the young upstart agents who thought they knew everything. Mac Nmir was one who dressed like a lawyer and acted like a politician. Those kinds of guys always wanted people to like them. The fucking little dot-head hadn't even indicted Tasker yet, and Dooley knew it was because Nmir liked the personable state cop and was looking for any reason not to arrest him. If it hadn't been for Dooley's maneuvering with the press and a few phony phone calls as a reporter to his boss, Nmir wouldn't be under any pressure at all to clear the case. Shit, even the bosses at FDLE were behind Tasker. They wanted him back at work as soon as he was cleared. They fully believed he was innocent. Dooley had never seen that kind of support from the Bureau before.

He had one more call to make, to a guy he knew with *The Palm Beach Post*. He figured that since Tasker was from there and had been in trouble a few years back, maybe a local reporter could stir up some shit.

Now there was nothing for him to do but wait for Sutter to come back to the office and see how reasonable he could be.

ALL MORNING, Tasker tried to put the pieces of the puzzle together. Things like: Who in the hell was Cole Hodges if he wasn't Cole Hodges? He had a dozen newspaper clippings, a *Tropic* article, a *Palm Beach Life* photo and a brochure from the CCR. He now realized how badly he missed one of the most important aspects of a large investigative agency: a criminal intelligence analyst.

FDLE was widely viewed as having the best, most creative criminal intelligence analysts, and Tasker was friendly with most of them. The problem was they had a network better than NBC. If he spoke to one, he spoke to all. Unless he wanted his investigation to become common knowledge, he had to think this through. Then he knew exactly whom to call. The one analyst who could make sense out of this and keep his mouth shut. He picked up his phone and punched in the main FDLE Miami number. After three rings he heard the familiar, tired voice with a tinge of a Latin accent saying, 'FDLE, may I help you?'

Tasker tried to lower his voice just in case the receptionist recognized it. 'Jerry Ristin, please.'

'One mom—' The phone switching cut her off.

After that he heard the raspy voice of his sixty-year-old friend. 'Ristin. What do you want?'

'Jerry, it's Bill Tasker.'

'Billy, why aren't you on the French Riviera?'

'Funny.'

'You could at least share with your friends.'

'Jerry ...'

'Billy, relax, we all know you're not a crook.'

Tasker chuckled into the phone. 'Jerry, I need a favor.'

'Name of a good attorney?'

'I need your professional talents.'

'My analytical skills? What the hell for?' After a pause. 'You're not working on this bank thing yourself, are you?'

'Got to.'

'The Bureau will have your balls if they find out.'

'They got them now. Will you help me?'

'Yes, you know I will. What do you need?'

Tasker gave him everything he had on Hodges, along with his suspicions.

Ristin finally said, 'So? I mean, who'll care if that asshole is really some other asshole?'

'Because he may have taken the cash.'

'I'll look into missing persons from the mid-eighties, unsolved patterns, that sort of thing, but trying to match this with the current Mr. Hodges is one hell of a long shot.'

'It may be all I have.'

TWO HOURS LATER, Tasker sat at a large corner booth with Derrick Sutter, taking the chance to speak privately with him before Tina and her sister showed up. He appreciated the chance Sutter was taking meeting him in a restaurant with the FBI surveillance continuing. Although it wasn't the hardest job in the world to lose those guys whenever he wanted to go someplace unescorted.

Sutter took a long drink of Coke and said, 'You still doing all right?'

Tasker nodded. 'I know I have to do something myself, but I don't know what.'

'It'd be nice if we could find the money.'

'You still think Dooley's got it in temporary evidence?'

'Nope.'

Tasker looked at him. 'Where is it, then?'

Sutter shrugged. 'He moved whatever was in the locker yesterday. He had a bag in his hand.'

'What'd the bag look like?'

'Just a plastic garbage bag.'

'You see him leave with it?'

'He walked out, then I saw him talking to a woman.'

'Someone from the task force?'

'No, a tourist or something. Looked like she was asking directions. I mean she was some kind of knockout.'

'And you haven't seen our fat FBI friend since?'

'Nope. I haven't been by the task force yet. But I got you other leads, too.'

'Like what?'

'The crack dealer who claimed you were at the bank. That'd be a place to start.'

Tasker just nodded, knowing the Miami cop was right. 'The Bureau already talked to him. He's the only one they did talk to.'

Sutter said, 'What about your girlfriend? Can she help?'

'I wouldn't put Tina in that position.'

'But you said you already told her my suspicions about Dooley and the money. You involved her.'

'I needed someone to talk to. She's got a good career, I don't want to ruin it. She's not used to dealing with snakes like the ones on this case.'

Before Sutter could answer, Tasker stood and welcomed Tina Wiggins, saying, 'Speak of an angel and she appears.'

Tina put her arm around the shoulder of her sister and said, 'This is my sister, Jeanie.'

Jeanie was stunning in a tight midriff top. The similarities with Tina were obvious, but the differences were even greater. The much larger and more proudly displayed boobs, the exposed stomach and the tattoo of a flaming ring around her navel spoke more to her profession as a dancer. This would be a fun lunch. Tasker couldn't help but notice Sutter stare at Jeanie like he knew her.

twenty

D ERRICK SUTTER WALKED into the robbery task force office with his head still spinning from lunch. In the eight years he'd been in the Miami police department, he'd been stabbed, had shot three guys and had seen Madonna jogging and had still managed to take it all in stride. But today he'd been truly surprised. He'd kept his cool, but it wasn't easy. When he saw that Tasker's girlfriend's sister was the same girl who'd been talking to Dooley, he knew something was up. He didn't think Mr. Straight Arrow white-bread state cop was in on it, but his squeeze, Tina, had plans. She was either on the case or on the make. His guess was that she was in it for profit. He'd figure it out soon enough.

As he sat at his small metal desk and started to gather his intelligence briefs of current robberies, trying to make a stab at his legitimate paying job, he couldn't keep his mind off Tina and her sister, Jeanie. It bothered Sutter to know someone was up to something in his city. He was about to call Tasker and tell him Jeanie was the woman he'd seen talking to Dooley, when the fat FBI man burst into the empty squad bay, looked right at Sutter and said, 'We gotta talk, hotshot.'

'Why's that?' Sutter asked, barely containing his smile.

'You know why, you fucking smart-ass. C'mon, let's take a walk.'

'What's in it for me?'

'You won't know unless we talk.'

Sutter considered this, and a minute later found himself walking down the back row of the task force parking lot, with Dooley fidgeting and looking around for surveillance.

Sutter finally took hold of Dooley's wrinkled suit coat. 'Okay, Dooley, what's the problem?'

'The problem is you got something that's mine.'

Sutter smiled. Now he knew what Tina Wiggins and her sister were up to. He said, 'I do? What's that?'

'You know, smart-ass, I could fuck you up right now.'

Sutter started to laugh. To have a fat, middle-aged man threaten him in his own town was a joke. He looked up to see Dooley steam.

Dooley asked, 'What is so fucking funny?'

'Threats from you. You think I'm some street nigger you can push around. I'd kick your old, fat ass before you even thought about going for that piece-a-shit six-shooter.'

Dooley shut up for a minute, then said, 'I could make it tough for you to spend that cash.'

'What cash?'

'Don't give me that shit, Sutter. You know what cash and what the hell I'm talking about. Now how do we resolve this?'

'Where'd that cash come from again?'

Dooley glared at him. 'I've had enough of your shit. We can be partners or competitors. You decide.'

Sutter let loose with another easy smile as an idea popped into his head, and he said, 'I'll get back to you.'

TASKER SPENT a couple of hours getting what little life he had in order, cleaning out his bank account of the thirty-two hundred dollars he'd saved since the divorce and borrowing seventeen thousand more against his retirement fund, all to pay the attorney who, so far, had only told him to keep his mouth shut and be ready to 'lay down some shit' if they went to trial. In fairness to this guy, Tasker hadn't been very honest with him. He hadn't told the attorney about Mac Nmir's last visit or any of the information Derrick Sutter had provided. Although he had let him in on his private investigation, which the lawyer had said to cut out immediately. All Tasker wanted this attorney for was legal maneuverings which, until recently, he'd never actually thought would be necessary. With the federal grand jury scheduled to hear his case the following week, he felt time slipping away.

Donna hadn't returned since her surprise visit with the girls and he didn't push things. He intended to call her in the next day or so to arrange a visit with the girls, and he secretly hoped she'd be available, too.

As he waited to meet Jerry Ristin for lunch to go over his findings, he straightened up the house and occasionally looked out the window to see whose turn it was to watch him. Mac Nmir was in his Taurus sometimes, but usually it was a young Asian female in a Monte Carlo or a white guy with a crew cut in a Crown Victoria. At first he was self-conscious about his security blanket, but now it had almost a comforting effect. He figured that since Bema's death and with the grand jury about to convene, they needed tighter reins on him. He'd warned Tina, and that was why she liked meeting in other places. She seemed jumpier the past day or so, definitely wanting to shy away from FBI attention. He couldn't blame her.

As he was going through his file cabinet upstairs, looking for any other account he might be able to drain, he found the old pistol box he kept stored behind the files. He pulled out the blue plastic box and unsnapped the front locks. Inside was his first personally owned gun, a SIG Sauer nine-millimeter. He had turned in his issued Beretta when he was suspended, and completely forgot to tell the FBI it was here when they did their search. A search that Tasker could now see had been completely inadequate and shoddy. How does a real cop miss a gun during a search? And one in plain sight, not even hidden. He now understood why some of the tougher criminals were always so embarrassed to be grabbed by the FBI. Tasker laughed at the thought as he pulled out the pistol and racked the slide on the well-oiled empty gun.

LATER, AFTER not seeing any surveillance, Tasker headed over to La Carreta, the gold standard of Cuban restaurants. As soon as he walked in, he noticed Ristin's square form rooted in a booth. His thick glasses magnified the analyst's bloodshot eyes as he browsed the three-page menu.

Tasker slid in across from him. 'Hey, Jerry, what d'you got?'

'Nice to see you, too, kid,' the older man said, looking over his glasses at Tasker.

'Sorry, Jerry, I'm just turned all around.'

'Don't sweat it, kid.'

The waitress, a dark Latina with braided hair, came up to the table and smiled. 'And what today?'

Ristin looked across to Tasker. 'You buyin'?'

'Of course.'

Ristin looked up at the pretty waitress. 'Palamilla steak, maduros and a Diet Coke. And the same for my friend.'

Tasker smiled as she walked away.

Ristin picked up a folder from his side of the booth. 'I could lose my job over this.'

'I know, Jerry, and I appreciate it.'

'Besides, no one thinks you did it anyway. Not enough ambition.'

Tasker paused, thinking about it. 'So my friends think I'm innocent because I'm lazy?'

'Roughly, yes.'

'What do you have, Jerry?'

Ristin explained how smart he was to tie different lists together, then went into more detail. 'You see, Billy, the key is the description. Get a good age, or range of ages, and look at those missing that fit it. Wider the range, the bigger the list of possibles. I took all those missing from 1980 to 1985, when Mr. Hodges graduated from Broward, and then pared it down by changing the ranges. So you have this list.' He handed Tasker a small booklet. 'Which is everyone. Something like twenty-two hundred names. Using a smaller range in age, you get this.' He handed Tasker an eight-page list. 'Eight hundred names. Then, say the current Hodges is fifty to fifty-five years of age, description as not only a black male but a dark-complexioned black male, and weed out those missing from foreign countries or because of military accidents, and you get this list.' He handed Tasker one page with eight names and brief descriptions. Ristin smiled.

Tasker glanced over the page. 'There were only eight dark-black guys missing from these five years?'

Ristin shook his head. 'Oh, hell no. There are hundreds, I'm sure. Most aren't reported or are reported to the local police, who don't pass it on. But these are the ones missing that wouldn't want to be found. All evading legal problems. Five escaped convicts and three facing trial. It seemed logical to focus.'

Tasker skimmed over the descriptions. All about the same height, age and complexion, but that was because of the search. Two had tattoos listed, one was missing the end of his index finger. Next to that information was a note that said, 'Result of a homemade explosive in the Indiana State Prison.' Tasker wondered about Hodges's hands. The last name on the list, Luther Williams, had a scar on his elbow, but it didn't say which arm. The note next to it said, 'Result of an attack by a fellow inmate at the Missouri State Penitentiary.' Tasker committed all the information to memory, then looked up at the heavy, older man. 'You got photos on any of them?'

'Working on it, but it's not that easy. Photos aren't in the computer and you're talking about cases at least fifteen years old.'

Tasker nodded. 'I know, I know. But, Jerry, this is incredible. You're a genius.'

'That is, if you're even right in your assumption and if this information is correct, and then there's luck. What I'm saying, Billy, is that there's less guesswork on *Who Wants to Be a Millionaire* than on these lists. I wouldn't put much faith in them.'

Tasker looked at him and said, 'I have more faith in these than I do in the FBI.'

SLAYDA NMIR had earned the nickname 'Mac' while finishing his engineering degree at Tufts University, and until recently never believed it would be a reason for scorn. Just the way Tom Dooley looked at him when he called him 'Mac' indicated the contempt the former Boston cop held for the former student from Massachusetts. Mac had never even mentioned to Dooley that he had lived in the Boston area. Right now, with the red-faced, heavyset, fifty-three-year-old lousy FBI agent staring at him, Mac wished his fraternity brothers hadn't given him a nickname at all.

Dooley said, 'Okay, Mac, what's the scoop on your case against that asshole Tasker? I haven't bothered you on it, but this is ridiculous. You're killing my task force while this investigation goes on. Why isn't he indicted yet?'

Mac kept his usual calm demeanor and said, 'Still building the case.'

'Still building? Shit, your grandparents built the fucking Taj Mahal in less time.'

'I'm not Indian.'

'Whatever. What the hell else you need to finish your case against him?' Mac almost enjoyed making him stew by not answering immediately.

Dooley raised his voice. 'You hear me okay? What else do you need? You got witnesses, the cash from the search warrant, motive.'

Mac shrugged. 'Something in my gut says to keep looking.'

'Your gut! Your gut. You ain't been on the fucking job long enough to have gut.'

Mac suppressed his emotions, as he did on most issues. He disliked Dooley. That was as strong an emotion as he could muster for anyone. Not hate, not rage, just not really liking him. He did realize that by listening to the older man he could pick up not only information but also insights, and perhaps even some of his experience.

Mac looked at Dooley and said, 'There are a few things I wonder about.'

'Like what?'

'Tasker doesn't act like a crook. He lives quietly, seems pissed off he's a suspect. Not worried about jail, worried about his reputation.'

Dooley jumped on that one. 'It's an act. What about his past?'

'The allegation was he killed a former partner to hide his role in a shakedown scheme.'

'That is some serious shit.'

'He was completely cleared. Except by the media. That's why FDLE moved him down to Miami. Basically for his own good.'

'Doesn't this sound a little like that incident? He killed the bank manager and maybe even the Reverend Watson to hide his tracks.'

Mac considered that. He didn't want to admit it, but that was a possibility. Mac had set up a rapport with Tasker and been alone with him and he still couldn't say where the guy was coming from. He just had an odd way about him. Mac had given him chance after chance to fess up in a nonthreatening environment. Just like they taught in the academy. Mac liked using his technical training and applying it to human interaction. He knew the environment was right for talking with Tasker, so if the guy hadn't talked he might not be hiding anything.

Mac was knocked out of his thoughts by Dooley's voice. 'So when do we grab him?'

'I don't see the hurry. He's not going anywhere.'

'Neither is the task force till this case is closed. Shit, with Bema in the deep freeze and the FDLE not filling Tasker's position till this is resolved, all I got is that fucking hump from the city, and he's missing half the time.'

'Sutter? I noticed on our surveillances that he spends a lot of time out of the office.'

Dooley froze for a moment. Just long enough for Mac to catch the sudden shift of gears.

Then Dooley asked, 'You ever follow him?'

'This is not your case, Dooley.'

He smiled and lowered his tone. 'I'm sorry, pal, I just wanted to know if I'm working with one thief or in a den of thieves. I'm curious where the guy spends so much time. He's not around the task force. It may be a reliability issue.' Dooley smiled like he was letting Mac in on an Internal Affairs case.

Mac eased up, knowing that many of the local cops took advantage once they were assigned to a federal task force. 'You can't follow him the way he drives in the city. We did happen to pick him up on an incidental surveillance the other night.'

'Where was that?'

'You know Tasker's girlfriend, Tina?'

'I've heard of her.'

'Over at her apartment in the north end.'

'Sutter cutting in on his partner's action, huh?'

'No, she left right after he got there. He was with the other girl that lives there.'

'Then what happened?'

'Don't know. The team was following Tasker's girlfriend because they kept losing him.'

'She lead you to Tasker?'

'Why?'

'Curious, that's all.'

Mac smiled. 'You ever see Tasker's girlfriend?'

Dooley thought about it a moment and said, 'I've only seen her from a distance, and she's a looker.'

TASKER AGREED to meet Tina back at Chili's after he lost surveillance. Tasker saw no problem with that, but when he left, just after dark, there was still no team on him. At least none he could see, which meant no team at all. He cruised the couple of miles to Eighty-eighth Street, the central road in Kendall, and then to Chili's a few blocks west, making some unnecessary turns and stops just in case.

Tina rose with a smile as he walked in and then avoided his kiss on the lips with an offered cheek. Her eyes darted around the restaurant as the Cuban hostess led them to their seat. She kept a quick pace, slightly ahead of Tasker all the way to the booth.

By now he'd gotten the message and slid in across from her and didn't reach for a hand or push her too hard for a touch.

'Everything all right?' he asked quietly.

'This whole mess has started to get to me.'

'Tell me about it.'

'No, I mean it, Billy. Every part of my life seems like it's touched by your robbery task force.'

'How's that?'

'At work everyone knows I'm involved with you and no one is sure what's happening. I see how it's affected you when I'm not at work, and now that Miami cop Derrick is hitting on my sister.'

'Sutter? Really? Where'd he see her?'

'She gave him her number the other day at lunch and he went by and saw her dance at Pure Platinum. He's at our apartment right now.'

Tasker kept his mouth shut, but still let a small smile escape.

'Is he trustworthy?' Tina asked.

'The guy has helped me out.'

'He's not married, is he?'

'Nope.' He looked at her. 'It's not a black thing with you, is it?'

'Not at all. It's a snake thing. Jeanie never dates and he had her number without either you or me realizing it.' She looked into his face. 'What're you smiling about?'

'I knew he was smooth, but your sister is quite a prize.'

'What's that supposed to mean?'

'Nothing, nothing, except I don't know many men who'd be brave enough to go after a woman as beautiful as your sister.'

'Oh, so I guess I'm easy to obtain?'

'That's not what I meant.' He paused, realizing that conversations like this never turned better. He said, 'I'm sorry. I withhold any other comments.'

She smiled at his surrender. Then she took his hand and

looked him in the eyes. 'Billy, I'm serious, this whole thing is getting to be too much.'

'I know. I hope it'll be over soon.'

'Then maybe we can pick back up when it is.'

There it was, laid out on the table with no punches pulled. Of all the shit that had happened in the past three weeks, this may have cut the deepest. He didn't protest. He felt as if he'd screwed up something special, and as soon as he got out from under his current problems he'd make sure he had another shot with this wild, unpredictable girl.

He sucked in a breath and said, 'Let's eat.'

twenty-one

DERRICK SUTTER strutted into the robbery task force office right at nine o'clock, the first time he'd ever made it to the office on time in the five months the task force had been up and running. He'd been out a little late after taking Jeanie Wiggins to Mezza Notte for dinner. That girl could be an expensive habit, except for two things: he didn't expect to see her again, and the CCR's satchel he'd found hidden in Tina's bathroom cabinet. It'd been a little tricky looking through the house, but Jeanie didn't have the smarts to match her looks and couldn't hold her wine very well. Luckily, he'd split with the cash before her sister came in and before Jeanie sobered up. He had a good idea where he could stash the satchel and know it'd be safe.

Now he had to deal with Dooley. It could be tricky to make sure the crazy FBI agent didn't try anything stupid like telling Mac Nmir or just shooting him. Sutter liked this kind of thing. When he worked in narcotics he'd juked with dealers all the time and scammed the scammers investigating fraud. Dooley would be easy. Then he'd pay a visit to a buddy in Internal Affairs. He needed some info on the bank case and IA would have the inside track even though it was an FBI case. Those types always kept up on each other's cases, thinking every cop could be corrupted. Sutter had to make sure things went the way he needed them to go, because he wasn't following many rules for a while.

Tom Dooley, standing at the entrance to their squad bay, broke his concentration.

Dooley smirked. 'Look who dragged himself in on time. What's next? The Second Coming?'

'I'd say you feel more like Job about now.'

'Why?'

'God's been testing you with bad luck. Everybody's been cutting in on your action.'

'So you admit you got my money.'

'Nope, but I know what happened to it.'

'What?'

'You're a cop, or at least an FBI agent. I'll give you a lead.'

'I'm all ears.'

'I thought you were mostly fat, but I'll tell you anyway.' He paused, enjoying Dooley's reddening face. 'The girl that asked directions from you the other day ...'

'Yeah, go ahead.'

'She's Tasker's girlfriend's sister.' No emphasis, just fact.

Dooley kept quiet. Sutter could see the gears of his mind churning.

'That son-of-a-bitch cock-sucking prick-loving donkey-fucker took what he's accused of taking. I can't believe it.'

'That was a good curse, even for you.' Sutter let him stew for a moment. 'I don't think Bill knows a thing about it.'

'You're shitting me. She took it on her own? How'd she know where it was?'

'I might have let Tasker in on my suspicions and he told her. She's sharper than you, that's all. What'll be interesting is: how can you get it back?'

'What're you coming clean for? What's in this for you?'

'We'll talk about my fee later.'

Dooley nodded. 'You got it, pal. I got work to do now.' He turned and started away at a good pace.

Sutter called out to him, 'Dooley, one thing or all bets are off.'

'What's that?'

'You can't hurt anyone. Not the girl, not Tasker. No one.'

'Or?'

'Like you said to me, I could make it hard to spend that cash.'

'Understood,' Dooley said, resuming his trek out the door.

Sutter smiled, thinking, That should keep him and the Wiggins sisters busy till I do what I got to do.

TASKER HURRIED DOWN the stairs to answer the door, knowing it wasn't anyone he wanted to see. Both Tina and

Donna had already declared their distance from his apartment, at least until his troubles were over. Was this the knock that ended his freedom? Was it Mac Nmir and some FBI guys? The news media? Maybe Dooley to put a bullet in his head? At this point he didn't care and didn't check first, he just threw open the door to a smiling Derrick Sutter.

'What're you doing here?'

'Hello to you, too,' Sutter said, slipping past him and heading into the living room. 'It took me a good twenty minutes to make sure you didn't have surveillance on the house.'

'They're on a staggered schedule. Sometimes they're here, sometimes not.'

'Like most FBI agents. When they're around, they don't do much, and when they're not, they don't do much.'

Tasker laughed, then asked again, 'What brings you by?'

'You know, in the neighborhood.' Sutter shrugged.

'In Kendall? At eight-thirty at night? Give me a break.'

Sutter just smiled. 'Wanted to see how you are.'

'Not as good as you.'

'What d'you mean?'

'Tina told me about you and her sister. Very impressive.'

'Nice girl, nice girl.' He kept smiling, patting his belly like he'd just finished a good meal.

Tasker said, 'Have a seat while I sign off my computer upstairs. Only take a minute.'

Tasker hustled back upstairs and shut down his online connection. As he hit the keys, he thought he heard the front door open.

'Derrick?' he yelled down, but got no answer.

A minute later, he headed back down to an empty living room. Then he noticed Sutter reclining in a lounger on the patio.

Tasker opened the sliding glass door. 'What're you doing out here?'

Sutter, still smiling, said, 'Man, you are just a suspicious type. Why am I in Kendall? Why am I on the patio? It's nice out. Like the air. Harder for the FBI to plant a listening device.'

He said it so matter-of-factly that it took Tasker a second to realize what his concern was. 'Oh. Oh yeah.' He quickly sat in the lounger next to Sutter, facing his chair.

'I'm telling you, Derrick. Something's not right about Hodges.'

'Yeah, like he's a thief.'

'But there's something else. I think it's an alias.'

'Like half the people in Miami. Big deal?'

'I'm thinking of giving this information over to Nmir.'

Sutter shook his head. 'You're wasting your time.'

'Why?'

'Because Hodges doesn't have the cash.'

'How in the hell do you know that?'

'Look, there's something I gotta tell you.' Sutter sat up to lean in close.

Tasker said, 'I'm listening.'

Sutter took a second and looked around, then said, 'You never heard this.'

Tasker nodded.

'Dooley took the cash.'

'For sure?'

'Absolutely.'

Tasker put his hand on Sutter's arm. 'How do you know?'

Sutter shrugged. 'I just do.'

'Great, let's get ahold of Nmir.'

'Not so fast, my brother. Dooley doesn't have it with him right at this moment, and you know you got to have a slam dunk to convince an FBI man that another FBI man did something like this. You got some work to do first.'

'Go on.'

'First, there's the witness who said he seen you at the bank. He never said it was you, he said it was a white cop in a Buick Century.'

'They started on me based on that?'

'And what Dooley said. Anyways, this witness is a small, small crack dealer name Cedric Brown, known as "Spill" on the street. Hangs by the bank and near the Church's Fried Chicken on Seventh.'

Tasker was quiet while he thought this over.

Sutter broke his concentration. 'What're you thinkin' about? You need to grab this crackhead by the ears and rattle his brain. Find out who he saw. Then maybe Nmir will see what you turn up.'

'I don't know.'

'I've done what I can do, my brother. You have to fight or they'll bury you.'

Tasker had to sit on the edge of the lounger as his muscles gave way to the fear that pumped through them. Could Hodges have been nothing but a wild-goose chase? Was he any kind of cop?

Sutter said, 'You okay?'

Tasker nodded. 'Maybe I'm just getting what I should've gotten four years ago.' He let his upper body collapse onto the lounger and decided to write the rest of the night off.

DOOLEY BACKED his issued Buick out of its spot in front of the FBI's combined task force office on Miami Gardens Drive at the peak of rush hour. From three o'clock on, he'd spent his time finding out everything he could about Tina Wiggins and her slutty sister and roommate, Jeanie. Mac Nmir had come up with that identification, but Dooley saw the resemblance in the driver's license photos. He'd been forced to use less efficient means of finding this information because he didn't want anyone to know he was working on it. Usually he'd just hand a name to one of the nerdy, useless criminal intelligence analysts, and a day or two later he'd get a neat little package with all the pertinent information in some semblance of order. This time he had to dig through the computer files and databases, both on and off the Internet, to find out what he could.

He liked to lead people on about his lack of computer savvy, but only because he didn't want people giving him more work. If they thought he didn't know a mouse from a rat, they didn't bother him about anything computer-related. In reality, he did better than most, and much better than his contemporaries, on the computer. On a task like this, all that time on the computer paid off big.

Now it was time to put all that information to work. He had a plan this time and it didn't include any more fucking partners. Jesus, he was sick of people looking to make deals. He'd told Sutter no one would get hurt. And no one would if Sutter helped him get his money back and kept his yap shut. As a precaution, Dooley had strapped on an ankle holster with a little Smith five-shot in addition to his heavy model 13 in his trusty hip holster. His pockets rattled with three speed loaders and his cylinders were full, giving him twenty-four rounds in case of trouble. He couldn't say he was actually angry; he was tired of being pissed at everyone who tried to do exactly what he'd done: take the money. Technically he'd done the same to the late Reverend Watson.

Dooley swung east toward US 1 before he could track north toward the Wiggins sisters' apartment. With a couple of guns, he felt pretty confident in any part of Miami, so he cut through the one nasty housing project in the north end of Miami and then along the huge recreation fields that serviced the projects and surrounding neighborhoods.

He rolled to a stop at the only working light in the area and checked the paper with Tina Wiggins' address. As he took a moment to figure the fastest route over there, he heard a ping against the rear window of his car a second before he felt an impact on the rear of the car. He sat motionless for a moment, thinking how he could explain this to the Bureau, when he realized it wasn't an accident but an assault. The rear windows shattered from a bullet, and now a second round traveled just past his right ear and into the windshield.

Dooley rolled and squeezed under the dash as he drew his big revolver, then crouched even further. Another shot sent him toward the passenger door, somehow managing to force his girth through the tight quarters. Dooley's mind raced, first with how to get out, then with who was shooting at him. He reached with his left hand for the door handle, but couldn't get a decent grip. He squeezed forward an inch, the steering wheel cutting into his hip and the dash into his back. He grunted as he forced every fiber in his body to move toward the door. He reached again and this time another shot forced him back down.

'Shit,' he said out loud, then again out loud said, 'C'mon, Tom, reach.' His pudgy fingers wrapped around the handle and with one movement pulled it then shoved the door open, the dim light from outside visible beyond the open door. He shimmied out to the edge of the door jamb and reached his right hand with the gun out the door, firing two quick shots without aiming, then with great effort, threw himself out the passenger door, landing like a fallen helicopter on the road. Taking one quick glimpse to see his assailant, Dooley scrambled for cover at the front of the car. He hadn't seen enough of anything to know how many attackers there were, let alone who was attacking him.

Dooley popped his head over the hood, looking through the blown out windows. A larger dark vehicle was still jammed against his and then another shot pinged off his hood. He jerked his head back down and, panting, checked his pocket for the speed loaders. He found them right where he'd left them, so he took his pistol, popped up again, and this time he fired. Four shots across the grill and windshield of the vehicle. Then he heard someone call his name and he froze.

'Dooley,' came the unfamiliar male voice. 'Dooley, I'm not mad, my friend.' Then two more shots came across the hood.

Dooley tried to associate the voice with a face. Shit! Where were the cops when you needed them? How long had this been going on? It felt like hours until Dooley checked his watch. More like a minute. The cops probably wouldn't even get called in this neighborhood.

Dooley gathered his breath and croaked, 'Who's that?'

'You don't know?' came the reply, still from the same place; it didn't sound like the guy was trying to work his way around on him.

Dooley shouted back, 'I got time and ammo. You do what you want.'

'I want my damn money back.'

Dooley could kick himself. Damn Cole Hodges had crept up on him again. Dooley said to himself, 'I must be slippin' to let this jig do this a second time.'

'Dooley, give me the cash and keep a hundred grand for your persistence. We both keep quiet and come out ahead.'

Dooley thought that over. He'd negotiate if he had the cash. 'Maybe we could work something out, but I don't have it with me. You kill me and you'll never find it.'

'I can find you anywhere I need to. Your office, that nice house in South Miami, you name it, I've seen you there.'

Dooley was stunned. How did that son-of-a-bitch bastard jerk-off do that? He followed me and I never knew it.

'What's it gonna be, Dooley?'

Dooley thought about it. He had nothing now. No money, no guarantee someone wouldn't point the finger at him. He took a breath and made a decision. Leaning around the front of the car, he could see it was a pickup truck, probably the same one that had run down Bema. 'Give me a couple of days and I'll work it out.'

'Where?'

He thought about a neutral site. 'Pro Player Stadium, Thursday at nine.'

'Wednesday.'

'Done,' shouted Dooley. He stayed put for a few seconds until he heard the truck back away. Half a minute later, he saw it heading east across the playing fields.

Now he had to get the cash and then decide what to do about Hodges.

IT WAS an impulse more than anything else. He pulled the Jeep off I-95 in Hallandale and headed east. Playing around on the Internet, Tasker had come up with the bank manager's home address. He figured since he was on his way to West Palm Beach anyway, he would stop at the house and see if anyone was home. He knew Louis Kerpal, the deceased manager, wasn't married, but he might have a roommate or a girlfriend. Tasker found the small house in a nice but older neighborhood.

Before he was out of the Jeep, an elderly woman was in the front doorway.

'May I help you?' She had a tired voice that matched her looks.

Tasker showed her his badge from a distance. 'I was wondering if I could ask you a few questions, ma'am.'

'About my son, Louis?' She may have had a slight southern drawl.

'Yes, ma'am.' He'd figured out her relationship to the dead bank manager and wasn't to the house yet. Not bad. Tasker had talked to dozens of mourning relatives in his career. His understated manner helped in this circumstance.

Inside the small house, Tasker accepted a seat in an old high-backed chair while Mrs. Kerpal trudged into the kitchen for two glasses of orange juice. He noticed the photographs, mostly of Louis as he grew up. Tasker recognized some of the wall photos as ones given to the newspapers for stories on the robbery.

As Mrs. Kerpal sat on the edge of the sofa next to Tasker's chair, he sensed that she was still in a state of shock over her son's death. Although she smiled, it was without emotion; even though she looked alert, she didn't have it together. He decided to move this along.

'I just need a little information, Mrs. Kerpal, then I'll get out of your way.'

'I don't know what else I can add. The young man from the FBI spent a lot of time with me and I told him everything.'

'Did your son talk about work much?'

'Oh, yes, he loved the bank.'

'Had he ever been the victim of a robbery before?'

'He was mugged outside the bank after closing, but never a robbery.'

'Can you remember anything unusual he used to tell you?'

She spent a moment thinking about it. 'No, not really. He wanted to work downtown where the famous people popped in all the time. That was one of his only complaints.'

'He didn't have anyone famous in Overtown?'

'Just the man from the black group.'

Tasker froze. 'Which man?'

'I think his name was Hodges. Louis loved him. Every time the man was on the television, Louis would go on and on about how he banks at his branch.'

'Did he say anything else about Hodges?'

'He had a safe-deposit box that Louis got to look in every week. He loved being in on something like that.'

Tasker started to formulate a theory. Maybe Hodges had taken his own money. Maybe he'd been forced to. He was about to ask Mrs. Kerpal another question when he noticed an odd look on her face. Then her lower lip started to quiver.

'Are you all right, Mrs. Kerpal?'

'You're him.'

Tasker knew the game was up.

She pointed at him. 'You're the state policeman who killed my boy.'

'No, ma'am, it's not what you think.'

'I'm not senile, you know. Sometimes it just takes a minute for everything to come into focus. Why are you here?'

Tasker started to rise. 'I'm hoping to find who killed your son.'

'You want to cover your tracks.'

'No, ma'am. I ...'

'Get out.' She stood with surprising strength. 'Get out right this second. I'll have nothing to do with you.'

'But ...'

'Get out before I have the Hallandale police arrest you for trespassing.'

He scurried to his Jeep before he was arrested for witness-tampering.

HIS DRIVE from Mrs. Kerpal's house was brutal; he knew he'd fucked up. If Mrs. Kerpal called the cops, he could be a fugitive by nightfall. Tasker arrived at his former house in West Palm Beach just as the sun set. He'd told Donna he'd come by, but hadn't said when, so it was half of a surprise. He pulled in next to her minivan and could see the girls through the front bay window as they looked to see who their company was. Then he saw the recognition in their faces as they jumped and raced to the front door. He started to calm down from the drive.

After his reunion with the girls, he sought out Donna, who'd yet to make an appearance.

He walked slowly down the hall from the living room, calling, 'Donna, it's me.'

He stopped at the closed bedroom door. Their bedroom. At least, it was a few years ago. That simple thought made him see his mistake. Not in the shooting, but in how he'd reacted to it. He hadn't been in it alone. He'd acted like it was just him caught up in events around the shooting but it had really involved his whole family.

'Donna?' he said, knocking lightly on the door. No answer. When he turned to head back to the girls, the door opened, revealing Donna with a tear-streaked face.

'What is it?' asked Tasker.

She didn't answer, but motioned him into the room. She stopped him with a foghorn honk into a tissue.

His panic increased. 'Donna, what happened?'

'The newspaper…' was all she got out.

'What newspaper?'

'The *Post*. A reporter was waiting when we got home.' She broke down and cried again.

'What'd he say? Did he hurt you?'

'No, no, he's doing a story on you and your troubles. He's connecting the Sandersen shooting and these new allegations. Oh, Bill, it was horrible. I couldn't get rid of him. He just kept asking me things. It reminded me of last time. I can't do that again.' She broke down again.

'What was his name?'

She pointed to a business card and kept crying as he picked it up and stuffed it in his pocket.

He patted her on the back, saying, 'It's all right, Donna. It's over now.'

She looked up at him. 'No, it's not, Bill. It's not nearly over. And I can't risk the girls. If someone talks to them or teases them, it could be devastating.'

Tasker just looked at her, waiting for the rest.

'So until this is over, and I know it will be soon, I want you to stay away. Call the girls, but let's try and shield them as much as possible.'

He stared at her because there was nothing left to say.

BILL TASKER LOOKED at the page of notes that had all the pertinent information about his case on it. If Sutter was right, Dooley had the money. If Tasker was right, it was probably Hodges. The only lead anyone could follow now was the crack dealer/witness. As far as the FBI was concerned, that lead had already been worked. Even though they hadn't done much else. Even Tasker had to admit that with all the rumors floating around, Tom Dooley was his main suspect, but again the FBI wouldn't be interested in that kind of stuff. He had to do it. His life had been thrown into a purgatory until this was resolved. He couldn't see the girls, Tina didn't want to have anything to do with him until it was over, he couldn't even go to work if he wanted to. He now knew he had to get his old life back, not just the one from a month ago, the one he lost four years ago on a bloody floor of a ranch house near West Palm Beach. He turned and bounded up the stairs to his filing cabinet next to the computer in his spare bedroom. Opening the top drawer, he grabbed the box containing the old SIG Sauer nine-millimeter and pulled out the pistol. He loaded the magazine with bullets he had stashed in his closet, charged the gun and crammed it in his waistband without a holster. Now it was time to kick some ass.

twenty-two

AS BILL TASKER settled into his four-year-old Jeep Grand Cherokee, his first priority was to lose the FBI surveillance team. He'd noticed that they came on about four in the afternoon, so they were relatively fresh. It was the official-looking guy with the crew cut, the Asian female and a dark-haired female he'd never seen before. They had cars that reflected the FBI's conservative tastes: a Taurus and two Buick Centuries. He figured he could show them how a South Floridian could drive.

Tasker started slow, signaling turns, stopping at lights, just like always. He headed west toward the 826 expressway. At seven in the evening, the traffic on the north-south artery was tolerable. Checking his rearview mirror as all three cars came on the ramp and lined up behind him, a small smile crossed his face. It couldn't really be this easy. Could it?

He slowly increased his speed until he hit eighty. As he headed north, he passed the 836 expressway, which runs east and west, and the airport until he reached Fifty-eighth Street. He signaled and slowly crossed the lanes of traffic to his right to allow the FBI agents to follow. He wanted to lose them, but couldn't resist leading them into Hialeah first. Once the street numbers didn't match the rest of the county and the locals showed no interest in traffic rules, Tasker was certain these young agents would be tied up for a while. He even smiled at the thought of some poor guy from Iowa who mistakenly believed Hialeah was part of the continental United States.

He made sure they were behind him and ready, then he took a sharp left onto an avenue with a shopping center on each corner. Hitting the gas, he shot through the gauntlet of cars streaming out of the parking lot. There were some beeps and fingers, but there always were in this huge suburb of Miami. He noticed one of the Buicks didn't make it past the corner. Then Tasker hung a right into a neighborhood and zipped around a slow-moving pickup truck with a huge, homemade gas tank welded into the bed. This was a Cuban phenomenon where men sold gas for cars door to door. Only the Asian agent in the Century made it past and stayed with Tasker.

His final move was to cut through an Office Depot lot, then squirt into traffic over a curb. In less than a minute, he was eastbound toward the city without anyone in the federal government knowing where he was or where he was heading.

DRIVING DOWN Seventh Avenue near Fifty-fourth Street, Tasker felt as if everyone on the street had their eyes on him, a white guy in a nice car. They thought he was either looking for a prostitute, buying crack or lost coming from the Miami Heat Arena. He kept his hand on his gun as he scanned the area for trouble. He was a victim of the media portrayal of the area. Sometimes he had to remind himself that most people just live here and don't want any trouble. He relaxed now, focusing on the individuals, trying to get an idea if Cedric Brown, known on the street as 'Spill,' was anywhere in sight.

Tasker saw a thin, dark-skinned guy leaning against a bus stop, drinking a Coke from a McDonald's cup about a block from the Church's Fried Chicken. He eased the Jeep into the slot where the buses stopped to pick up passengers. The man gave him an uninterested look. His half-opened eyes barely raised to meet Tasker's.

'Whatcha need?' mumbled the man.

Tasker appraised him for a second.

The man came off the bus stop and said, 'I got twenties and fifties. I'll make a deal for anything over a hundred.' His eyes cut in both directions.

Tasker realized what he was talking about and said, 'You Spill?'

'I spill what?'

'Are you Cedric Brown?'

The man dropped his Coke and took off in an instant sprint west across a parking lot away from the street.

'Shit,' Tasker muttered, throwing the Jeep back into gear and bumping over the curb in pursuit. He never minded car chases when it was a state car he was tearing up, but he didn't like the sound of his undercarriage scraping the curb. Tasker knew these streets from surveillances and dope deals in the area. He drove a block past where he'd seen the man, pulled down the street and hopped out. He crept next to a walking trail that ran from Seventh to Twelfth Avenue. As he came to the trail, he saw the man slowing to a trot and looking behind him to see if anyone was following.

Tasker stepped up and shoved the man off his feet while he wasn't looking and said, 'Don't run again, shithead. I'm not looking to bust you for sales. I just need to ask you a question.'

The man looked up at Tasker, no longer uninterested, and asked, 'Why you want to talk to me?'

'You're Cedric, aren't you?'

'No, sir.'

'Cut the shit. I'm not interested in what you do, only what you saw.'

'I'm not Spill. He four or five inches smaller than me and he don't dress this nice.'

'Then why'd you run?'

'You the police, aren't you?'

'Yeah, that's my job.'

'And it's my job to run from the police.'

Tasker bent down and helped the man up. 'You seen Spill around tonight?'

The man nodded, looking at Tasker as he came to his feet.

'What's he wearing?'

The man shrugged. 'He probably got on some Black Power shirt. That's all he ever wear.'

'You drive around with me and point him out for ten bucks?'

'What about twenty?'

'Okay.'

'And a Church's dinner.'

'Okay.'

'And a pass the next time I get picked up for selling.'

Tasker looked hard at him. 'You got your pass tonight.'

The man smiled. 'You right.'

As they were starting to turn toward the Jeep, a figure came strolling down the path. The small man, about thirty-five, sipping a Schlitz beer, stopped and looked at them.

Tasker's assistant said, 'Shit.'

The new guy spilled his beer; Tasker smiled, handing his assistant a twenty. 'That's for the thought.'

Tasker realized that Spill had talked to him the day he'd gone to the bank to ask about the robbery. He looked at Cedric Brown's wet T-shirt that read 'Black Panthers are endangered, too,' and said, 'C'mon, Spill, we gotta talk.'

TOM DOOLEY DROVE his roughly patched-up Buick Century slowly down the street where Tina Wiggins's apartment building stood. He'd taped over the three bullet holes Hodges had put in his trunk and paid two-twenty-five to have the glass replaced. No way he was gonna tell the Bureau about this. The car now rattled and wind blew through it no matter what speed he went.

As he looked down at the paper with her address, he nearly drove off the road to avoid a Chevy Monte Carlo. Before he could curse, he realized his luck. Tina Wiggins was oblivious to him as she cut through the neighborhood toward the main road.

He had to make a snap decision and decided to pull another page out of Cole Hodges's playbook. The slick lawyer had definitely gotten his attention when he'd cornered Dooley near the ball fields. Dooley didn't want to waste any more time. He'd have this little bitch take him back to the money and then thank him for not killing her. Once she saw the gun, he knew she'd fold like a cheap lawn chair.

Dooley waited until she stopped at a four-way stop away from the traffic on Ives Dairy Road, then hit the gas, slamming into her with a pretty good thump. He saw her head snap, then twist to see what had happened. He already had his pistol up so she could see it, giving her a minute to realize what was going on. As he aimed, he flinched at the sound of his own windshield shattering. The pings of the rounds from Tina's automatic sounded like a fast Latin beat. He threw his car in reverse and hit the gas, seeing for the first time the female FDLE agent holding her big Beretta nine-millimeter in both hands, shooting over her seat. She hadn't even hesitated to blow out her back window and then destroy his brand-new windshield. She kept up the fire until Dooley had taken the corner in reverse. As soon as he swung the car around and stopped, he took a couple of panting breaths and surveyed his car. It had ten new bullet holes and the right mirror had been blown off. He felt the sweat pour from his forehead and wiped it off, noticing the blood from all the flying glass embedded in his face.

He checked his face in the mirror. 'Shit!' he said out loud.

Then, without warning Tina's Monte Carlo whipped around the corner, tires squealing, and bore down on him.

Dooley threw the car into drive, even though he was facing her, and hit the gas. Swerving hard, he rolled through a front yard as Tina passed by, popping off a couple more shots as she approached. Dooley lost the rear driver's window to that barrage.

He laid on the gas and fled toward Ives Dairy Road before that crazy bitch came back.

SLAYDA 'MAC' NMIR lay half asleep, going over all the facts in the case. David Letterman talked quietly on a small TV across from his comfortable bed. The facts of the case said Bill Tasker had committed the robbery and stashed at least part of the cash at his Kendall town house. But Mac's instincts told him this guy wasn't a thief, much less a killer. This was difficult reasoning for a person with a degree in engineering who looked only at facts and figures. He found it hard to ignore those facts and go with his feelings. He went through it all again and then was zapped out of his dozing by a pounding on his front door. He stopped long enough to put on the safety chain before opening the door.

The door caught on the four-inch chain and he peered through, speechless for a second. 'How did you get this address?'

Bill Tasker smiled and said, 'I still got friends.'

'How'd you get past the gate?' Mac asked, still secure behind the door.

'There's no gate,' Tasker said, then added, 'anymore.' Tasker stepped back from the door. 'Listen, I just need to talk to you.'

Mac relaxed a little. 'So what's this all about?'

'About getting me off the hook. You know I didn't have anything to do with that robbery or murder.'

'Explain the money in your grill.'

'We can go round and round or you can come out to my Jeep and meet someone. In fact, I wouldn't mind bringing him to you because so far he's ruined my Jeep's interior.'

'Who is it?' Mac tried to look past Tasker but couldn't see anyone.

'Come and see for yourself.'

Mac thought it over and figured if this guy wanted him dead, he could've shot through the door. 'Okay, I'll tell you what. Give me a few minutes to get myself together and I'll meet you over at the park in front of my complex. The kids playing late basketball will be my insurance against any funny business.'

Tasker smiled and said, 'You watch too much TV.'

DERRICK SUTTER had plans. No one knew what they were, maybe not even himself, but he had plans. He sat at his kitchen counter in his small Miami Beach apartment that looked over one of the old diners that was now considered a new café and tripled its prices, writing down a few notes on what his story would be once the FBI rounded up all the players in this drama he'd bought into. He knew someone was going down, mainly because he couldn't let a guy like Bill Tasker take the fall for something he had no part of. No matter who went – Dooley, Tina Wiggins – they would talk and someone would mention his name. He knew the score. No one stood tall for too long. Right now he could just deny, but sooner or later someone would look for the cash. He knew it was safe for now, but that wouldn't last long either.

He wrote out a scenario on how he could help Tasker and not incriminate himself, then tore up the paper when he saw a flaw. He did this twice more, then cursed and threw the pad across the room. His line of shit would carry him when the time came because he had the goal and the ball and all he needed was a little interference.

TASKER HAD SAT quietly listening while Mac Nmir went through some stock questions with Cedric Brown, known to the residents of Liberty City as Spill. During the interview, Spill had managed to splash coffee on both himself and Mac. He'd been reluctant to go into detail with the FBI man at first, but, like he had when Tasker questioned him, he opened up.

Mac asked again, 'You certain that when you said you saw a cop in front of the bank, it wasn't Agent Tasker?'

Spill nodded. 'Yeah.'

'Why didn't you say that when we first interviewed you?'

'You didn't ax me about him.'

'But you said all cops look alike to you.'

'Yeah, but not that much alike. The other guy was fat and old.'

Mac paused, making a note.

Tasker cut in. 'Sound like anyone we know?'

Mac looked up at him. 'Be careful there, you're inferring that a federal agent was involved in these crimes.'

Inside, Tasker had been maintaining his composure. His nerves were shot. He looked at Mac Nmir and said, 'You can't ...' Before he could finish his thoughts, he balled his fist and threw it into Mac's stomach, knocking him backward and then onto the ground.

Mac gasped for air a second, then scrambled to his knee in case there was going to be a follow-up attack. He looked confused as he realized that Tasker hadn't moved.

Tasker went on. 'Stay over there in case I can't control myself again. You seem like an okay guy, but this pompous attitude that the FBI is king has got to stop. Have you ever looked around your office?'

Mac nodded cautiously.

'You got a lot of good people, but you've got your share of slugs, too. You were awful quick to assume I was a crook, but you can't think the same of Dooley? Give me a break.'

Mac finally got enough air to speak. 'But you had a track record.'

'That's a long story and really none of your business. Now the question is, if you thought this witness was credible enough to investigate me, he must be credible enough to look at Dooley. Christ, Mac, I'm not even saying arrest him, just check out this story and see what he held in evidence, see about his finances, do something, don't just say it's impossible.'

Mac stared at him, then looked over to a clearly overwhelmed Spill, trying to distance himself from this whole situation. Mac raised his hands in front of him. 'Okay, Tasker. I'll admit I see your point. I'll poke around, but without letting the Bureau know until I turn up something.'

'We'll talk to Sutter together.'

Mac said, 'I don't know.'

Tasker leaned forward. 'I do.'

Mac shrugged his acceptance.

Tasker realized that not only did he feel better, he liked being rude. It was fun. Suddenly he understood South Florida much better.

TINA WIGGINS PACED next to the service counter of Artie's Auto Glass as Artie wrote up an estimate for her blown-out rear window. She dialed her cell phone for the fourth time and squeezed the end button in frustration when there was no answer. Ever since that asshole FBI agent had tried to ambush her, nothing had gone right. She had fought with her sister over Derrick Sutter's true nature, searched fruitlessly for him and was now wasting time having this moron replace her window. She looked up when Artie cleared his massive throat.

The wildly obese man smiled, wiping the sweat from his upper lip. 'I'll tell you what. I'll do the whole thing for one-seventy-five. That's less than the other cop paid. You guys must be going through some glass.'

Tina leaned in. 'What other cop?'

'Didn't get his name. He waited just like you, but it was a white Buick. He come in twice. Once for windshield and rear window and then just this morning I replaced them both again. Said it was kids in the neighborhood fuckin' with him.'

Tina forced a smile. 'Yeah, me too. They never quit.'

'That's for sure. I got a couple of teenagers. You know what? They—'

Tina cut in. 'Can you tell me after you put in the glass, I'm in a hurry.'

'Sure, doll, anything you want.'

As he walked past, her thin but muscular arm reached out and grabbed his shoulder, twisting him toward her. 'And if you call me "doll" again, you'll have a personal rear-window problem.'

The guy knew better than to answer back.

She walked out the bay garage door and punched in the number she'd been trying. This time she got a 'Hello.'

Tina said, 'Do you know who this is?'

The voice said, 'I can't talk. Give me a number and I'll call you in two minutes.'

Tina gave in and waited, still pacing from one end of the short lot to the other, occasionally looking in at her car where Artie and three other guys were busy pushing in foam rubber around the newly seated window. The phone rang in her hand and she answered it immediately.

'Yeah,' she said, walking away from the garage.

'What did you want?' came the voice.

'C'mon, Sutter, you know why I'm calling.'

'No, tell me.' Derrick Sutter's voice was broken over the cell phone but clear enough.

'We have issues, Sutter. You took something that belongs to my family, and you broke my little sister's heart.'

'I'm sorry about your sister, but I didn't take anything of yours.'

Tina hesitated as she kept walking. 'Okay, be that way, but we need to talk. Pick some place away from your office. I don't want an encounter with that fat son of a bitch Dooley.'

Sutter paused so long she thought the line had gone dead, then his voice filled the receiver again. 'Okay, okay. I'll meet you, but I don't have anything that's yours.'

'Whatever,' said Tina. Then, 'Where?'

'How 'bout tonight, around six.' He paused again, then said, 'Make that seven. Seven at the north end of the Aventura Mall.'

'I'll be there, but you better be serious. This could get ugly.'

'I'll be there, but I still don't have a clue what you're talking about.'

She hung up rather than saying what she thought and pissing him out of meeting her. She needed him within grabbing range and he needed to understand the value of a partner.

BILL TASKER SAT with Mac Nmir in the conference room of the robbery task force, still in shock that Derrick Sutter was on the phone talking to Tasker's ex-girlfriend about her role in a bank robbery. Both Tasker and Mac had been skeptical when Sutter laid out his whole theory on Dooley and the money and how Tina and her sister had it now. Then, out of the blue, Tina had called. The vice cop mentality in Sutter thought fast enough for him to put off the call for a minute or two to set up a recorder and let the other two men sit in on the call. Tasker could only shake his head. He now understood some of Tina's questions and the timing of her breakup with him.

As Sutter hung up, he looked at Mac. 'Now do you believe me, Mr. FBI?'

Mac nodded. 'I would say this adds credibility to your statement. But we still don't have the money. Where is it?'

Sutter shrugged. 'Maybe Dooley figured it out and got it back. Maybe he has partners. Shit, who knows? We'll have a better idea tonight.'

Tasker finally composed himself enough to speak up. 'Maybe it's a mix-up, a misunderstanding?'

Mac looked at him. 'Is that what it looks like to you? Not to me.'

'You were wrong at least once before.'

'What do you want, Tasker? You want off the hook or not? Someone has the cash and whoever does can tell us how they got it. We got about seven hours to try and track down Dooley and get a better idea of what's going on. You with me?'

Tasker thought about how he'd been wrong about Hodges, then looked at Nmir and Sutter. He nodded, starting to feel the effects of being up all night and the shock of learning Tina was involved.

twenty-three

BILL TASKER DOZED for a few minutes while Mac Nmir ran into the FBI office to see if Dooley had been at work the past few days. Mac had parked a block away in the Howard Johnson's parking lot to be certain no one saw Tasker in the Bureau car. Tasker knew the FBI man's heart was in the right place, but his brain hadn't completely committed to the plan they had laid out. It was as if a voice in his head kept telling him another FBI agent like Dooley could not have done something like this.

Tasker let his exhaustion sweep over him as he waited for Mac's return. He figured Mac would recruit the necessary help to cover the deal they had set up for that night and all the preliminary things that needed to be done first. Mainly, finding Tom Dooley.

As he slipped into a comfortable rest with his head propped against the closed window, his mind kept working toward Tina Wiggins. There had to be a logical explanation for her involvement in this bizarre turn of events. Maybe Derrick Sutter had confused things and Tina had been helping to clear his name. Maybe it was just a misunderstanding. God knows that's how he had gotten tangled up in the whole mess. A misunderstanding and Dooley's attention to detail in framing him.

Tasker snapped back to consciousness when Mac opened the door and slipped inside. Checking all around, more like countersurveillance than checking for traffic, Mac threw the car into reverse and backed out. They were westbound on the 826 before he spoke.

Mac said, 'No one's seen him in a couple of days.'

Tasker nodded.

Mac held up a piece of paper. 'But I got his home address.'

Tasker said, 'Great. Who's helping us?'

'What do you mean?'

'I mean, did you get some more agents to cover the deal tonight?'

'No.'

'Why not? We don't know who might show up besides Tina. We've gotta make sure Sutter is protected while he's undercover.'

'I think we can handle Tina Wiggins.'

'Number one, I doubt we could, and number two, if someone thinks Sutter has that cash they might be after it, too.'

'I can't ask for help yet.'

Tasker just looked at him hard.

'I still don't have enough to ruin a guy's whole career. If he's dirty, we'll get him. If he's not, we can save a lot of heartache.'

'You mean like all the heartache you saved me?'

'Please allow that I made a mistake and would prefer not to make it again.'

That shut Tasker up. Maybe the guy was straight up.

AFTER FAILING to find Dooley at any of his expected hangouts, the uneasy partners headed toward downtown Miami and then on to the Aventura Mall and Sutter. Tasker felt as if Mac had been hinting about a subject for the past twenty minutes, but couldn't figure out what it could be. Then he spoke up.

Mac asked, 'What did you mean by needing more agents to cover Sutter?'

Tasker looked at him, not sure what he meant. 'You know, in case of trouble. To make sure he doesn't get hurt.'

'He can look after himself.'

'Maybe he can, but a UC should never be alone.'

Mac remained silent.

Tasker asked, 'Haven't you ever been undercover?'

Mac shook his head.

'But you've covered a deal like this before, right?'

'No, mostly I've done financial and robbery stuff.'

'How long you been on the job?'

'Four years.'

'And you've never done any kind of undercover work? What about surveillance?'

'Not much.'

Suddenly Tasker wasn't as proud of losing his FBI surveillance the night before.

Tasker said, 'We need to keep an eye on Sutter while he meets Tina. She might be the one who wants the cash, but she might not. It could be Dooley showing up. We don't know, so we have to prepare like it is and help Sutter if he gets in any kind of trouble.'

Mac nodded. 'You got a gun?'

Tasker pulled the SIG Sauer from his waistband.

'Where'd you get that?'

'That's in my lesson on search warrants.' He smiled and caught sight of Derrick Sutter waiting in his car near the back of the mall parking lot.

TINA WIGGINS SAT on the edge of her couch, consoling her sister.

Tina said, 'It's a business meeting, not a social.'

Jeanie blew her nose into a paper towel and looked up from streaked mascara. 'He said he'd never met anyone like me and I believed him.'

'I know you want to see him, but we need the money and I can't look after you while I'm dealing with him.'

'Will you ask him if I'll ever see him again?'

'C'mon, Jeanie, he used you. He burglarized our house. You don't want to ever see him again.'

She burst out in a sob again. 'No, I do, really. Just once to clear the air.'

'Let's clear our finances first, then we'll worry about our love lives.'

Jeanie straightened up. 'Didn't you use Billy? I mean, he gave you the information to get the cash.'

'That's different,' Tina said, turning away.

'How?'

'I liked Bill before the money. I just took an opportunity.'

'You really think someone couldn't like me for me? You think they all flock to you but are only interested in me if they can get something?'

Tina had heard this argument before somewhere. She didn't have time to get into it now.

'I'll see you around nine, sis.'

Tina quick-stepped out the front door as another wave of sobs swept over her sister.

TOM DOOLEY was much more careful following Tina Wiggins this time. He watched her pull out of her complex and head east toward the water. He hung way back, looking through his third windshield in four days. He had plans for this bitch tonight and he didn't care how he got the money back. The days of being Mr. Nice Guy were over. If the loopy broad shot at him again, he'd shove the pistol so far up her ass her kids would spit lead.

He kept well back as she turned onto US 1 and headed south toward Aventura. Dooley's heartbeat rose and he instinctively put a hand on his Smith & Wesson model 13 on his hip. He had his little backup on his ankle and was prepared to trade fire tonight if it came to that. There was a lot he was prepared to do now that he wouldn't have done a few days ago, because now the stakes were too high. And after this, at some point he had Cole Hodges to deal with and he knew that wouldn't be pretty either.

COLE HODGES EASED the gold Acura he'd stolen from in front of the Federal Courthouse into the street. The car had obviously belonged to some kind of U.S. marshal employee because of the paraphernalia in the car and the small SIG Sauer P-230 pistol in the glove compartment. Hodges took the gun and the extra magazine of seven .380 bullets and slipped them into his pocket. Looking through the painfully dirty windshield, he could see Tom Dooley's beat-up Buick Century head down Ives Dairy Road toward US 1. Hodges didn't know where the FBI man was headed or whom he'd been watching for the past three hours, but he knew he'd given the fat man more than enough time to get things together and turn it all over to him even if it was a day before their scheduled meeting at Pro Player Stadium. Hodges had plenty of firepower to make his point, and if it didn't work out he intended to hightail it over to South Miami and detain Dooley's son, Andy. Seemed like a nice young man and wouldn't put up much of a fight. It was almost too bad the Reverend Watson wasn't around. He would've liked the boy, and that would've been one more thing to encourage Dooley to deliver the cash.

He turned south on US 1 with Dooley. The FBI agent obviously didn't recognize the Acura and couldn't see who was driving.

'This will be sweet,' Hodges said with a smile as he stayed with Dooley and they passed into Aventura.

twenty-four

THE AVENTURA MALL spread out like many South Florida shopping centers across a wide and deep lot east of US 1. The modern mall had the usual big anchor stores, Bloomingdale's on one end and JCPenney on the opposite side. In between were the normal clothing, gift and electronic stores associated with an upscale, yuppie neighborhood. Aside from the food court, a T.G.I. Friday's, Johnny Rockets and a new Cheesecake Factory provided places to feed the hungry shoppers, who were more locals and American tourists than in the other malls in Dade County.

Tasker had never spent any time at the mall, so he and Mac had been circling the sprawling structure for the past ten minutes, getting an idea of the layout and making sure Tina Wiggins hadn't slipped in early. Tasker still had a hard time believing he was part of the surveillance of a girl for whom he had strong feelings. He couldn't call it love, but it had been way more than friendship. He hoped there was another explanation and that she was just trying to help him, but deep inside he knew that was unlikely.

They drove back and met Sutter at his car almost an hour before Tina was supposed to show up. In normal circumstances, Tasker wouldn't meet at the same place as a suspect, but normally he wouldn't be trying to make a case on his girlfriend or be facing an indictment if it didn't work out. He'd accepted that the normal rules of police investigation had been suspended since sometime the night before.

Inside the T.G.I. Friday's they grabbed a table near the main window. Tasker took a minute to catch his breath.

Across from him, Derrick Sutter shook his head for the fourth time, explaining to Mac and Tasker how he wasn't mixed up, confused or lying.

Sutter said, 'The bitch used her sister to distract fat boy and she took the cash.'

Tasker said, 'And she told you this?'

'No, I said that Dooley explained it. He thought I had it then, and when I saw Jeanie I knew the score. Dooley just confirmed it.'

Mac pulled a black microcassette recorder slightly bigger than a pack of cigarettes from his pants pocket and slid it across the table toward Sutter.

Sutter picked it up in his bony hand and said, 'What's this, J. Edgar?'

'Recorder.'

'No shit. What do you want me to do with it?'

Mac cut loose for the first time since Tasker had known him. 'Stick it up your ass so I know how you're feeling during the deal.' He paused without smiling. 'You've got to record the whole conversation.'

Sutter rolled his eyes. 'You dumbshit, she's a cop. That's the first thing she'll check.'

'Maybe in your pocket?' suggested Màc.

This time Tasker shook his head, reluctant to enter a conversation about gathering evidence on Tina. 'We won't hear shit if it's in his pocket. And if we tape it to his chest, she'll find it.'

Mac asked, 'What do you suggest?'

Tasker took the recorder from Sutter and held it up to the paper napkin dispenser on the table. Then he took out a handful of napkins and stuck the recorder inside, pushing the record button as he did it. He replaced the napkins and said, 'That should work. One, two, three, that should work.' He retrieved the recorder and started to play back his test, then realized it had no internal speaker to save on size. He looked at Mac. 'You have the speaker?'

Mac shrugged. 'At the office.'

Tasker's face flushed. 'How'd you manage to make a case on me?'

That brought laughter from Sutter, but a glare from Mac's dark face.

Tasker said, 'We'll have to trust it works,' and handed the recorder back to Sutter. Then he said, 'I want this recorded because I hope you've screwed up what she said or what Dooley meant. You'll see she's okay.'

Sutter nodded. 'I believe she's okay. I just think she stole the cash. Too bad it's a crime, that's all.'

Tasker said, 'We'll see.'

Mac stood up and looked down at Sutter. 'Make sure you hold this table when you go to wait for her and don't forget to turn that thing on.'

Sutter nodded. 'Where will you guys be?'

Mac said, 'I'll stay on foot close by. Bill will be in the lot in the car. If you get into trouble, we'll be right there.'

Sutter smiled. 'The day I can't get out of trouble and the FBI needs to save me is the day I quit police work.'

DERRICK SUTTER SAT alone at the restaurant table, staring at the small recorder in his hand. He'd tried to get out of recording his meeting with Tina Wiggins. That would've been the easiest thing to do. Then when he testified, as he knew someday he would, he wouldn't implicate himself, could clear Tasker and make his statements vague enough so that Tina and her stupid sister wouldn't face prison either. That way everyone would come out ahead. He could make up some lame story about the recorder malfunctioning, but even the FBI was getting wise to that scam.

Sutter checked his fake Rolex Aviator and saw it was seven on the nose. He'd told Tina he'd be standing outside the Friday's now. He couldn't see the street in front of the restaurant, so he decided to go outside and wait. He looked once more at the small recorder, then, sighing, mashed the tiny red record button. He could see the spindles turn slowly. He took out about ten napkins and placed the recorder inside, then replaced the napkins. It looked natural; he just had to remember to sit on this side and not use extra napkins.

As the young waitress walked past the table, he caught her attention. She'd seemed a little annoyed every time Mac had told her to come back when they were talking and she wanted to take their order. Now it was up to Sutter to convince her to hold the table while he stepped outside. Luckily, God had given him the gift of charm and he knew how to use it. He smiled, then looked up at the buxom waitress.

'Excuse me.' He touched her name tag like he needed to see it. 'Shelly. But would it be possible to hold this table for a few minutes while I catch the attention of someone outside?'

She looked around at the crowded room, then back at Sutter without saying a word.

'Shelly, that's a pretty name. What's your last name?'

'Lipstein,' she said without emotion. 'How pretty is that?'

'It goes with you. Now how about it, Shell? Can I keep the table?'

'Let me make sure I understand this great offer. You and your cheap friends take up this table for forty-five minutes without ordering a thing. Then the other two split. Now you want to tie it up longer while you look for someone. Is that the plan, slick?'

Sutter pulled a fifty from his imitation alligator money clip and said, 'Yeah and you get this on top of everything else.'

Shelly Lipstein smiled and said, 'No problem.'

AFTER ONLY a moment of settling into the Ford Taurus, Tasker saw Derrick Sutter come out onto the sidewalk and wait by the street. A big part of Tasker didn't want Tina to show up. Even though she'd dumped him and, in all likelihood, used his information to steal the cash, Tasker didn't want to think about the consequences for her. He sighed and continued watching Sutter.

After ten minutes, he saw her pull up in her state-issued Monte Carlo. If he ever had to testify, he couldn't be more clear. He saw her behind the wheel, wearing a blue top and her hair pulled back into a dark ponytail. She didn't smile as she stopped in front of Sutter. They exchanged some words and she peeled the tires as she cut into the parking lot. Tasker could see her two rows away after she got out and marched toward Sutter, who was still outside the restaurant. Tasker's heart sank a little when he saw her give his partner a long, friendly hug, then a decent kiss.

TINA RAN her arms over Derrick Sutter's tight ribs and back. This man is built, she thought. She ended the hug by running her hands across his waist, then she leaned forward, kissed him and discreetly put her left hand on his crotch, even rubbing his penis for a second.

Sutter pushed her away. 'Damn, girl, Jeanie been tellin' you stories?'

'Funny. Now let me see that phone.'

Sutter eyed her silently.

'You want to talk, I need to see that cell phone.'

Sutter shrugged and unclipped his small Nextel I-90 cellular phone and handed it to her, waiting quietly as she flipped it around in her hand, then took out the battery, slipping it into her pocket.

Tina said, 'I can never tell if they fit a recorder in these or not. If this works out, you'll get your battery back.' She paused, then added, 'Even though I know you can afford a new one.'

He nodded.

She handed him the dead cell phone and said, 'You're not in such demand that you can't be out of touch for a few minutes.'

Sutter smiled and said, 'You'd be surprised.'

She eyed him up and down and realized she wouldn't be surprised by anything this guy could come up with.

TOM DOOLEY swung his car into a spot near the T.G.I. Friday's where he'd dropped his first hint to the Channel Eleven reporter about the Tasker investigation. He'd been stunned when Tina Wiggins met Derrick Sutter out front with a big hug and kiss. Not stunned that they met, only stunned that he'd believed that no-good son-of-a-bitch dick-sucking whore asshole Sutter when he'd told him Tina had stolen his cash. He should've known that slick cop had been involved. Mother-fucking shit-packing jerk-off. This really pissed him off. He sat in the car, staring through the new windshield at the entrance the two had just walked through. He could go in and make a scene but, as he considered consequences and actions and remembering how quick on the trigger the broad was, he decided to wait till they came out and then maybe reason with them. Maybe, between the three of them they could neutralize damn Cole Hodges, who Dooley knew would turn up sooner or later.

COLE HODGES didn't figure it out until Dooley parked and stayed in the car; then he knew the FBI man was following someone. He didn't see who it was but he guessed it was whoever lived in the apartment Dooley had watched all afternoon and that it had to do with the CCR's money. Hodges had had all he could stand of being treated like some kind of street thug. Smacked around by that cocky Cuban roadkill and having his cash taken twice by that ton-of-lard federal agent. It was time to clean this shit up and quick.

All bets were off. Once he had the cash he was outta here. Too much had happened for him to stay around South Florida. He leaned back in the Acura he'd picked up and laid his .357 revolver across his lap, and the .380 he had found in the glove compartment was still in his pocket. He'd know when it was time to act.

SLAYDA 'MAC' NMIR, second-generation American, four-year veteran of the FBI, was in the first situation in his whole life where he had gone outside the rules. He had failed to notify anyone at the Bureau that they might have a bad agent. His supervisor didn't know what he was up to, and in the FBI, control was a big thing. And lastly he had no idea what he was doing. If Tina pulled a gun, he didn't know what to do. If she admitted to everything, he wasn't sure how to handle it. And when this was all over, he'd have to explain it to someone and that wouldn't be pretty. He'd be reviewing wiretap transcripts for another two years if things didn't happen to fall his way. How did he ever get so far in over his head?

He lingered by the eastern mall entrance, looking across the small courtyard, relieved that there weren't more patrons.

As he was about to make a short walk around the nearby stores to avoid looking like some kind of stalker, he caught a car out of the corner of his eye. He could just see the Buick and maybe someone moving inside through the back window. It looked like Dooley's car, but he didn't see why he'd be here. He had no way of knowing about this meeting. Mac had a twinge in his stomach and wondered if this was what real cops felt when they had a hunch.

twenty-five

D ERRICK SUTTER had managed to make it to the table without raising Tina's suspicions by saying he had saved a table. Then he remembered to sit on the correct side of the napkin holder, all while maintaining his friendly, easygoing smile. This was going to be tough and he knew it. One wrong word and everyone and their brother would know he had the money.

Tina slid in and faced him across the clean table.

The waitress, Shelly, came up. 'Can I get you something to drink?'

Tina looked up and said curtly, 'Just water for now.'

The waitress wandered off as she muttered, 'Figures.'

Sutter tried to look Tina right in the eyes. She was a fine-looking woman. Not as fly as her sister, but nice.

Sutter said, 'Why'd you have to check me for a wire? What have you got to hide?'

'I know you took our money, but I don't know why. Could be profit, maybe it's something else.'

'Don't know what you're talking about,' Sutter answered, staying calm.

'You see, you're smart and cold. You could be laying a defense for later.' Her dark eyes cut around the room once, then fell, sharply, back onto Sutter.

Sutter smiled. 'I'll take smart, but cold? No way.'

Tina shook her head. 'You broke Jeanie's heart and I'm pissed about it. But if you give me back our money, I think we can all be friends again.'

'I'm not saying I know what you're talking about or not, but I'm not clear how you had so much money to lose.' He eyed the napkin holder even though his mind said keep looking into those dark brown eyes.

'That was easy. Men have a weakness for Jeanie. Once the FBI guy, Dooley, saw her, he forgot about leaving the cash in his car.'

'How'd you know Dooley had the cash?'

'This is why I know you're full of shit. Billy Tasker told me that you thought he had the money in temporary evidence at the task force. A couple of days' surveillance and he comes out with a plastic bag. We took a chance and it worked. If it'd been something else in the bag, we were gonna hire one of the girls that dance with Jeanie to distract him the next time and keep doing it until we had the money.'

'What if he caught on?'

'Men never think that pretty women are a setup. They always think that women are just attracted to them.'

Sutter nodded, knowing he had enough on tape and that he was safe. He flinched when she reached for a napkin from her side of the holder. She patted her lips then dipped the napkin in her water, splashing a little on the table. She immediately reached for some more napkins. Sutter stayed cool and watched, then, without warning she pulled out the last napkin on her side and with one fluid motion turned the holder around so the hidden recorder faced her. She pulled out a couple more napkins and mopped up the spill.

Tina looked up. 'So what's the verdict? You gonna play ball or do things get ugly?'

Sutter's eyes reflexively shifted from her to the napkin holder. 'It sounds like fat boy Dooley found you out and took it back.'

She hesitated and Sutter caught it.

'What is it?' asked Sutter.

She still paused, then took out another napkin and patted her forehead.

Sutter held his breath. The recorder had to be nearly visible by now.

Tina said, 'He knows something, 'cause I had a run-in with him yesterday.'

'What kind of run-in?'

'A nasty one.' She reached for another napkin.

Before Sutter could think of something to say, the waitress walked up. 'You guys ready yet?'

Tina answered, 'No, still thinking.'

The waitress looked at Sutter. 'You're gonna have to leave if you don't order soon. I mean, this is a prime table and you and the other two tied it up for almost an hour, now this.'

Sutter nodded. 'Yeah, yeah, I know, thanks.'

Tina stared at the waitress, then at Sutter. 'What other two? You got partners? Is this a setup?' She reached in her purse and kept her right hand in there. 'Don't move, Derrick. You know what's in here.'

He nodded slowly.

'Now we're gonna walk outside and figure this whole thing out.'

'Okay with me,' said Sutter.

DOOLEY WATCHED as Sutter walked out with the girl right beside him. This was it. He had to act while they were together. Hash it all out right now. If they didn't pay, they could worry about him talking. He knew he couldn't shoot it out with both of them, but he was ready if someone drew.

He hopped out of the car and started across the lot toward them.

TASKER SAW Sutter and Tina come out the front door but immediately knew something was wrong. Sutter didn't have his normal strut and he looked around like he expected someone else. Then, as Tasker reasoned this out, Sutter raised both his hands like he was being robbed. Something was up. Tasker opened the car door but hesitated. He couldn't believe Tina would be holding a gun on him. He paused until he noticed someone heading toward them from the parking lot farther south. It took him a second to recognize Tom Dooley, before he realized he had to act and act fast. He raced across the lot, pulling his pistol from his waist.

SUTTER FELT his heart race as he raised his hands. He knew it would only last a second but hoped someone caught on to his problem.

Tina said, 'Put your hands down, I'm not robbing you.'

'Habit when someone holds a gun on me.'

Tina stayed calm. 'Break the habit. We're in public.'

'What's the plan now?' Sutter asked as he lowered his hands.

'We go get my money and you explain who your friends were in the restaurant.'

'What if I told you it was Billy?'

'And who else?'

'The FBI agent Mac Nmir.'

'You're full of shit. Billy wouldn't come out on this.'

'You know, you're the cold one. You'd let Billy go to jail to keep that money.'

'He's not involved. They wouldn't even take him to trial. Now level with me, who was in the restaurant?'

Before Sutter could formulate an answer, he heard someone else's voice.

'Look at the two lovebirds. I shoulda figured.' It was Tom Dooley coming up onto the sidewalk.

Sutter still didn't answer when a black guy behind Dooley said, 'Do these young people have my money, Agent Dooley?'

Dooley twisted as the black guy pulled out a big revolver and leveled it at him.

Sutter felt Tina step away and bring the small .380 out of her purse. As he moved toward the street, she popped off two quick rounds at the black guy. The noise almost deafened Sutter as he dove for the curb and what little cover it offered. He heard Dooley yell, 'Hodges, you son-of-a-bitch turd.' Then Dooley had a revolver out, too. Sutter now recognized the black guy as Cole Hodges and knew exactly what was going down.

From the mall side, Mac Nmir came running with a small automatic in his hand.

The noise of the shots seemed to blend into one another as fire came from at least three weapons. He could see the others spread out to find cover, then from the other side of the street he saw Bill Tasker coming toward him, firing on the run at Dooley, trying to cover Sutter as well as he could.

This shit was getting thick.

TASKER DIDN'T FEEL anger as he yanked the trigger of his pistol, causing every round to miss the fat profile of Tom Dooley; he just wanted Sutter to get to safety. By the time he reached the sidewalk, everyone had backed to a neutral corner and was firing from behind cover. Tasker closed on Sutter.

'You okay? You okay?' Tasker asked, crouching toward the prone Sutter.

'Yeah.'

Tasker grabbed Sutter's belt at the rear of his pants, lifted the thin detective to a crouch and said, 'Let's get outta here. Over to the bench.'

They scrambled to a heavy cement bench and turned it on its side. Now Sutter fumbled for his own pistol on his ankle. Tasker could see the civilians racing away from their location. Most Miamians knew what to do in a gunfight and usually had their own gun, but these rich people didn't move as fast. He prayed no innocent people had been hit.

Tasker looked over and saw the black guy who had started this whole thing against the wall to the east mall entrance. He looked like he'd been hit and was done shooting for now.

Tasker leaned behind the bench again and asked Sutter, 'Who the hell is that guy?'

'Cole Hodges.'

'I told you he's involved!'

Sutter nodded.

'Here for his own cash. I knew he was a crook.'

Sutter said, 'You and everyone else.'

'How'd he know who had it?'

Sutter turned to him. 'How the fuck does anyone know anything around here? Right now I just don't want to be shot.'

Tasker nodded his agreement, then he heard Mac's voice.

'This is the FBI. Throw down your weapons and surrender.'

This brought fire from at least two positions.

Sutter rolled his eyes. 'He's not serious, is he?'

Tasker leaned up again and saw Tina, now bent over but running toward the injured Hodges.

'No, Tina,' Tasker yelled, standing and charging in the same direction. No one fired and he realized he had no idea where Dooley was holed up. He could see Mac come from the entrance as he ran, and heard Sutter following behind him. He turned the corner Tina had just disappeared behind and found her with her pistol on Hodges. Tasker raised his gun.

'Please don't, Tina.' His voice cracked.

She looked at him. 'I'm sorry, Billy,' she said without lowering her gun.

He shuffled closer with his pistol now only four feet from her head. 'Drop the gun, Tina.'

Hodges crouched on the ground with his hands over his head.

She didn't move and Tasker tightened his finger on the trigger.

From behind him, Sutter said, 'Drop it, bitch, or you're dead meat.'

Now Tina looked up at the two guns and the angry black face and let the gun fall from her hand.

Tasker slid forward to kick it out of the way and noticed the blood spreading on the ground from Hodges.

As Mac came racing up, Sutter said, 'Get fire rescue now.'

twenty-six

TASKER FELL into Mac as the ambulance took the corner toward North Miami Regional Hospital. The young surfer-looking driver leaned back and asked, 'Is everyone still alive?' Mac grunted, 'Yes,' and pulled himself back onto the small bench next to Tasker. As soon as the Aventura cops had arrived at the mall, Mac flashed his badge and left Sutter to explain things. Tasker knew they were in the ambulance not only to get Cole Hodges's statement, but to avoid detention by other FBI men when they arrived. Mac was coming around.

Mac said, 'Your girlfriend looked pissed in the back of that patrol car.'

Tasker ignored him.

Mac looked down at Hodges as the attendant checked the IV drip. Mac said, 'Mr. Hodges, you know what's going on. I'm an FBI agent and you're screwed.'

Hodges turned his head slightly. 'Dooley's FBI, too. I'm not impressed.'

Mac nodded. 'Touché, Mr. Hodges, but you've got a lot of explaining to do.'

Tasker could see this wasn't getting through to the guy. 'Look, Cole, what my formal friend here is saying is that you've got one chance to jump on board and make a statement or you get no consideration when the indictments start to fly. If you haven't started talking by the time this ambulance pulls into the hospital, you won't get another chance. Understood?' Tasker waited for it to sink into this guy's head.

Hodges lay silently, looking at Tasker. 'Well stated, young man. However, I'm a victim.' He looked across to Mac, then back and asked, 'Am I under arrest?' He maintained the same calm, slow, clear speech.

'Yes,' answered both Mac and Tasker at the same time.

'May I inquire as to the charge?' He gave a faint smile.

Mac paused as Tasker jumped in. 'Aggravated assault with a firearm. Attempted robbery and related charges from your little gun battle at the most exclusive mall in the county.'

Hodges nodded. 'Oh yes. That unfortunate incident. I shall claim self-defense. You will not overcome this defense. In fact, I am already considering a civil rights suit against you should you detain or question me further.'

Mac appeared horrified at the threat. Tasker looked at the older black man more reclining than lying in the stretcher. He really didn't seem concerned. Was that the lawyer in him or something else? Tasker looked closely at his face, searching for something to unnerve him. As Tasker turned in his seat, he bumped an IV running down to Hodges's arm, causing the tape on his arm to come up slightly.

'Sorry,' Tasker mumbled, as he leaned down to smooth out the tape. When he held Hodges's arm, he noticed a significant old scar on the lawyer's right arm. Tasker thought back to the list of possible identities he'd been given the week before. He patted his shirt pockets, knowing he still had it on him, then reached in his rear pocket and pulled out the single sheet. The eighth name down, Luther Williams, had a description that included a scar on his elbow from an attack received at the Missouri State Penitentiary. Tasker figured it was probably a shiv stuck in him while he took a shower. Could this be the scar from a sharpened metal stick years ago?

Mac looked at Hodges. 'So what's it going to be?'

Hodges let out a sharp laugh. 'I've already explained it. You have nothing and you never will.' He turned his head in the other direction for effect. He was saying that the interview was over and it looked like Mac accepted that.

Tasker couldn't let it end like this; he had nothing to lose. He leaned closer to Hodges, but tapped Mac on the arm so he'd pay attention.

'Okay, let's cut the shit.' He waited for Hodges to slowly turn his head toward him, showing he was barely interested. Tasker continued. 'We're not all the idiots you think we are.'

Hodges grunted, 'You couldn't be as stupid as I think you are. No one could.'

'Tell me, did you develop this attitude while you were in the Missouri pen?'

Hodges reacted. His head jerked before he could try to compose himself.

Tasker touched his scar. 'That's right, I know about the fight in the shower, I know it all.'

Now Mac looked confused, but he saw Hodges's obvious reaction and jumped in. 'That's right, we know exactly what's going on.'

Tasker kept it up. 'So, Mr. Williams, or do you prefer to be called Luther? What's it going to be? You with us or not?'

Hodges considered this. 'So I am in custody regardless.'

'You are.'

Hodges nodded to himself, then with a surprisingly strong voice asked, 'What's the deal?'

Mac said, 'Just consideration. We'll speak on your behalf and you get to tell your side first.'

The ambulance took another corner and tossed everyone except Hodges to the rear. He took a moment to reflect. The expressions on his face passed through determination to doubt to resignation, then he said in a quick, sharp tone, 'Okay, gentlemen, here's the thumb-nail sketch of the situation.'

Mac and Tasker sat, spellbound.

'Reverend Al Watson apparently withheld some cash from the CCR. Shortly after he retrieved it, Mr. Dooley stole it and the good reverend vanished. I'll let you look into that. It was my intent to recover the cash from Dooley when all this unpleasantness took place.'

Tasker said, 'And you expect us to believe that?'

'For now, yes.'

Mac asked, 'Who took the cash from the bank?'

'I assume Reverend Watson.'

Mac kept it up. 'And he killed the manager?'

'That would not be out of his character.'

'Did you see any of the news reports about the investigation into the robbery?'

'I heard a few where some cop was a suspect. I know nothing of this. Mr. Dooley had clearly been interested in the cash for some time and we knew it. It wasn't hard to figure out who took it.'

The ambulance bumped over the entrance to the hospital.

Tasker eyed the injured man cautiously. 'What are you holding back?'

Hodges grimaced at a bump and said, 'I think you've found out the most important facts, young man.'

AN HOUR AFTER arriving at the hospital, Mac slammed down a pay phone and turned to Tasker.

The dark-skinned young man said, 'We're as good as fugitives.'

'What?' asked a startled Tasker.

'Don't worry, I'm talking figuratively, not literally. If we show up back at the mall or at my office, we'll be delayed for hours while we answer questions about procedure, not about the case. They know Dooley's a crook and they've got guys processing the scene. So to avoid all that, we're on the run and not checking in. How's that sound?'

'Like you're becoming a cop.'

'What's our next move?'

Tasker thought about it. 'We need more help. Let's get Sutter; we can trust him and he doesn't give a damn about FBI procedure.'

'Okay, Hodges won't be out of ICU for another four or five hours anyway. The Bureau is sending over someone to watch him. I suggest we disappear prior to their arrival.'

Tasker nodded and then, hesitantly, asked, 'What about Tina?'

'She's being processed at the office. She's asked for an attorney and isn't saying anything.'

'What'll happen to her?'

'Depends. Right now we have her for unlawful detention of Sutter.'

'Kidnapping?'

'Yeah, related charge and they're working on the money charges. They've even sent some agents to talk to her sister. What will she say?'

Tasker nodded slowly, staring straight ahead. 'She'll talk.'

'Then I'd start looking for a new girlfriend.'

Tasker said, 'That decision was made for me.'

*

THE TRICK in getting back to the mall and recovering Mac's car was not being seen by any of the Bureau bigwigs. The place looked like a movie set, with the extra lights and people milling about. There were four separate TV satellite trucks. Tasker couldn't help staring at the Channel Eleven truck with the young female reporter who'd broken the story reporting him as the suspect in the bank robbery. As Mac paid the cabbie and stood back, surveying the scene, Tasker felt compelled to talk to the reporter. He started toward her.

Mac said, 'Hey, come back.'

'I'll only be a minute.'

'Where are you going?'

Tasker ignored him as he marched up to the young woman. He asked, 'You recognize me?'

She cast uninterested eyes on him. 'No, you recognize me, though.'

'I'm Bill Tasker.'

'So.'

'The name's not even familiar?'

'No, now I'm busy, so get lost.'

'When you report this story, make sure you point out that I didn't rob the Overtown bank and that you were wrong when you reported it.' He turned; this woman clearly wasn't worth his time and it felt good to realize that.

As he headed toward Mac and the car, he heard the reporter say, 'Oh shit, wait a minute, Mr. Tasker. Hurry up, guys, get the camera online.' Tasker heard her scurry toward him. 'Please wait, Mr. Tasker.' She stopped and turned to her crew. 'Would you assholes c'mon.' She turned back toward him. 'Mr. Task—' She was cut short by a microphone wire wrapped around her leg that pulled her off balance with such power she smashed her chin into the asphalt, opening a nasty cut that filled the road with blood.

Mac asked, 'What was that all about?'

Tasker said, 'If I was a recovering alcoholic, it would have been one of my twelve steps. Did you find out where Sutter is?'

Mac nodded. 'He went home about ten minutes ago.'

Tasker nodded with authority now. 'Let's go.'

THE SHORT RIDE across the William Lehman Causeway to Sunny Isles gave Tasker a few minutes to gather himself and let it sink in that this most recent nightmare was almost over. Once Dooley was safely in custody, things might start to get back to normal. That didn't mean he was over all his problems, but it was a start.

No matter his feelings on the case against him being over, Tasker couldn't help but worry for Tina and her safety. By now she had to realize she was not getting out of this and that he knew all about her role in the cash. That was the one thing he wished he could change. Tina should still be innocent because it was her association with him that had gotten her in this predicament in the first place.

He stared out the window silently as Mac made phone call after phone call on a tiny cell phone. The sights of Collins Avenue passed by while Tasker's mind raced over the events again and again. His mind was surprisingly calm as he looked forward to Sutter's help in the case. After they found Dooley, there was still the question of the cash. Where was it and who took it? He felt confident these questions would be answered in the coming days.

Tasker sat up as they came closer to South Beach and Sutter's apartment.

'Over there, over there,' Tasker said as Mac ended a call.

They parked and headed up the single staircase to the second-story landing, where Sutter's apartment was the only one of four without an ocean view.

. Mac knocked and they waited. After a minute, Mac said, 'Maybe he's not here.'

'His car's out front.'

Mac knocked again and heard a muffled, 'Hang on.' After another twenty seconds, the door opened and Derrick Sutter, still in the clothes he'd worn at the mall, stood frowning.

He asked, 'What's up?'

Tasker started to answer, when Mac threw his entire weight into the door and kicked Sutter back off his feet.

Before Tasker could react, he heard two shots. He pulled his pistol and barreled into the dark room as two more shots went off. He turned to see Mac locked in a bear hug with Tom Dooley. The larger man clearly had the advantage, but Mac had hold of his gun hand and was making a fight of it. Tasker sprang up, throwing his whole body into a block that sent all three men into the tiny walk-in kitchen and bouncing off an old refrigerator. They fell on the ground in a heap, Dooley's gun spiraling across the floor. Tasker lost hold of his gun but managed to kick it under the stove. He then grabbed hold of Dooley's throat and swung hard with his left hand. With Mac still locked between them, the blow didn't do much harm. He swung again.

Mac yelled, 'Christ, Bill, wait a second.' Then he squirmed out of the way. 'Now hit him.'

Tasker opened up with a series of four quick, hard blows. Dooley went limp under the barrage as Tasker slowly worked himself free and stood over the fallen man.

Mac picked up his small automatic, then reached under the stove for Tasker's nine-millimeter. Tasker warily backed away from Dooley and then, tripping over the big .357, retrieved Dooley's pistol.

'You okay?' Tasker asked Mac.

Mac nodded. 'You?'

Tasker, still gasping for air, nodded. 'What about you, Derrick?'

There was no response. Tasker looked over at the Miami detective and before he saw him clearly, he saw the blood seeping into the green carpet.

twenty-seven

'THINK HE'LL MAKE IT?' Tom Dooley asked, as he sat on the couch with a bloody dishrag on his mouth where Tasker had split open his lip.

'He better. Either way you're screwed.' Tasker had all he could stand of this creep. He gripped the handle of his Beretta but kept his finger off the trigger. He didn't want to risk inadvertently tightening his finger. Not that he'd miss Dooley. No one would. But if he killed the fat man, he'd be in the same fix he'd been in with Sandersen. Everyone would think he'd killed Dooley to keep him from talking. Right now Tasker would give his own life to make sure Dooley stayed safe. When the FBI man shifted his weight on the couch, Tasker raised the pistol like he would hit him with it. 'Don't move, asshole.'

'Ohh, the Boy Scout swears.'

Tasker ignored him and leaned against the front door, waiting for the local cops he'd called for backup. It had been less than three minutes since Mac had raced Derrick Sutter to Cedars-Sinai with a bullet in his upper chest and Tasker figured it'd be another five until the locals showed. Sutter had lost a lot of blood and even Mac Nmir had suggested it wouldn't be a tragedy if something happened to Dooley before he went to jail. That was a bad sign for the overweight FBI agent sitting on the couch ten feet in front of him.

Dooley cleared his throat and said, 'No, seriously, I'm worried about Sutter. He took my cash, but I sorta liked him.'

'How do you know he took your cash?'

'I saw him with the FDLE broad. You know, Tina.'

'How did you know she had it?'

'Look, I know the score. I'm done, that's all. Don't worry about trying to get me to confess.'

214

'I'm not. How did you know Tina had the cash?'

Dooley looked off into space and said, 'You can't know what it's like to spend so long with an outfit and have nothing to show for it. In the new mother-fucking cock-sucking economy I coulda been rich.'

'How'd you figure out who had the money?' Tasker asked.

'You know who'll be hurt by all this? My son, Andy. He's the victim in all this. That's what hurts. Thinking about my boy.'

Tasker finally ignored him as he rambled. He turned toward the window waiting for the locals. He had Dooley's revolver in the small of his back. He hadn't let Dooley move from the couch because he had no idea how many guns Sutter had stashed around the apartment. His shoulder hurt from the fight but he was more or less intact.

Dooley shut up and stared at Tasker for a few moments.

Finally unnerved, Tasker said, 'What? What is it?'

Dooley shook his head. 'I hope you realize it was nothing personal.'

'Was to me.'

'I'm sure, but I mean, it was just a stroke of luck I got to shove the blame on you.'

'Great.'

'Really. You're a good cop and a regular guy. You were the last guy I wanted to cause any trouble for. It just worked out that you had to take the blame.'

Tasker just nodded.

Dooley said quietly, 'You know I'm done.'

Tasker smiled. 'Sutter would say, "You're done like a Christmas turkey."'

'What's that supposed to mean?'

Tasker smiled. 'I don't know, but it's nice to have a laugh at your expense.'

'Yeah, yeah, everyone likes to kick you when you're down.' He stretched his arms high over his head and leaned forward, stretching from the waist, still on the couch. 'I'm tellin' you, Billy, you shouldn't beat up on an old man like me. You fucked me up.'

Tasker watched him, but Dooley made no attempt to get off the deep, soft couch.

Then Dooley said, 'Oh great, I hear the Miami Beach cops using their sirens. This will be embarrassing.'

Tasker turned and looked out the window. He hadn't heard anything, but his ears were still ringing from the fight. As he turned back to Dooley, he saw the FBI agent sitting up from a deep waist bend with a small revolver in his hand. Tasker brought up his gun as Dooley cranked off a round.

Tasker darted to the side, amazed at the speed of Dooley, who rolled off the couch and headed for the doorway to the bedroom. Tasker aimed but didn't fire, watching as Dooley disappeared into the room. A second later, he heard the fat man catch his breath and yell out to him.

'Not bad for an old man, huh, Billy?' he panted a couple of times. 'You didn't expect a backup on my ankle. You kids with the automatics never worry about a little extra firepower. Experience counts, my young friend.'

Tasker's mind raced. He could wait for the locals and let them deal with him. That way no one could accuse him of trying to silence Dooley or say they were accomplices. Then the FBI man shouted from the bedroom again.

'What to do? What to do?' He paused. 'I can't wait for a SWAT team to flush me out, Billy. And you know if you shoot me, it'll look like you were eliminating another witness.'

Tasker froze.

'That's right, I have access to all kinds of files. Little Mac Nmir left shit on his desk all the time. I guess he thought the FBI office was secure.' Dooley laughed. 'Now I need to go. You can let me out the front and no one gets hurt, or we can shoot it out. You're off the hook if I get away. Shit, they'll catch me anyway in a few days. Why not do us both a favor?'

Tasker crouched by the refrigerator, aiming his pistol at the open doorway.

MAC NMIR threw the Taurus into a powerslide to make the turn west toward Cedars-Sinai. Sutter sat slumped in the front seat, still holding his chest and shoulder. The bloody towel seemed to have stemmed the blood flow.

Sutter said, 'You saved my ass up there. How'd you know?'

'Saw it on TV.'

'You're shittin' me?'

'Nope. *Magnum, P.I.* or something like that.'

Sutter coughed. 'Doesn't matter. You kicked ass and I appreciate it.'

'You gonna quit police work now that an FBI agent saved you?'

'Don't think it counts, because an FBI agent was holding me hostage.'

Mac nodded. 'Good point.'

After a moment, when the hospital was in sight, Sutter said, 'I gotta tell you something.'

'Hang on, Sutter, we'll be there in a few seconds.'

'This is important, about the money.'

'Hang on.' Only this time Mac meant for him to hang onto something literally because he misjudged a turn and was sliding over a curb at high speed.

The impact knocked Sutter completely unconscious as Mac brought the car to a stop in front of the emergency room. He hit the gas once more and had an orderly help him with the limp Sutter.

TASKER HAD a choice: Let Dooley escape and hope he was captured or shoot him as soon as he came through the door and get accused of the same thing as in West Palm Beach. He raised the gun again and shouted, 'Dooley, everyone knows you framed me. If you don't toss out the gun and come out that door with your hands up, I'll shoot you and I won't care if you live or die.'

'I don't care, either, Billy. I'd never make it on the inside.'

Tasker tensed. He didn't know how the furniture was laid out in the other room or if there was a fire escape on the window. All he could focus on was the door. Then it hit him. Here he was doing nothing again. He had to act, and act decisively.

Tasker stood up, using his right hand to keep his Beretta aimed at the door, and grabbed one of the small wooden kitchen chairs with his left. He crept forward toward the empty doorway. From the other side of the wall, he heard Dooley again.

'What about it, Billy? Can I walk?'

When he was next to the door, Tasker pointed the gun at the wall a few feet from the door and pulled the trigger. He fired one round, then aimed a few inches closer to the door and fired again, then again.

Dooley yelled, 'Shit!' and appeared at the open door as Tasker swung the chair hard at his head. Before Dooley could react, the chair shattered across his head and he tumbled back into the bedroom as his small revolver dropped straight to the ground.

Tasker stepped into the doorway and looked at Dooley as he rolled on the ground holding his head.

Tasker said, 'That was option three.' He relaxed as he heard the police sirens in the distance.

twenty-eight

BILL TASKER, special agent with the Florida Department of Law Enforcement, sat on his porch listening to the morning songs of the tropical birds and the annoying shrieks of the state bird, the mockingbird. In the six days since the shoot-out at the Aventura Mall, as the media referred to it, Tasker felt like he'd slept over half the time. Deep sleep, without dreams. Probably the best sleep he'd had in more than four years.

Now he sat gently stretching his right leg as he cooled down after a decent morning run of five miles through the quiet streets of Kendall. He wanted to shower before Mac Nmir came by at nine. One thing Tasker had learned was that if Mac gave you a time, he meant that exact time. He rose for one more stretch when he heard a knock on the front door. He could hardly believe Mac was twenty minutes early but strode to the door, flexing his legs as he went.

A smile swept across his face. 'Thought you were on bed rest at home another three days.'

Derrick Sutter shook his head as he came inside, turning so his right arm in a sling didn't bump the door frame. 'Four days at the hospital was two too many; I couldn't face more than a couple on my couch.'

'What brings you all the way out here?'

Sutter settled into the recliner next to the couch. 'Just bored, needed to talk to someone.'

'I woulda visited you again. I thought I was wearing you out.'

'Kinda wanted to talk here.'

Tasker shrugged, sliding into the kitchen. 'Okay.' He grabbed a small bottle of Powerade from the refrigerator. 'Want anything?'

'Nah, I'm cool.' Sutter waited for Tasker to sit down across from him at the end of the couch. 'Anything new with the case?'

'Not much. No one's talking but Hodges, or I should say, Luther Williams.' Once the Bureau figured out that they'd watched a fugitive on TV dozens of times, they clamped down on him. He was still saying it was all Dooley.

'Dooley's sitting at MCC on firearm and civil rights charges on the grounds he used his official position to further the crime and tried to shoot you and Tina.'

'What do you mean, "tried"?' Sutter asked, touching his tender chest and shoulder. 'I heard the Bureau doesn't want to give you credit for figuring the whole thing out. That jackass would still be on the street if it weren't for you.'

Tasker shrugged. 'I'm just happy they're not looking at me like a crook anymore.'

Sutter nodded. 'What about the girls?'

'Tina is being held on the unlawful detention charges and official misconduct, too. She hasn't said a word and has got a good attorney.'

'And her sister?'

'Jeanie said that she doesn't know anything about the money and wishes that Dooley would've killed you.'

'So she's free?'

'Yep.'

'Good.' Sutter nodded as he slowly worked his way up and out of the recliner, then strolled through the open sliding glass door. 'Looks like the case is all wrapped up.'

Tasker said, 'Not quite. There's still the money. No one knows where it is.'

Sutter nodded. 'No one knows if it really exists. All you have is the statement of a fugitive who probably stole it in the first place.'

'True.'

'Bill, what would you do if you had that money?'

Tasker eyed him carefully. 'Why?'

'I mean, you wouldn't turn it in to the FBI or anything stupid like that, would you?'

'Again, I'd have to ask why?'

Sutter ignored him. 'Because they'd just tie it up in forfeiture, then turn it over to a government general fund. No one would even notice it. Everyone involved with it is either dead or in jail on enough charges to keep them locked up a long time. It has no value other than being a million and a half bucks.'

'I don't like where this is going, so I'll ask one more time: Why?'

Sutter took one step to the side and lifted the lid to the grill. 'This is why.'

Tasker stared at the clean grate and empty grill. 'So?'

Sutter looked down at the grill. 'Oh shit!'

'What? Jesus, Derrick, what the hell have you been talkin' about?'

Sutter moved to the front of the grill and opened the lid again like it was a magic trick. Then he did it again.

Tasker asked, 'What're you doing?'

Sutter took three long steps into the living room and sat down in the recliner. 'Bill, I gotta tell you something.'

'Go ahead.'

'Remember when I came by about three nights before the shit at the mall?'

'Yeah.'

'When you were upstairs, I hid the cash in your grill.'

'You planted more cash in my grill?'

Sutter stood, raising his hands in defense. 'No, no, man. Nothing like that. I figured the FBI had searched this place already, so it was safe. That's all.'

'You *did* take the cash from Tina and Jeanie.'

'I thought how everyone was after it but you, and you were the only one on the hook for it. You deserved it for a legal fund. Now I say you still earned it, so you could do what you want with it.'

Tasker cocked his head. 'Isn't that illegal?'

'No, it's fair. All the shit you been through, you definitely earned it.'

Tasker sat down now, looking toward Sutter. 'You know Mac is coming by in about five minutes.'

'Yeah, that's why I came by now, so I could say hey to both of you.'

'And implicate me in a felony.' Tasker stared at him straight-faced.

'You're missing a big point, Bill.'

'What's that?'

'Where'd the cash go?'

Now Tasker smiled.

Sutter's eyes snapped open. 'You found it. You took it.'

Tasker continued to smile, his laugh lines filling out.

Sutter shook his head. 'I'm in the presence of greatness. Where is it?'

'I can't tell you, but I know where it will be '

Now Sutter broke into a broad grin. 'You sneaky sly dog.'

'You think I'd be home for a week and not cook out?'

Sutter said, 'I didn't expect to be laid up a week when I hid it there. Now, where is it?'

Before Tasker could answer, there was a knock on the door. Tasker purposely didn't say anything to Sutter as he opened the door for a sharply dressed Mac Nmir.

Mac nodded to Tasker and smiled at the sight of Sutter. 'What're you doin' here, slick?'

Tasker said, 'You don't want to know.'

'That's good enough for me.' Mac sat on the couch.

Sutter said, 'Actually, I came by to talk to both of you.'

Mac asked, 'Oh yeah, what about?'

Tasker's stomach tightened.

'You remember the night you took out Dooley?'

Mac said, 'That was the same night you said that the day the FBI saved you was the day you quit police work.'

'Exactly. That's what I wanted to say.'

Tasker looked at him, amazed. 'You're quitting the job?'

Sutter nodded. 'Yep, I put in an application with the FBI. A minority, experience, I'm betting they pay me a signing bonus.'

Tasker couldn't contain his smile as Mac tried to keep his customary cool.

Sutter kept it up. 'I've seen enough excitement. I'm ready to slow down.'

Mac asked, 'You're serious?'

Sutter handed him his neatly typed application. 'And I listed you as a reference.'

TASKER WAS STILL laughing to himself over Sutter's announcement when he pulled his Cherokee to a stop in front of the downtown Miami strip mall later in the day. The well-kept inner-city mall had a mini-mart, a dry cleaner and the new offices of the Committee for Community Relief.

Tasker grabbed the satchel off the seat and walked through the front door of the four-room office, which, unlike the old office, bustled with activity.

A middle-aged woman with her hair held back by a series of rainbow clips smiled at him. 'May I help you?'

Tasker returned the smile. 'The director is expecting me.'

She led him back to the small office in the rear and then backed away silently.

Tasker waited for the new director to look up from his cluttered desk.

The sixty year-old extremely fit-looking man smiled at his old friend.

'Hello, Billy. What brings you over here?' asked Deac Kowal.

'Wanted to see how retirement was treating you.'

'Never busier.'

'How's the CCR?'

'Could be better. For all the fund raising that snake Watson did, he spent even more. We've sold everything extravagant and now we're almost in the black. It'll take a while, but we'll be able to help the area.'

'This might speed things up,' Tasker said, handing the satchel across the desk.

Deac looked in it and then closed it up quick. He kept his small round face neutral, saying in a low voice, 'Billy, tell me this isn't what I think it is.'

'If you think it's an anonymous donation that could be wasted sitting in evidence or could be put to use by you instead, you're right.'

'You didn't ...'

'No, Deac, I didn't. But someone did and I ended up with it and the cash belongs to the community. That's why it's called the Committee for Community Relief.' Tasker smiled like he had won a debate.

Deac kept his face calm, then slowly reached up and rubbed his gray temples. Finally, a smile spread over his face and he said, 'God bless you, Billy.'

Tasker smiled. 'I think he forgave me, Deac, and that's one big blessing.'

After his visit, Tasker trotted out to his Cherokee and jumped onto I-95 northbound toward West Palm Beach.

*

DEAC KOWAL, twenty-nine-year veteran of the Miami Police Department, five weeks into his retirement, could not keep his eyes off the cash inside the canvas satchel. It was a little over one and a half million bucks. It danced in his head like a green-tinted cartoon. He could give half to the CCR and still have a hell of a retirement. Maybe give five hundred thousand to the CCR and really live it up.

He scooped up the satchel and headed out to his battered Mercury Sable, tossing the money into the backseat. He headed down Fifty-fourth Street waving to a couple of people he knew on the sidewalk. He passed that goofy kid Cedric Brown everyone called 'Spill,' in his 'Black Power Forever' shirt, and even waved to him. He turned south on Seventh Avenue, headed toward his small house. He needed some time to decide what to do with the cash. He thought of it as taking the money for a little walk.